Secrets of Winter

by

JP Barry

The Fall of Winters Trilogy

Secrets of Winter

COPYRIGHT © 2025 by JP Barry

Cover Art by *The Wild Rose Press, Inc.*

The Wild Rose Press, Inc.
PO Box 708
Adams Basin, NY 14410-0708
Visit us at www.thewildrosepress.com

Publishing History
First Edition, 2025
Trade Paperback ISBN 978-1-5092-6134-5
Digital ISBN 978-1-5092-6135-2

The Fall of Winters Trilogy
Published in the United States of America

Dedication

For my husband & daughter - Everything is limitless, especially you.

Chapter One

Beau

"Please raise your right hand. Do you swear or affirm the testimony you're about to give will be the truth, the whole truth, and nothing but the truth, so help you God?" the stern-faced, portly, well past his prime, gray-haired judge asked.

Maybe. Let's see where this goes first, Judge Stone, and let's not forget who has the power to strip you of your title should you piss me off.

"I do."

"Head over to the witness stand and take a seat," he further instructed, pointing his crooked, right index finger at a walnut-stained, wooden chair, atop a wide podium. The eerie sound of furniture scraping against the scuffed lacquer floor sent a chill up my spine.

"You may proceed, Counselor," Stone added once everyone was in position.

Concealing my buzzing nerves had become a full-time job. The motion to not allow cameras in the courtroom had been denied, so here I was, fully exposed to the prying eyes of the people who once believed the Winters family to be perfect royalty. However, if I'm to be fair, it's all a lie. It's always been one epic tale of smoke and mirrors. Do you want to know the truth, the whole truth, and nothing but the God damn truth? Are you curious as to how a true politician *really* feels about their constituents? If you can help us, you're in. If you can't, you don't exist, unless there's a photo op. Sorry to break the bad news to you, but it is what it is, and it always will be—don't *ever* forget that. When your usefulness wears thin, you're gone. Plain and simple. Perhaps you'll be placed neatly on a shelf in a closet—door firmly shut of course, for potential use at a later date, but don't hold your breath. Who leads in the polls matters. Who wins matters. Pushing personal agendas matters. Making obscene amounts of money matters. Everything in between is insignificant. Smile bright. Nod your head a lot. Kiss some babies. Shake a few hands. Present the illusion people's concerns mean something to you and your approval rating will skyrocket. My popularity ranking is well over ninety percent. The kicker? I haven't played an active role for the government in almost two decades. Do you really think I give a rat's ass about what I had to do to get here? Fat chance.

I'm an eighty-year-old former attorney, town councilman, congressman, senator, vice president, and currently a political consultant. These days, my time is spent schooling my moronic grandson, Jackson, on how to have a successful presidential run. The only reason he stands a snowball's chance in Hell is because of *me* and *my* name. Other than that, he's an idiot. The nitwit doesn't realize the subtle art of a successful side deal, or how financially gainful it can be. He has no clue how to manipulate the wealthy to donate to his campaign, or how to schmooze powerful politicians with clout to throw you their support. All of those times I made headlines by crossing party lines—it sure as shit wasn't for the greater good. It was for me, my likability, my name highlighted in the papers, and for the hefty payout. Thankfully, his two sisters, brother, and cousins weren't as stupid. However, since I'm attempting to be truthful, the only one of my grandchildren that I ever truly felt anything for was my Nicky. That kid is the apple of my eye. Though a screw up if I ever met one, he was a living, breathing reminder good people did exist. When he informed me years ago he wanted nothing to do with politics, I'd never been prouder.

That boy grew up to become a world-renowned psychotherapist who refused to take any of my son and daughter-in-law's bullshit. The way he stood up to them was impressive. Even Nicky's wife, Jillian, I enjoyed. That bitch was a real ballbuster who'd stop at nothing to get what she wanted. God love 'em both. The problem is, she knows too much. Actually, if I'm pressed to tell the *absolute* truth, there are several people who share that very same boat with her. That's where I stand now. Initially, I thought I'd be the one having to craft a clever idea on how to silence them, but as luck would have it, someone beat me to the punch. To date, Jillian, along with Madison Santino, Marco Santino, Liam Stevens, and Salvatore D'Angelo have all been missing in action for about six months. With a little support on my end, the Feds were able to tie it all back to Luca Santino, but frankly he's not the bad guy. He's the shmuck currently standing trial for crimes he didn't commit. Once he's locked up for life, I'll have to find a way to tie up a few loose ends, because Frank Santino and his thugs will definitely be coming after me to seek revenge. Nicky will have to be shut up too, which pains me, but so be it. My family's secrets must be protected at all costs. Period. Sorry, grandson.

"Good morning, Mr. Vice President," Joshua Lyman, the Nassau County District Attorney, said.

"Good morning," I said.

"Can you state your full name for the record?"

"Beau Lincoln Winters."

"Can you tell the court your credentials?"

"Of course. I am the former Vice President of the United States of America. I also hold a Juris Doctorate from Yale University, and was a Town Councilman on Long Island, a congressman for the state of New York, as well as a Senator for the State of New York. Currently, I'm a political consultant."

"That's an impressive career in public service. Why did you get out of politics?"

"I wouldn't say *I got out* of politics. As I said, I'm a political consultant, but I left public office due to severe health issues. I didn't feel I could do this country the justice it deserved while recovering from a major heart attack," I explained, making sure to soften my baby blues and look down to reflect a sense of tremendous sadness—a classic Beau Winters move.

"Totally understandable and commendable. Right now, I'd like to draw your attention to May twenty-seventh of last year. Do you remember that day?"

"Yes."

The easy part is over. Here comes the coverup.

"Can you walk us through your day starting from the time you exited The Grind Coffee Bean?"

"I left the coffee shop and planned to head home. It was my driver's day off, so I had driven myself. I was walking to my car, which was parked in the municipal lot located about one block east from The Grind Coffee Bean. Luca Santino approached me and strongly urged we take a walk. He pressed the barrel of a gun to my back while he forcefully shoved me down a dark alley."

"Objection. Calls for speculation. If an item was pressed to Vice President Winters' back, how could he possibly know what it was? Does he have eyes in the back of his head?" Ally Newman, the defense's counsel objected. Though I never personally retained her, I knew of many who had—Nicky included. The woman was cutthroat. A true beast of a broad who was merciless and trained her associates to act in a similar ruthless fashion. The fact Frank Santino's son worked for her was news to me. I only found out when Nicky informed me Luca Santino would be representing him for his custody battle. Back then I held my breath because I didn't want to raise suspicions over my ties to the Santino Crime Family. In the end it all worked out in Nicky's favor so, no harm no foul, or so I initially thought.

"Sustained," the judge answered.

"I apologize. Luca Santino held a narrow, hard object against my back. He and three other men led me to a secluded alley. Mr. Santino proceeded to verbally threaten me over a picture he received, eventually showing it to me. The graphic photograph revealed an odious crime scene. A man and a woman were lying dead on a floor. There was blood everywhere. It appeared both had been shot. While he was doing this, he held his forearm against my throat. The more I told him I had no idea what he was talking about, the more force he used. At several points, I couldn't breathe. One of the men he was with warned him many times to stand down, but Mr. Santino refused. Words like *consigliere* and *il capo* were used to calm him. Eventually, he released his hold and took off. A few seconds later, I felt a sharp, stabbing pain in my left arm which shot up to my jaw. My chest tightened and I hit the ground. The next thing I can remember is waking up in the hospital attached to all sorts of machines. Later that evening, my cardiologist, Doctor Pierce Rothchild, informed me that I'd suffered another major heart attack. I was admitted to the hospital and remained there for two weeks. I am still under the strict care and watchful eye of Doctor Rothchild, and his team of highly skilled assistants."

"I am so sorry you were forced to endure another serious cardiac event, Mr. Vice President. If at any point you need or require a break, medical attention, or feel as if you cannot go on for any reason whatsoever, please let me know. Are you all right to continue?"

"I sincerely appreciate your concern and if necessary I will take you up on that offer, but for now, I believe this old man can carry on so justice can be served in the timely manner our legal system grants for our citizens."

"Fair enough. Moving along. Is Luca Santino here in this courtroom today?"

"Yes."

"Can you identify him and describe what he's wearing?"

"Yes. He's sitting beside Ms. Newman. He's wearing a jet black, three-piece suit, a white dress shirt, a crimson tie and pocket square, black socks, and heavily polished dark shoes. Mr. Santino is also wearing glasses and is holding a blue ballpoint pen and writing on a canary yellow legal pad."

"Let the record show Vice President Winters clearly identified Luca Santino."

"Noted," the judge said.

"Do you see any of the other men who were at The Grind Coffee Bean on May twenty-seventh here today?"

"No, I do not."

"Prior to Mr. Santino's violent assault—" Lyman began.

"Objection. Hearsay, prejudicial, speculation, opinion. I could go on if you'd like, Your Honor. *Everything* about Mr. Lyman's accusation of my client assaulting Vice President Winters is flat out bias and loaded with incorrect information. With all of the bologna the prosecution is throwing around, we don't have to adjourn for lunch," Newman huffed.

"Sustained."

"I'll rephrase. Prior to your impromptu conversation with Mr. Santino, have you ever had any business dealings or communication with him?"

"No."

"Didn't Luca Santino represent your grandson, Doctor Nicholas Winters and his wife, Jillian Winters, for a previous legal matter?"

"I was not privileged to the details of the case in question." *Total lie.*

"You weren't aware that your grandson retained Newman and Associates?"

"No. Nicky never shared that information with me. I knew he was dealing with a legal matter, but I didn't press him for any information. If he needed my help, he knew he could come to me, but he chose not to, and my wife and I do not force anyone to do anything that makes them feel uncomfortable." *Epic lie.*

"Nicky?"

"My apologies. Doctor Nicholas Winters, my grandson. To my beautiful wife and I he's our Nicky."

Hey! Finally the truth!

"Are you familiar with the Santino Crime Family?"

"No."

"Objection," Newman yelled, throwing her hands up in the air. "Permission to approach, please, Your Honor?"

"Granted."

With the swagger of a man, Newman marched up to the judge's bench. With each wild bodily gesture, the judge's face grew angrier. Though I couldn't hear exactly what they were discussing, one could only imagine. After he put Lyman in his place, Newman returned to her seat.

"The jury is to disregard the comment made by Mr. Lyman about the Santino Crime Family. The Santino Family is not on trial. Only Luca Santino is."

"Mr. Vice President, are you familiar with any other member of the Santino Family? Have you ever met or conducted business with them?"

"No. Absolutely not. Never." Massive, mega, humongous lie, but it was told with a straight, honest face. Glancing at Frank Santino, I could see that only the whites of his eyes were visible. It was his Mafioso way of warning me of his displeasure. I suppose I'd be enraged too if I were in his position. His kid had nothing to do with what happened. Mine on the other hand...*well*... Once convicted, Luca's life would be over, which was a pity because he had an attractive wife and a small child, but I couldn't let the Winters dynasty go down for this. We'd be ruined. Destroyed with no hope of a bounce back ever. As long as everyone's focus remained firmly locked on the young Santino fellow, who cared? Let the cops and Feds do their job and figure out what actually happened, which they won't.

My dealings with Frank Santino began a touch over a decade ago. I'd dealt with scandals in the past, but this particular time I couldn't use my usual cleanup crew because I lacked confidence in their abilities to keep this situation securely under wraps. In politics you can trust no one, and this incident had to do with my Nicky. Late one balmy summer night, the blaring ring from my bedside phone woke me from a deep slumber. Removing my black, silk sleep mask, my fingers grappled for the receiver.

"Hello?" I said gruffly, attempting to conceal the fact I'd been out cold. Whoever was on the other line had to think I was powerful enough to not require sleep.

"Grandpa?"

"Nicky? What time is it?" I asked, sitting up and turning to check on Maris. Thankfully, she'd grown so accustomed to the phone ringing at all hours it no longer served as a disruption to her rest.

"I'm sorry for bothering you at this hour, but I have a problem. A big problem that I have no idea how to get out of. I need help, please," he replied. An edgy anxiousness dripped from each word he spoke.

"Are you okay? Is it Jillian?"

"She caught me."

"She who? Jillian?"

"Yeah."

"Exactly what did Jillian catch you doing?" My brain was still hazy with sleep, and I was too old to be playing guessing games.

Cut to the chase kid so Grandpa can go back to bed.

"I was in Louisiana promoting my new book, and Jill showed up out of the blue. The stupid desk clerk gave her the key to my room without alerting me first. When she got to my suite, she saw me and my assistant in bed together," he explained.

"Kelly?"

"Yes."

"Never dip your pen in the company ink, Nicky. Didn't I teach you better?"

"I know. I know. Can you please fix this? Jillian doesn't seem mad, but she also hasn't said anything, *yet*. She just walked out of the hotel. We haven't spoken since. I'm due home in two days."

"You didn't go after your wife?"

"No. If I had, when I caught up to her, what would I have even said?"

Oh, I don't know, kid. I'm sorry? It was a mistake? Please forgive me? I love you? Perhaps reach into your chest, rip out your heart, then hand it to her on a platinum platter from Tiffany's?

"Define *fix*. Do you want to stay with Jillian, or would you rather be with this other woman?"

"Of course I want to stay with my wife. I love her. Kelly was just a warm body to screw around with when Jill wasn't available. I have no feelings or emotions for her whatsoever. Give up Jill for some random southern slut? Hardly," Nick scoffed.

If you loved your wife so damn much you wouldn't have been messing around with someone else behind her back.

I may have been a lot of things, but never once during my sixty years of marriage to Maris did I ever consider stepping out. Don't get me wrong—there were opportunities, plenty of them, but the bond between a husband and wife was sacred. Good or bad, ups or downs, your wife was your wife and damn it, you better respect and revere her. The right partner supported you, elevated you, and was the only person you could fully rely on.

"All right. Take a breath, Nicky. Text me Kelly's full name, address, and phone number. I'll handle it, but Nicky, this crap ends. I will not bail you out of this type of situation again. Make it work with Jillian. I don't care what you have to do. I never, ever, want to hear you tell me you're leaving her. Jillian is perfect for you. I couldn't have found a better wife for you myself. By the time you get home, Kelly will be handled. Apologize to Jillian—beg her to take you back if that's what it takes. Buy her something nice and expensive. Take her on a vacation, and while you're on said holiday, make a baby."

"Thank you so much, Grandpa." Nick paused. "Please don't tell Mom and Dad."

He hadn't heard one thing I said after I told him I'd figure out his little situation. "That's what grandpas are for. Don't worry about Tag and Miranda, or anyone else for that matter. This will remain between us."

After hanging up, my body tossed and turned for hours.

How on God's green Earth was I supposed to fix this? Who the hell do I even call?

My mind went into overdrive as I attempted to think of anyone to reach out to until finally the answer presented itself. While flipping through the newspaper over my morning coffee, I saw it, plain as day. The answer to my problem stared back at me in the form of a black and white photograph—Frank Santino, notorious New York Mafia Crime Boss. He'd recently skirted yet another criminal incident without a scratch. The man was like Teflon. Nothing ever stuck to him, his family, or associates. Briskly making my way into my home office, a few keyboard strokes later, I found and dialed his number. Some real uneducated man with a heavy Brooklyn accent, Salvatore, took down my information, scheduling a meeting for later that day.

The conference location was a real low class, trailer trash, greasy spoon somewhere in Queens, but Santino and his buddy fit right in. He wore an off the rack, cheap suit, and his friend donned a white tracksuit with a purple stripe running up the side of the pants. We filed into a decrepit booth in the back, and an hour later, crisis averted. Santino and his cohort said they'd make it so Kelly would no longer be an issue. A week later, Frank and Salvatore requested another chat at the same shithole eatery.

"We offered Ms. Greenly half a million dollars, a condo in Los Angeles, a new car, and a job as a secretary at a law firm. In exchange, she agreed to never speak to the press, or anyone for that matter, about what happened between her and your grandson. She will also abstain from reaching out to him. As far as she's concerned, it didn't happen and your grandson doesn't exist. Case closed," Salvatore informed.

Money? A condo? A car? A job? That was their grand plan to make this woman disappear? I could've done that myself without having to consort with these criminal thugs.

"Who's to say she'll live up to her end of the bargain?" I challenged.

"She will," Frank assured.

"That's not good enough. I want her gone. Erased.

Eliminated. Whacked. Whatever it is *people* like *you* do, do it," I demanded.

"We're done here, Mr. Winters," Frank said sternly, then stood.

"Fine," I replied.

"Payment?" Salvatore said.

"When you complete the job, you'll get paid. You haven't, so go take a hike." These slime balls weren't about to bully me.

"It was an affair. Your grandson is just as much at fault as the girl. No one got hurt. No damage was done. The wife found out and got mad. So what? She'll either get over it or divorce him. Tomorrow morning, the girl will board a plane, never to return to New York again. In my opinion, this is a non-issue. Rearview mirror material for all parties involved." Frank paused. "You've been given the wrong impression over exactly what my family and associates do."

"No. No, I don't think I have, but you are right about one thing. We are done here," I said, rising and leaving the diner.

Much later that night, I reached out to a former New York City detective contact of mine, who put me in touch with an anonymous source. A quarter of a million dollars transferred to an offshore account later, Ms. Greenly never made it to Kennedy Airport the following morning. *That's* how you solve a problem.

Fast forward to three years ago. Again with Nicky. This time he vanished into thin air. For the record, I had nothing to do with any aspect of that situation, nor did I know who Warren Lessor was. Horrified after watching the press conference Jillian gave, I feared I'd suffer another major heart attack. My chest tightened, my breathing shortened, and I collapsed on the sofa in my home office. Maris found me moments later, promptly calling nine-one-one. Though not a cardiac event, the emergency room doctor called it a panic attack brought on by sudden stress. After a call from my public relations representative, because this would make for great headlines, I found myself pissed off at Jillian for not reaching out to me first, but I completely understood why she hadn't. Tag and Miranda always treated her like a dog who just soiled their priceless Persian rug. Shame too. Jillian wasn't as bad as they painted her. If they only had treated her with an ounce of kindness, dignity, and respect, she would've been quite the asset to the Winters family. *Especially* for them.

Stuffing aside the offense of finding out when everyone else in the damn world had, I knew something needed to be done and quickly. Yes, the police and FBI were involved, but that meant squat. They were as useless as tits on bulls. Giving it a few days to see if anyone reached out with a worthwhile tip proved wasteful. Even with Jillian's one-million-dollar reward nothing of substance surfaced. At home Maris refused to allow me to do anything other than lie in bed, read books of her choosing, or go over the notes for my autobiography which was being ghostwritten. No television. No cell phone. No computer. No tablets. Absolutely no stress. Of course she kept me updated on Nicky, but she wouldn't share much else. The boiling point was when Tag and Miranda swung by for a visit. Obviously I questioned the hell out of them, but they didn't seem to give a tiny rat's ass. All they saw was a publicity stunt in the making. In fact they only showed up to tell me my and Maris's presence was required at a presser they were holding at their home the following day.

The second they left I knew only one option was available—Frank Santino. Surely he had friends in low places who'd be able to locate Nicky, hopefully alive. When Maris left to run errands, I snuck into my office and made the call. Initially, Salvatore was reluctant to provide any sort of assistance, but a sizable cash payout changed his mind quickly. Quietly, under the deep cover of night, I met them outside of my home. In order to ensure they'd help, I handed Salvatore a brown envelope with half of the payment. The following day, before Tag's press conference, Frank's son, Marco, snuck in with some reporters. He casually slipped me a small piece of paper and whispered, *"Your grandson is alive and at this location."* The address he provided was for some place all the way out on the east end of Long Island. Before I could process anything or confirm the validity of this lead, it was time for the Winters family to show a public united front for the media. Staying off to the side with Maris, we allowed Tag to act as our spokesperson. The press went wild. The Winters became America's favorite family again. Our tragedy had become theirs.

Checking out the address the younger Santino provided was a bit tricky. I had to make up an excuse in order for Maris to allow me to leave the house. Hesitantly, she agreed that I could run a few errands for a change of scenery and some fresh air, but only if I had my chief of security, Marshal, come along. Happily, I accepted her terms, because after decades of loyal service, Marshal proved trustworthy. He wouldn't breathe a word of this to anyone, ever. A few hours later, I had Marshal park on the side of the road a little ways down from the address. On the outside the place appeared neat and tidy. The large home didn't seem threatening in the least. Armed with a pair of binoculars we sat, waiting, until eventually several people emerged from the house. One of them was in fact Nicky. Dressed in all white, he picked up an axe and chopped wood.

Two choices presented. I could call the police or I could ignore what I'd seen, privately knowing Nicky was alive and well. To any typical person the only option would be to call the authorities right then and there, but I had the rest of my family to consider. The press we received boosted Jackson's lead in the preliminary polls almost ensuring he'd obtain the party nomination. Tag's name was circulating again in a positive light. The career advancements my other grandchildren were seeking were now within their reach, and all of my past accomplishments were being talked about, with me being hailed a hero. Maris and I were viewed as the deeply worried, fragile grandparents. Who cared that Jillian was forced to take the brunt of the media's negativity? Not me. Besides, she was young, bright, and strong. Once this came to a head, she'd recover just fine. Telling Marshal to turn the car around was one of my best choices to date. Eventually Jillian figured it out, like I knew she would, and Nicky came home. Sure, he suffered a gunshot wound, but it wasn't fatal, and yes, Jillian murdered a man and maimed a woman, but she wasn't charged with the crimes—no harm, no foul. In less than six months Nicky had healed completely. Though he refused to engage in any family activities, he more-or-less wrote his parents and siblings off, he remained in contact with Maris and me. A win in my book. A little while later, Salvatore came nosing around for the second half of his payment, but I made sure he was blocked from any face-to-face contact. He backed down after a while, disappearing into the shadows where the thug belonged. Everything was coming up aces, until last year.

Again, Nicky was the culprit. However this time he didn't come crying to me. He didn't want help, but rather he was seeking advice. While abducted he'd been forced to sleep with one of the women in the house—the same one Jillian had shot in the foot. Surprise, surprise, the girl ended up pregnant. Apparently she'd been blackmailing him and Jillian. Nicky wanted it to end and asked me how I'd go about it. Never once did he request I clean up the mess. This impressed the hell out of me. He'd finally grown up and had become the man I always knew he could be. Long gone was the weak little boy who'd called me in the middle of the night, begging that I solve his adultery drama. But, I suppose after what he'd been through, and now being a father to a sweet baby girl, it was bound to happen. Not wanting to steer him in the wrong direction, I advised he speak to one of his lawyers about the matter. The moment he left, gut instinct caused me to pick up the phone and dial Frank Santino for one last favor.

Going into it I was sure the brute wouldn't be too thrilled to hear from me. Our past two transactions hadn't gone smoothly, and I did owe him quite a bit of money, but maybe I'd be able to squeeze help out of him if I offered to pay upfront. The conversation went over as well as rain on your wedding day—a total disaster. Salvatore didn't even allow me a chance to get halfway through what I had to say before he hung up, but not before telling me to lose his number and to never bother him or his family again. Who needed them anyway? They were total losers. I never liked them in the first place.

Nicky went ahead and retained Ally Newman, and all appeared well. His legal team went straight to work. A few weeks later, during a lunch strategy meeting at my home with Tag and Jackson, five greasy slime balls bullied their way past Marshal and his security team. They came slamming into my dining room. Within seconds, two of the men had Tag and Jackson paralyzed against the wall while Frank Santino's son, Marco, practically lifted me off of the chair I sat in. The low life demanded I tell him everything I knew about Warren and Noah Lessor, some woman I never heard of—Sarah Davis, another woman I couldn't tell you anything about—Madison Langmore, and his brother, Frank's other son, Luca. Truthfully? I had no idea what he was ranting about.

Evidently Madison Langmore, who happened to be Luca's girlfriend, had been kidnapped by Noah Lessor, who was tied to Sarah Davis—the mother of Nicky's possible child. These criminals boldly threatened my and my family's lives if I didn't cough up any information. All I could share was the brief conversation I had with Nicky several weeks prior. It seemed to do the trick because they left, but not before threatening me that if they found out I lied, they'd end the Winters entirely. The happening shook Tag and Jackson up so much they benched me. My assistance was no longer required. This aggravated me beyond words. I had the power to make that weasel President of the United States—*not* Tag, who even on a good day struggled to decipher his ass from his elbow. Who the hell do you think dragged his sorry ass across the finish line? Me. He was the frigging Speaker of the House because of me, damn it.

Some days later while I was getting a cup of coffee at a local café, a newspaper headline caught my eye. It stated Nicky and Jillian had adopted a son. I snatched the periodical from the rack. The article—an obvious fluff piece carefully crafted by their personal relations team-- gushed over their happiness, suggesting their family was now complete. A snapshot of the four of them in their home revealed the happy couple laughing with their now two children. Though I was proud of Nicky and Jillian for carefully concealing the truth while spinning unnecessary drama in their favor, a certain amount of annoyance overrode the positive. Why hadn't they called to tell me about my new great-grandson, Ethan? Between Tag and Jackson's dismissal and now this, I felt like an outdated, useless relic. A year and a half after that, someone touched my shoulder as I walked to my car.

"Let's take a walk," a masculine voice requested.

Unsure of how to respond, I kept smiling and doing as told. I'd given Marshal the day off, so I was alone. Sure, we were in an area that encompassed many witnesses, but who the hell pays attention to what's going on around them? Not many, if any at all. The man, who I'd yet to identify, escorted me by my elbow down a dark side alley behind a strip of offices. I didn't feel anything pressing into my back. That's not to say the men were unarmed, they more than likely were, but at that moment I wasn't being held at gunpoint.

When we stopped moving, the man aggressively spun me around and slammed my back against a brick wall. His and the faces of several others—all familiar, came into view. The original culprit was Luca Santino.

Behind him were two of Frank's lackies, the very same two who'd threatened me in my home, and Frank's other son, Marco.

"What do you know about this?" Luca demanded as Marco shoved a black and white picture in my face. Luca's massive forearm was pressed against my throat causing my breath to catch in my windpipe. His other hand gripped my right shoulder. He positioned his knee between my legs applying a considerable amount of pressure on my groin. There was no escaping this hold. Once my eyes were able to focus on the photograph, it appeared it was a police crime scene snapshot. There were two bodies—one male, the other female. Both were lying on the floor. Blood had seeped onto a throw rug, and a gun rested nearby. Small triangle markers were strategically placed around the space.

"Nothing. I swear I have no idea what you're talking about, or what this picture is even of," I panted, struggling for air.

"Don't lie *to me*," Luca hissed. His grip grew firmer. His eyes were white with rage. Though his body was rigid, he was still forcefully in control.

"I know nothing," I insisted, because frankly, I didn't.

"Ease up, *fratellino*. You're giving him too much juice. Remember what Pop always says—dead men can't talk," Marco warned Luca.

"True, but should my elbow slip causing me to snap this shit bag's neck, would you really care?"

"If it were up to us we'd let you do whatever you'd like with this *coglione*, but you'll piss off *il capo* and no one wants that, *consigliere*. Trust us," one of the men standing behind Luca said.

When his hold released, my body collapsed, and I gasped for even an ounce of oxygen. "Look, I have no clue what that picture is of, who is in it, or why you're showing it to me," I said, desperately attempting to regain my composure.

The four-man gang simply stood stone still while they stared me down. A fear so deep ensconced my soul. Profuse, terrifying sweat dripped down my forehead, stinging my eyes.

"Here. Take it," I said, reaching into my back pocket for my wallet. Extracting all of the cash inside of it, I stretched my arm out trying to hand it to them, but no one would take it. "I know I owe Frank more. I'll get it to him by tonight. Just let me go."

"Nobody wants your money," Marco replied with an air of disgust in his voice.

"You better hope to God you're telling the truth, because if you're not and anything happens to my wife or family, I'll kill you myself. Bare hands and all," Luca sneered. He turned on his heel and walked away with the others, leaving me in the alley alone.

A sudden pang of sharp pain shot through my jaw and down my arm. Once again my breathing became labored, but this time it wasn't because someone's arm was pressed against my neck. I'm unsure of what followed after my knees finally gave out and my body hit the ground. The next thing I was aware of was waking in the hospital, hooked up to half a dozen machines. One could suppose this is where our story begins.

Chapter Two

Frank

I should've been pacing the house anxiously waiting for my sons and Salvatore's two kids to return, but I wasn't. They knew what they were doing. A certain amount of confidence they'd handle the situation properly quieted any scattered thoughts—I hoped. Unaware of how many years I had left to lead this family, my boys needed to be thrown into the fire so I could make sure they could deal with everything when I took a step back. My only worry was Luca. You'd think it would be Marco, my hot headed, shoot first ask questions never son, but it wasn't.

Something had changed inside of my youngest during, but especially after, Madison's abduction. On the outside he appeared the same, but internally his once bright light had darkened. If anyone so much as glanced at his wife or son he'd lose his shit. Armed with a violent temper, we all kept a watchful eye on Luca. His behavior only grew worse after he received an anonymous note attached to a picture of the Noah Lessor/Sarah Davis crime scene. Though he wasn't the one who pulled the trigger, Lessor offed himself and I had the privilege of silencing Davis after she went after Salvatore with a butcher knife; he'd been the only one targeted. Whenever anyone mentioned the Winters Family or anything having to do with the kidnapping, if you looked into his eyes one could clearly see squirrels juggling chainsaws. Only his wife possessed the ability to calm his weary, angry, anxious soul. She kept his ass in firm check daily, but for how long could she maintain that control?

A few days ago, Luca reached the end of his fuse. He stormed into my home in a fit of fury, screaming and ranting over how we still hadn't figured out who was behind the mystery threat. He accused us of doing nothing aside from sitting on our lazy asses. Not true at all. We were biding time. After Marco calmed him down—a long walk around the block, two shots of tequila, and a half a pack of cigarettes later—we sat in the basement discussing our immediate course of action. A macabre sense of satisfaction resided inside of my heart. Beau. I knew eventually he'd reveal his involvement in the abduction. It never sat well with me that he didn't have his hands on Madison's situation. My gut always believed that bastard played a role. I could never prove it though. Now, a chance had presented itself. I only wished I had more concrete evidence that he was without a shadow of a doubt the true culprit. So, to shut Luca up, I sent Salvatore's two kids, Tony and Jimmy, along with Marco and Luca to have a little chat with good 'ole Beau. I'd have preferred to bench Luca, but the way he was acting there wasn't a chance in Hell he'd listen.

"Beau says he had nothing to do with it and I believe him, *but* I've got a feeling his family is involved in this. I don't know which member, but one of them is. It doesn't matter though. Beau will do all of the work for us. He'll lead us to whoever is at the root. I'd bet my life on the fact that if he hasn't already, he will be in contact with the culprit shortly. I'll get Sammy or Rocco to keep an eye on him and hawk his every move in stealth," Marco informed.

"What about Maddy?" I asked.

"What about *my* wife?" Luca questioned in full rage mode.

"We should have her investigate this," I suggested.

Slamming his fist into the nearest basement sheetrock wall, a string of obscenities flew out of his mouth. Carefully approaching him from behind, Marco put his arm around Luca's broad shoulders. He whispered something into his ear before pressing his forehead to his brother's. With that, Luca touched the side of Marco's face and took off out of the back door.

"Marco, *vieni qui*," I said, using my right hand to guide him up the stairs and into the kitchen.

"Yeah, Pop. What's up?" he asked while opening the refrigerator.

"What did you tell your brother?"

"To be cool, walk it off so Maddy and Frankie don't pick up on his tension. That we went in hoping to wrap this up today, but were aware it would probably become a thing we'd have to pick at a little more." He paused. "He's new at this, Pop. Add that to the raw emotions that go along with receiving a veiled threat and having a wife and child to protect. It would drive any man batty with fear. Even the strong ones, like us. I'm aware of why we've put a pin in this Beau bullshit. I know why we haven't made a move yet—we don't have proof. The fact I've been pounding the pavement searching high and low for even the tiniest scrap of rock solid evidence for months now isn't registering in Luca's brain. He's wound so tight nothing we say or do will matter. Plus,

Maddy's been on his ass about making another baby."

"Do you think he'll be all right or should I have a chat with him?"

"I've got him on a leash. A rather short one. The same way you controlled me when I started working with you is how I've been dealing with him. He's learning to trust and listen to me. Let me handle this, okay?"

With a sigh, I exited the kitchen and padded to the living room. Picking up the television remote, I flipped it on. As my ass prepared to make its final descent onto the recliner, a female newscaster's voice caught my attention, drawing me away from resting and thrusting me back into fight mode.

"Sources have confirmed that former Vice President Beau Winters has been hospitalized. We're unsure of what happened or his current condition, but we'll keep you updated with the latest when information becomes available."

"What did Luca do to Beau?" I demanded, stomping back into the kitchen.

"Threatened him a little, but that's about it," Marco said, looking up from his cell phone.

"He's in the hospital, Marco."

"Who? Beau?"

"Yeah. So I'll ask again. What did Luca, or anyone of you, do to him?" I pressed harshly.

"Nothing, Pop. Luca pinned him against an alley wall. I mean sure the guy struggled a bit to breathe because Luca had his arm against his throat, but when we walked away, he was totally fine. He was panting a little and visibly in shock, but he wasn't lying dead on the ground or in any sort of medical distress. Had he been, one of us would've called the paramedics."

"And Luca hasn't been out of your sight since then?"

"He was glued to my ass the entire time and there's no way he could've done anything over the course of the past twenty minutes since he left here. In order to get back to Beau, he'd have to get on the Belt Parkway which at this time is a freaking parking lot. You asked me to keep an eye on him. I have." He paused thoughtfully before picking up his cell phone and dialing a number. "Hey, Paulie, it's Marco. How've you been, man?"

I had no idea who the hell Paulie was, and it infuriated me that I couldn't hear what he was saying.

"Congrats, man. That's awesome. We'll have to get a drink and catch up. Listen, I need a favor."

More inaudible chatter.

"Was Beau Winters admitted to any of the hospitals today?"

I sat across from him shocked but impressed by his actions.

"Oh, yeah? Interesting. Do me another favor? Keep me posted?" Marco said as he jutted his chin out at me while his fingers toyed with the tines of a fork.

"You're the best, *amico*. Meet me at Gabriel's Pub tonight around ten, okay? I'll take care of you." After a series of easy laughs and goodbyes he hung up. "Beau was admitted to the hospital, the one in Manhasset. He's in the Cardiac Care Unit—heart attack. Paulie is an ER doctor, Doctor Paul Costa. He stitches me up from time to time. He said the old shit should be okay. Apparently, someone found him on the ground when they were taking trash to a dumpster and called nine-one-one. When they questioned him as to why he was behind a store, and about the events that led up to the episode, he told the staff he couldn't remember anything. He won't sing. He's too scared. Well, for the moment anyway. I'll hook up with Paulie later. Throw him a few bucks so he keeps us informed. As for Luca—him, Maddy, and Frankie are swinging by later for dinner. I'll handle him. Problem solved, Pop. Now go sit down and take it easy. I got this."

With a 'hmmm,' a half smile, and a light, side face tap against Marco's scruffy cheek, I'd never had more confidence in Marco than right then and there. My hot-headed boy had become a skilled, confident leader in the making. After all these years he'd listened, learned, and was now applying controlled practices.

"*Sei un uomo buono, Figliolo. Sono orgoglioso di te*," I said.

"I'm all right, but thanks, Pop."

"What about Madison?" I asked.

"What about her?" Marco's attention returned to his sandwich.

"You may have addressed one problem, but we still have to deal with whomever sent the picture to Luca."

"Please, let me handle this."

"She's untouchable at what she does."

"Did you not just see your son slam his fist into the basement wall? Did you not hear him lose his mind the moment Madison's name was mentioned?"

"What Luca doesn't know won't hurt him."

"True, but it might kill all of us." He paused. "Please, I'm begging you. Let me take the lead on this one. I have some irons in the fire and I'm working an angle. I suspect this matter will wrap up shortly, but you've got to trust me."

"When is your next trip?" For some years now every month Marco would disappear for either a long weekend or the entire week. I never questioned his whereabouts mainly because it wasn't my business and quite frankly, I didn't want to know. He always stayed in touch and would return with a bit of a fresh kick in his step— happier, lighter, at peace with the world. Logic suggested he had a steady girl on the side, but he never brought anyone special home for us to meet. I suppose he could've been seeing a man and wished to keep his secret locked away from his family. Perhaps the string of bimbos he often hung around with were decoys.

"Couple weeks. This should be over and done with by then. Don't worry."

With a brief nod I contemplated if I should share my inner thoughts with him. Yes, Marco was being groomed to take over the family when the time came, but he was still my son and there were lines parents and children should never cross. Deciding this wasn't the time to hold back I spoke again. "Marco…"

"I'm not gay, Pop," Marco said. His focus remained firmly on his cell phone. It was as if he could read my mind at times.

"What or who you do in your free time is none of my business, but if you were, your mother and I wouldn't care. Neither would your siblings or anyone in this family. However, that's not what's keeping me in this room."

"All right, then what is it?" he answered with a heavy sigh, establishing eye contact. The kid wanted to run point on this so badly. My meddling was driving him insane, but he kept his patience and remained calm. Ten years ago this wouldn't have been the case.

"Since day one I've always felt Beau's hands were all over this. I understand why he left his grandson high and dry when he could've helped him after Warren Lessor abducted him. I don't agree with it, but I get it. It was free press and publicity. His crap family's name was back in the headlines in a positive way. I don't believe he directly played a role in *that* situation. Then there was the Luca/Madison fiasco. He swore he wasn't involved, and he may not have been, but again, my gut reaction was that he was an indirect player in the game. Now this with Luca and the anonymous envelope. This ties back to him, Marco. I just don't know how, but I promise it does. If anyone can connect the dots it's Madison. Once we have the smoking gun I can end this."

Marco sat scribbling on a piece of Gina's telephone scratch pad. "You're right, Pop. It's *not* Beau. I know who we're looking for," he said, heading for the front door.

"Where are you going?"

"To fix this. I'll be back later. Tell Mom I won't be home for dinner," he answered, then he exited the house.

Before my brain could even begin to process what he was up to, Madison and Frankie walked through the back door. It was time to put on a smile so as to not worry her any more than she already was. Keeping Luca in check these days was a fulltime job. Between that, a baby, and working for me, I refused to add more to her plate. Besides, Marco had this figured out, I hoped. I prayed.

"Where's Marco off to in such a rush?" Madison asked as she handed me my grandson.

"You know Marco. Could be anywhere," I replied as casually as possible.

She turned and looked me straight in the eyes. As amazing of a private investigator Madison was, she excelled at one particularly annoying talent—people reading. "Try again," she challenged.

"I really don't know, *tesoro*."

"What were you two talking about before he left?"

With a sigh I spoke. Madison Santino wasn't going to let this one go. If I brushed her off she'd press and press until she got what she so desired. "The envelope. Marco believes he knows who sent it. He scribbled something down on a notepad and left."

"This pad right here?" she inquired.

"Yes. Why?"

Grabbing a pencil from the junk drawer she lightly stroked the side of the lead against the blank sheet. As she picked it up, her eyes went wide. "Damn it, Marco," she hissed.

"What's the matter?" A healthy sense of concern filled my tone.

"I have to go. Watch Frankie. Tell Luca I had to run to the store. I'll be right back," she said rushed, racing out of the door with Marco's note crumpled in her hand.

I stood in the kitchen baffled, but with a keen awareness whatever they were up to wasn't good.

Chapter Three

Madison

Smashing the gas while merging onto the highway, I darted my eyes left and right in a desperate attempt to spot Marco's car. In spite of me telling him I was onto something, urging him to wait until we spoke later at dinner, of course he didn't listen. I had a strong feeling he too figured it out or at least had a solid inkling as to whom the real culprit was. After countless hours of sneaking around behind Luca's back, Marco and I worked in stealth—not even Frank was aware of what we were doing. It wasn't until early this morning that the pieces to this shady, insane puzzle slammed together inside of my brain. Though I wasn't one hundred percent certain, my theory was at least practical and sound. Dialing his cell, the line rang several times before he picked up.

"Hello?"

"Marco," I hissed into the air aimed at the speakers in my SUV.

"Kind of busy right now, Mads. Can I call you later?" He asked. His voice sounded a touch off. Besides that, he never called me 'Mads.' Only Luca did.

"Everything all right?" I asked cautiously.

"Oh, yeah. Of course. Mom asked if I could pick up some *popsicles* for the kids."

Popsicles...Crap.

He used our safe word. A word no one else besides us knew about.

"Okay. One quick thing before I let you get back to your errands. Could you grab me a box of that *winter green* tea I like when you're at the store or have you already gone? My sinuses are acting up. It's the only thing that helps." Marco was quick on his feet. If anyone would pick up on the winter green tea bait it was him. Obviously 'winter' referred to the Winters family.

"Haven't made it to the market yet, but *of course* I'll grab that tea for you. Listen, Mads, I have to go. Catch up later? Maybe we could grab a drink at The Tipsy Leprechaun? A nice hot toddy or Long Island iced tea should clear those sinuses right up."

"Always with the Long Island jab. We all can't be Brooklyn boys." I laughed. A sense of relief washed over me. He'd provided enough hints for me to figure out exactly where he was. "All right, my favorite brother-in-law. I'll see you shortly. Love you." Hanging up, I aggressively crossed three lanes of traffic. Spotting a strip mall parking lot to the right of the exit ramp, I pulled in. Slamming the vehicle into park, I grabbed a receipt from a bag in the back seat, frantically scribbling down Marco's clues before I forgot them.

Winter Green.

Long Island Iced Tea.

Hot Toddy.

The Tipsy Leprechaun.

Connecting Winters to Long Island was the easy part. Beau and Maris, Tag and Miranda, Nick and Jillian all lived there. Jackson and Keira lived in Maryland. The two older sisters lived out of state as well—Connecticut, I believed. But Hot Toddy and The Tipsy Leprechaun threw me for a quick second. Digging deep in an attempt to recall every last detail about that family took a minute. I was amped up. Someone had Marco and who knew how much time I had on the clock to locate him before it was too late?

Think, Santino. You can do this.

According to the news from earlier Beau has been hospitalized. The broadcaster didn't say where, what hospital, or what was wrong, so obviously he's not home, and his wife is more than likely with him. Scratch them.

Tag and Miranda are probably with them as well as it's his father who's ill, and he's undoubtedly concerned for Beau's welfare while trolling around for a photo opportunity or interview.

Jackson and the sisters don't reside in New York, but it's not out of the realm of possibility they're here visiting. Where would they stay if they were? With their parents, grandparents, or at a hotel? Did any of them have second homes in New York?

The Tipsy Leprechaun...it's obviously a bar, but where?

After doing a quick internet search, I found that the pub in question was located in Port Washington, New York—the North Shore of Long Island. Tag and Miranda owned a home in Sands Point—the next town over. Their house—Todd Lane. Marco had to be there. Inputting the address into the GPS, shoving the gear shift into drive, I took off like a bat straight out of Hell. I was still in Brooklyn meaning I was about an hour away with moderate traffic. He could hold on. I knew he could.

"Incoming call from Luca Santino," the car assistant's voice spoke through the speakers.

"Hey, babe," I said, struggling to remain as calm as

possible.

"Where are you, Mads?" Noticeable traces of worry and annoyance hung from each word.

"Running a few errands. You?" I lied.

"At my parents' house. When will you be back?"

"Stay on the Jackie Robinson Parkway for the next two point seven miles, then merge onto the Grand Central Parkway," the damn assistant informed blowing my cover.

"Where the hell are you going, Madison?" Luca demanded.

"I'm working, Luca. Okay? I have something I have to do. Depending upon what time I wrap things up, I'll meet you back at either your parents' house or our home," I replied firmly, digging my heels in. If I told him what was up he'd lose the plot and freak out. I loved my husband, dearly, but since the mysterious photograph and note arrived he hadn't been himself. He'd turned into someone I wasn't a huge fan of.

I remember that damn day with extreme clarity. Heavily pregnant, exhausted, and drained from the summer heat, I'd just sat down on the couch. An alert pinged from my cell phone stating someone was at the front door. The thought of having to hoist myself up again and deal with a person caused me to ignore it. The bell never rang, so I assumed it was a delivery. Not wanting to leave anything boxed outside on the porch, with a huff, I begrudgingly retrieved the envelope noting it was addressed to Luca and tossed it on the center island in the kitchen. Then I dozed off waking up to the sounds of a panicked Luca. The video feed from the front camera revealed a young man dressed in a tan courier uniform. After reaching out to the company and speaking with the delivery guy, the parcel in question had been dropped off at one of their many locations. Hours of scanning far too many surveillance cameras revealed absolutely nothing.

"Working for whom because my father insists he has you working on nothing at the moment."

"Listen, babe, I'm doing a favor for Marco. He asked me to look into something and I am. I'll be back before you know it. I have to go so I can focus on the road. I love you and will see you and Frankie soon," I said before clicking the off button. I couldn't be having this conversation with him now. Of course I wanted to tell him the truth, but this way was the only option. Once the Winters were handled and this nightmare came to a close, I'd share everything. Until then, my lips were sealed.

Pressing the gas a little harder, I maneuvered through a sea of cars. My brain needed to quickly formulate what my next move would be once I got to Tag and Miranda's home.

Chapter Four

Jillian

"They're both finally asleep." I sighed, collapsing on the bed beside Nick.

"What did it take?" Nick questioned, raising an eyebrow.

"Three stories, a bunch of songs, and when that didn't work, I bribed them with a trip to the toy store tomorrow. That seemed to do the trick."

"Normally I'd say we shouldn't resort to bribery, but in this case you could've offered them a million bucks a piece *and* my soul and I would've been totally okay with it. Hell, this morning I promised them ice cream for breakfast if they listened to me and got ready quickly, which incidentally is what they ate. Sorry. It had to be done."

Before I could reply, Nick's phone rang. Glancing at the caller ID he exhaled heavily while rolling his eyes.

"Dad. How are you?" he said into the receiver. He rose from the bed and began pacing the length of the room.

Though I couldn't hear exactly what Tag was saying, I didn't need to. Looking at the television, I saw a picture of Beau on the screen. Scrolling below it read Beau had been rushed to the hospital for an undisclosed, sudden illness. Standing, I moved closer to the entertainment unit. My jaw dropped. Nick's fingers ran through his thick salt and pepper hair. His head was down. Reaching for my own phone I dialed Liam. If any new details or gossip had come over the wire he'd be the first to know.

"You've reached Liam Stevens. I'm sorry I can't come to the phone right now, but if you leave your name, a call back number, and a detailed message I will return your call as soon as possible. In the interim have a good day."

Damn it. Freaking voicemail.

"Hey, Liam. It's Jill. Nick's grandfather was taken to the hospital. It's all over the news. If you hear anything, anything at all, shoot me a call or a text. Thanks. Talk soon."

As patiently as possible I waited for Nick to end his conversation with Tag. The second he pulled the phone away from his ear, I pounced.

"What's going on?" I asked. For a while we shared suspicions Beau was up to something and had his hands somehow on the abduction—both abductions, Madison Santino's and Nick's, but we could never figure out how or why. Maybe it was because we really didn't want to know the truth. Ignorance is bliss right? However, aside from that accusatory thought, I had nothing against Maris or Beau. They never treated be poorly like Tag, Miranda, and Nick's siblings had *and* still do. Those shits even treated our children unfairly. Granted, Jordyn was the product of our marriage, whereas Ethan was a reminder of an unavoidable, extra marital affair on Nick's part, but that didn't make Ethan any less mine or related to them. He still had Winters blood coursing through his veins.

To avoid a public relations nightmare, our team

crafted a somewhat fact-based story about Ethan. We gave an interview with a popular celebrity magazine stating Ethan had been adopted and now our family was complete. It wasn't a total lie. I had adopted Ethan and Ally Newman drew up papers stating Nick had as well. We also had his birth certificate changed to read our names. Luca and Madison Santino, the only two known individuals with knowledge of the truth, agreed to and signed a non-disclosure agreement. Our secret was safe. It was no one's business except ours as to how we gained the beautiful little boy in our lives. In spite of Ethan, formally Tanner, being biologically tied to Sarah Davis, the reality was, the moment I found out Nick had a child I instantly wanted and loved them. That desire grew stronger when I heard Sarah had been killed. No child should have to suffer because of the sins of their parents. Nick kept prodding if I was truly okay with him fathering Sarah's baby, but Ethan wasn't the result of conscious adultery.

Public relations felt it best to not only introduce our family in print, but to have Jordyn and Ethan pop up every now and again on *This Just In*. Viewers loved those segments and so did we. Every single time Lyla would let go of Jordyn and Ethan's little hands and they'd come running to me—always me first, then to Nick, I fell in love with them all over again. The life I'd dreamed of was finally mine.

"Apparently Beau collapsed in an alley. A passerby saw him and called nine-one-one. The doctors say they believe he suffered a major heart attack." Nick appeared caught somewhere between shocked, concerned, and a touch detached from the situation in general.

"Is he going to be okay?"

"He's conscious now. They are pumping him full of medication to keep him stabilized. Heart surgery isn't out of the question. My parents are with him. I offered to go to the hospital, but they told me not to—that they'll keep me posted." Nick's tone revealed a deep sadness.

"If you want to go, go, Nick. They don't control your actions. If you're worried, let's head up to the hospital so you can see what's happening for yourself. I realize it's the nanny's night off, but she's in her room downstairs. If we tell her it's an emergency, throw some money at the problem, and give her tomorrow night off, she'll help out," I urged.

"I don't know, Jill," Nick said, rubbing his temples.

"You do know. Come on," I said while giving myself a quick once over in the dressing mirror.

With a small, brief smile, he followed me out of our bedroom.

****

"I'm going to stay the night," Nick said as we exited Beau's hospital room.

By the time we arrived, Tag, Miranda, and Maris were preparing to leave. Beau was in the cardiac care unit tucked away from the public in a heavily guarded suite. He was receiving round the clock attention and was in extremely capable hands. However, Beau was severely weak, which was causing him to fade in and out of consciousness. Perhaps it was the medication or his age, but he looked frail lying in a hospital bed with IVs and all sorts of machines hooked up to him. The moment Nick saw him, my husband's face knotted with intense anxious apprehension. The doctors were still unsure if he'd require an operation and warned that he was far from out of the woods. When Nick attempted to press

Beau about what led up to this, Beau mumbled a few words which triggered Miranda to jump down Nick's throat over how inappropriate his line of questioning was. Backing down, we stood in the farthest corner of the room until they left.

"I'll stay with you," I offered.

"No. The kids need you more. Be there for them when they wake up. I'll keep in touch with any updates. Please, Jill."

If Nick wasn't as broken and down I would've argued, but now wasn't the time.

"I'll call Liam and tell him to run a repeat for tomorrow's show. Keep me posted," I said softly, kissing his lips.

"Thank you. I'll be home soon."

With that, I headed to the valet booth. Digging in my purse for the ticket, I looked up to hand it to someone, but no one was there.

"Damn it. Tell me they're closed for the night and I have to break into the key cabinet, then schlep through a parking garage to find my freaking car," I groaned.

"That won't be necessary, Jillian," a familiar voice spoke. Before I could positively confirm the owner, he spoke again. "This is my lucky day. Four birds. One stone. Only a handful left to collect, but I'm confident that will happen real soon, especially now that I have you. Get your ass in the fucking car and you better not make a sound or I swear to God I'll make you pay dearly."

"Jackson?" I questioned completely confused over what was going down.

"Get in the fucking car, Jillian," he grunted.

My eyes rapidly darted left then right. What the hell

was going on?

"No. Not until you tell me why," I demanded.

"You've got two choices, lady. The easy way where you do as you're told, or the hard way where I make you do what I want. The choice is yours, but that offer expires in about ten seconds," he warned, removing a silver handgun from the glovebox, then pushing the passenger side door open.

Not allowing any part of my being to show fear, I took a deep breath before speaking. "Where's Nick? Is he still with your grandfather or is he in the trunk?" I asked flat out, dead serious.

"My brother is fine. I'll deal with him and his tree hugging bullshit later. Times up, Jillian."

For some reason I believed his words. Jackson was a lot of things—sneaky, shady, slimy, stupid, and spoke out of both sides of his mouth like most politicians, but his expression and body language suggested he currently was telling the absolute truth. Making sure to drop my valet ticket on a sticky piece of discard gum on the ground, I placed my hand behind my back, quickly signing the letters to Jackson's name. I wasn't sure if there was an exterior camera, but I was certain there was one in the lobby I stood in front of. Once Liam realized I was missing—possibly Nick as well, he'd make damn sure he reviewed whatever close circuit television footage was available. He'd read the cues and figure it out from there.

"All right. You win," I said, sliding into the vehicle. Once on the road, I turned in my seat to face him. "First, congratulations on the party nomination. With Beau as your grandfather and campaign manager you're a shoe in for president. Second, what are you doing, Jackson?

Have you lost your mind? I'm acutely aware you and your family can't stomach me and that's totally fine—rule of thumb, never take criticism from anyone you wouldn't take advice from, but what do Nick and I have to do with your life? We live in our own bubble far away from yours. We never comment on or criticize the Winters Family, ever. If it's our vote you're after, well, earn it like every other politician has to."

"What's my problem? First, you and Nick know far too much. Second, you're damn right. I fully intend on winning and will, once I tidy everything up." His eyes remained firmly fixed on the road.

"What's to tidy? Again, Nick and I don't bother you, nor do we interfere with your business," I reiterated.

"Just shut up, Jillian. Look out the damn window and be quiet for once in your fucking life," he spat.

Not wanting to rock the boat any more than I already had, I followed his direction. I knew exactly where we were going—Tag and Miranda's house. He and Keira moved into their pool house immediately after he received the nomination. Granted, it had been some time since I'd been to their home, but I still remembered the way. I mean, who could forget the road leading to Hell's threshold? Not many.

Once the massive wrought iron gates opened, he navigated the car around to the back of the main house.

"Get out," he barked.

"Once you do whatever it is you plan on doing to me and then Nick, what are you going to do to Ethan and Jordyn?"

"Who?"

A sudden panic gripped me. If something happened to both Nick and me, who would care for our children?

"My son and daughter. Your niece and nephew."

"They'll make for fantastic press and photo ops. Now, get out."

"And go where?" I replied in the most uncaring tenor one could muster. This son of a bitch just suggested my flesh and blood would become props in his sick game.

"You're one royal pain in the ass, as well as queen of the bitches."

"Many wouldn't view that as a compliment, but I do, so thanks. Now again, where are we going? Why am I here? And what do you want? I've played by your rules. It's time for some answers, or the Glock in my purse will find its way into my hand and I will not utilize any control as my finger pulls the trigger. Self-defense, baby. Charles Downey got me off once. I'm confident he can do it again," I threatened.

"You're not doing anything other than what I tell you. Try something funny and I'll be the one shouting self-defense, *baby*," he warned, roughly taking hold of my left arm. He snatched and tossed my pocketbook into the backseat of his vehicle. With his other hand, he pressed something deep into my lower back. One could only assume it was his weapon.

Forcefully shoving me around the back of Tag's house, he stopped by the pool house's front door. Releasing his grip, he fumbled for the keys in his pocket. Inserting them into the lock, he pushed me through. Practically dragging my frame through a door in the kitchen, he led me down into the finished basement. There, sitting in what resembled a living room with their hands and feet zip tied together was Liam, Marco Santino, and Madison Santino.

"Welcome to the party, Jill," Liam muttered as a fat drop of blood slid down his cheek, hitting the white tiled floor.

Chapter Five

Madison

"What the hell?" Jillian Winters hissed. Her mouth dropped open as she took in the situation she'd just walked into.

She was shoved into the chair next to mine and received the same treatment as we all had—zip tied wrists and ankles compliments of Jackson Winters. After satisfied with his work, Jackson returned to the stairs.

"I'll be back. While I'm away, it's highly advised you don't try anything funny. There's no way out of here, so there's no point. I have all of your cell phones, wallets, purses, keys, vehicles—everything, which means *I*, not you, own your lives," he warned before exiting.

"Is everyone okay?" Jillian asked calmly.

"Oh yeah. Living the dream, lady," Marco snapped.

"We're not doing this again, Marco," Liam replied. "Get your head in the game because we don't know how much time we have before he returns, nor do we know what his next move will be. You can be pissed later. Does anyone know where you are, Jill?"

"No. I left Nick at the hospital with Beau. He thinks I'm on my way home. I'm going to assume when he gets back to the house later tonight or tomorrow morning the nanny will tell him I never got there." She paused. "Any idea what's going on?"

"Really? For starters, your brother-in-law

kidnapped us. Why, you ask? Easy. We're his '*October Surprise*.' How does a shady politician avoid skeletons flying out of his closet right before their big inaugural day? He takes a bullet to our heads, then buries us in shallow graves. Some months, maybe years later while the cops search for some missing rich girl, cadaver dogs will dig up our rotted corpses. Hopefully there will be enough of each of us left so the authorities can identify us, and our families can lay whatever pieces were found to rest. I don't give a shit about anyone in this room, me included, besides Maddy. So, my goal is to get her the fuck out of here, then deal with your whack job family. As long as my sister-in-law gets home safely to my brother and nephew, I'm good," Marco ranted.

The touching sentiment over how his focus was on me and my wellbeing temporarily warmed my heart. Marco Santino may have been a lot of things both good and bad, and he may not have been the most educated man in the world, but his fierce protection and loyalty to his family was beyond anything I'd ever witnessed. It was stronger than his father's, which was something I didn't think was possible. However, I knew Marco, well. He was frustrated and angry. When he'd get like this nothing good ever came of things. While Marco and Liam conversed, I spent the time quietly loosening my wrist and ankle ties. I could've commiserated with them, but why? What good would that have done? Emotions cloud better judgement and clear thinking which is exactly what led me to walking right into this mess.

Once I reached Tag's house the PI in me snooped around. Jackson nailed me from behind kicking the back of my knees causing me to fall. Once I was on the ground, he grabbed me by my hair and dragged me into the pool house basement where Marco and another man sat. After exchanging a warning look with Marco, I opted to keep my mouth shut and not demand answers of any kind. The other person in question introduced himself as Liam Stevens. Having intimate knowledge of the Nick and Jillian Winters case I knew who he was. Liam wasn't fuming or enraged, but rather calm and focused. Marco, on the other hand, was another story. He thrashed around the moment Jackson left in an attempt to break the chair or sever his ties.

"You're wasting your time," Liam suggested.

"Maybe, but sitting around and waiting to see what happens next isn't going to work for me, especially not when my sister-in-law is now a part of this," Marco replied, still slamming the chair legs against the tile.

"Liam is right. We have to go about this smart," I added, finally freeing my wrists.

"Okay, so what's the plan?" Marco's tone dripped with annoyance that I'd beat him to the punch of freeing my limbs first.

"I don't know, *yet*. What I do know for sure is we're all connected to this jackass. I suggest we figure that out first before formulating any sort of escape strategy."

"Jackson is just going to tie you back up when he returns. I'm also fairly confident when I say that he'll be pissed off as well," Liam stated.

"There's not a handcuff, zip tie, chain—whatever, that I can't get out of," I shot back, freeing everyone except Liam. "I can leave you the way you are if you'd like. Dealer's choice."

"Let me out. There's safety in numbers," he replied with a heavy sigh.

Once everyone had been freed I began an initial

investigation of the space. Several small rectangular windows adorned the top perimeter of the main room. Unsure if anyone of us could squeeze out, I had Marco hoist me up to examine the structure. The frame was far too narrow for even my son to crawl out of. The basement appeared to be set up as an apartment for perhaps out of town visitors. The main area was tastefully decorated with an oversized, L shaped, cream leather, reclining couch. Two similar fabric rockers were placed on each side. A glass coffee table and two end tables were positioned around the furniture, all which faced a light oak entertainment unit.

"Check out what's in there, Marco. Maybe there's a television, cable box, or WIFI wires we can do something with," I requested pointing to the cabinet.

Exploring farther down the short hallway off of the living room, I discovered there were two bedrooms—one with two twin sized beds and one with a queen-sized bed. Again, each area was decorated with time, care, and thought. Though simple and plain décor had been used, nothing appeared threatening about anything. A Jack and Jill bathroom was found through one of the bedroom doors.

"Could you nose around in the bedrooms, Liam? Look in the closets, drawers, under the bed—basically look everywhere," I asked.

With a nod, Liam disappeared into the master bedroom.

"Jillian, would you mind doing the same with the bathroom?" Even though nothing appeared out of the ordinary—the space encompassed a toilet, double vanity, large garden style tub, and a standalone shower the entire Santino family could've gotten into, it was worth a shot.

Lastly, there was an open, airy, eat-in kitchen off to the other side of the living room. Maple cabinets lined one wall. On the other side was a fridge beside a long, taupe, marble countertop. A sink/garbage disposal combo, a dishwasher, and stove were on the main exterior wall. Opening the refrigerator, I saw it was fully stocked with essentials—as were the cabinets. Dishes, flatware, pots, pans—whatever necessary to create a simple meal was neatly stored. Behind two accordion doors was a washer and dryer. To the naked eye this was the perfect place to kick back and relax while visiting family or friends. Private, quiet, and far away from the world's prying eyes.

"Anything?" I questioned when everyone returned to the main area.

"There's a television with a traditional cable hookup. Nothing special. It turns on," Marco answered flipping through a series of channels. "No Wi-Fi hardline or router. Unless these people live in the Stone Age, I suspect they have internet, but it's wireless. Without a password or a device it's useless."

"The bedrooms are just that—bedrooms. Clean, with nothing in the dressers or closets," Liam reported.

"Same with the bathroom. It's stocked with toiletries, but otherwise nothing of interest exists inside of it. No secrets. Anyone sweep for bugs?" Jillian inquired.

"Yeah. It's clean out here," Marco said.

"Same," Liam added.

"The kitchen is a kitchen. Stocked with food, but no visible wire taps or cameras," I said.

"Well, for starters this place is not up to code. Any

inhabitable space requires two forms of egress. There's one there which takes you to the main floor, but a cricket couldn't squeeze out of these windows. So that means this apartment is either illegal, which could be the case for regular people like us, but not for the Winters family—that's all a wealthy, in your face all the time political family needs; a front-page story about how they skirted town codes and laws, or there's another hidden door somewhere. Have you ever been here, Jill?" Liam asked.

"A few times many years ago when Nick and I were dating, but I was never down here. This is without a doubt Tag and Miranda's home—the pool house more specifically. In fact, this property was Nick's predominant residence when he was growing up. Beau and Maris don't live too terribly far from here, but you already know that, Marco, based off a previous visit to him some years ago. You should've popped a cap up Beau, Tag, and Jackson's asses then. What a wasted opportunity, but I digress. We need to try to find the other door or a large window if there is one."

"Who died and made you the boss?" Marco snarked.

"I realize when your father dies you actually become *the boss*, but down here in the trenches you're one of us. We can either go at each other's throats accomplishing nothing, or work as a team. I vote for the latter," Jillian replied, raising one well-manicured eyebrow.

Moving to Marco's side, I placed a hand on his shoulder, compressing the area gently. "*Non abbiamo scelta*," I whispered.

With a nod he positioned his hand on top of mine.

"Who hit you?" Marco directed his question at Liam.

"Jackson. I was leaving the studio from the back lot. I went in off the clock to make sure the equipment and set were put back in proper order because new flooring was installed the night before. All I remember was taking my key fob out of my pocket, then someone clocked me square in the jaw. They put a blindfold over my eyes, shoved me in the back seat of a somewhat small car—I only know that fact because I couldn't move around, nor stretch my legs, and here I am. When the scarf was removed, I realized it was Jackson. I tried to prod him for answers, but he was in a hurry and ignored me. Next came you about two hours later, then Madison, and lastly Jill. You said he nabbed you at a gas station when you were buying cigarettes."

"Yeah. I was heading here actually because I was confident Jackson was the one that's been screwing with my brother. I stopped at a gas station, went inside to grab a pack of smokes, then exited. As I approached my car, I saw that all four tires had been slashed. A few seconds later, someone pressed a gun to my back and ordered me into their vehicle. And, here I am."

"How did you know Marco was here?" Liam asked me.

"I called him to see where he was. We've been working for months on closing in on whoever was threatening my husband. I was following a paper and money trail, while Marco was canvassing enemies of the Winters family. We knew what happened to Luca had something to do with them, but we couldn't pin it on anyone without concrete evidence. Once we had what we needed, we planned to deal with the issue head on. When I spoke with Marco earlier he subtly dropped clues. It wasn't too terribly difficult to connect the dots."

"Jackson let you keep your phone?" Liam asked Marco.

"No. I spotted Jackson as I exited the gas station convenient store. Then, I noticed my car. I was still standing in from of the store when Maddy called. Like she said, I dropped a few hints I knew she'd be able to string together, though right now a part of me wishes I hadn't. The last thing I intended was for her to end up in harm's way. Jackson took my phone the second I got into his vehicle—which you are correct, is a small sports car. I went without a fight because the only one who could provide me with rock solid evidence was him, and I was hoping to obtain that. Unfortunately, hindsight is twenty/twenty and I should've beaten him to death right then and there. Just to clarify, Jackson took everyone's wallets, purses, and mobile devices?"

Everyone nodded in agreement.

"Okay. Let's sum total this mess. I was abducted from the station's back parking lot. There are no cameras back there, but my car might still be in the lot. Marco gets taken from a gas station which may or may not have cameras, but his car could still be there as well. Madison gets caught sneaking around here, which means your vehicle is pretty close by, but nevertheless, abandoned. I'd bet my sweet black ass this place is chockfull of security devices. And lastly, Jill was taken from the hospital so your SUV is possibly still in a hospital parking garage and hospitals are typically under constant surveillance. Unless Jackson is working with other people who are running around disposing of vehicles, he's got a lag time. That could help us."

"When I left the emergency room I spotted four cameras in the lobby. I didn't see any outside mainly because my attention was on finding a valet to get my SUV, then my focus shifted to Jackson. However, before I got into his car I signed his name behind my back in ASL. I did that because I knew you'd go looking for me and would check security footage first. Sadly, that plan will not pan out," Jillian said.

"Luca," I whispered to no one in particular. Sudden realization struck that Luca might be next, or Jackson would go after him and possibly Frank to murder them. Maybe Salvatore or another Santino was his new prime target. Quite possibly he'd abduct my son. Anxiety broke free within me causing a panic attack of epic proportions to overtake my once levelheaded mind. I raced up the steps to the locked door; every ounce of energy inside of me yanking on the knob. When that didn't work, I resorted to pounding my fists on the wall and screaming.

"Hey, hey, hey," Marco said, taking hold of my waist from behind. "Shhh. Deep breaths, sweetheart." Slowly he turned my body to face his.

"Luca," I yelled in his face.

"Luca, Pop, Mom, *Zio*, the boys, our sisters, Frankie, your family—everyone is going to be okay. Luca is a beast. He's smart, a skilled fighter, and one hell of a shot. The guy can withstand a beating and walk away just fine if need be. Pop is exactly the same. Luca will realize we're MIA soon, if he hasn't already. He will deploy *Zio*, who will get our soldiers out pounding the pavement. Pop will put two and two together real fast and reach out to the other *families* in the area. Luca will file a missing person report for us. Our family as well as the other four families will be hyper vigilant and go into lockdown mode. There are parts of this business you don't know about yet. There's a protocol to follow when something like this happens. All will be well, but I need you to trust me. Can you do that for me, sweetheart?"

With a nod, he pulled me into a tight embrace. Though his words provided some comfort, intense worry still lingered within my bones.

"We're going to figure this out, Madison," Liam said in his most comforting voice once I returned to the living area. "Hopefully a camera picked up something from one of us. I'm going to get the ball rolling here and assume, apologies if I'm wrong or out of line, we're all here because we've crossed the Winters family at some point. For Jill and me, aside from her being the most hated daughter-in-law in existence, it was because of the Warren Lessor fiasco. For Marco and Madison, I'd bet it has to do with them and Luca uncovering or knowing something they shouldn't. Perhaps they dug something up when they were trying to find Madison when she went missing. It's not out of the realm of possibility to speculate the Santino and Winters families might have engaged in a business crossover at some point within recent years. Politicians and the Mafia are often tied together. No offence, Marco," Liam said.

"What the hell with everyone's obsession with calling my family a *Mafia Crime Organization*? We're in real-estate investments and waste management," Marco scoffed, still close by my side, lovingly rubbing my shoulders. Perhaps it was his way of keeping my body stationary. Whatever the case, his touch continued to soothe my soul.

"I like what you did there—waste management. Cute. However, what your family is or is not, is not the point of the story, and lying about who and what we really are isn't going to help get us out of here any quicker. You're the *Don's* son, next in line for the throne. Your brother, her husband, will more than likely become your underboss when your father retires, but Luca Santino is currently acting as your family's *consigliere*. Personally I don't care. Do you, Jill?"

"Old news," Jillian answered, casually flopping onto the couch.

"Once we bust the hell out of here, I can assure that none of us will be inviting the others over for a dinner party or ringing anyone to hang out. We'll go back to our lives and everyone's secret will remain buried deep within this room. If we don't work together we've got nothing. If that's the case, we may as well all lay down and die right now," Liam rationalized. "Cards on the table time. Let's start with the Santinos, then work our way out to the Winters, because the Stevens don't know anything. I'm simply collateral damage."

I exchanged a look with Marco, who nodded in response.

"What do you want to know?" I asked.

Chapter Six

Jillian

"How are our families connected, because I know they are?" I asked.

During the Madison Langmore abduction I attempted to pump the information out of Madison's then paramour Luca Santino, but he refused to budge. People like him were often hesitant about trusting others, but more so when negative pasts were involved. Without realizing it his lack of response spoke volumes.

"Are you *sure* you want to be made aware of the *entire* truth, or would you prefer an edited version? Marco and I sincerely want to be completely transparent with you, but I also don't want to hurt you with certain details. Sometimes people make mistakes and those mistakes trickle down crushing the hearts and souls of others. I've been on both sides of that equation and I wouldn't wish to inflict that pain on anyone," Madison said. A sweet, kind, understanding softness filled her jewel green eyes.

Marco's hands remained decisively attached to her slender shoulders. I wasn't sure if he was protecting her or if he had intimate feelings for her. Their shared body language suggested a more than familiar connection. Picking up on my assessment of her and her brother-in-law, she spoke again. "Despite what you may believe of my family—that we're Mafia trash, we're not. Yes, we are all members of the Santino Family and yes, Frank Santino is known as the *Don* of our clan, but we're all good, upstanding members of society. My father-in-law is an amazing man who gives back so much to his community every chance he can, but since the papers never report on that, no one knows. Personally, I think he likes it that way, but that's all part of his charm—charm you've never been privileged to experience. My husband is a talented, remarkable, brilliant, established attorney who worked his ass off for every cent he's ever earned. And this man right here, my brother-in-law, well, there's no one in this world who could hold a candle to him. He's incredible. Marco would throw himself on a live grenade to save the ones he loves, no questions asked. He'd go to Hell and back if necessary to help those around him. He also happens to be my and my husband's best friend. Don't mistake loyalty and family for lust and adultery. I hope one day you'll be able to experience unfettered faith in someone other than your spouse. We're Mafia, not adulterers or criminals." With her declaration Marco pulled her closer.

"I appreciate your empathy and desire to protect my feelings, but I'm a big girl who can withstand any shot that's aimed at me," I said, actively choosing to not respond to her assessment of my unspoken assessment.

"As you wish, but if at any point you want for me to stop, just say the word. Years ago, after you caught Nick in bed with Kelly Greenly, he ran to Beau to fix the problem. Beau hired my father-in-law to make the situation go away. Frank and one of his associates, Salvatore—I believe you've met, found her and offered her a brand-new life in a brand-new state with a new job, car, condo, and a crap ton of cash in exchange for her silence. She happily agreed. However, this wasn't enough for Beau. He wanted my father-in-law to *whack* Kelly, which is something we, as a family and organization do not do. Because of movies and the freaking media what we do has been depicted incorrectly. We're here to help when the police and Feds don't or can't. We don't sell drugs, there's no prostitution, and we most certainly are not murderers for hire. Anyway, Beau was pissed off when Frank said no. As far as I'm aware, Kelly was offed by someone Beau commissioned *after* Frank told him to screw off. Beau also conveniently never paid Frank for his time. Fast forward a bit to Nick's abduction. Your grandfather-in-law called upon Frank again. Guess what? Marco located Nick within less than twenty-four hours. How? I don't know. Marco has his ways. Ways not even I as a private investigator are familiar with. Marco found Beau, told him, and provided him with the address to that house of horrors. What did Beau do? He stood like a little bitch in front of the cameras for a press conference ten minutes later. He always knew where Nick was—*always*. He did nothing to help though because for the first time in a while the Winters name was back on top. Once again he screwed my family out of their rightfully earned money. Sometime later Beau called upon Frank for a third time—right before I was abducted, over Sarah Davis blackmailing Nick. This time Frank told him to go scratch," Madison explained. A certain amount of venom resided within her voice, but her loyalty to the Santinos rang through loud and clear.

"Okay. I understand how we're connected, but that doesn't explain why we're all here now," I said. To be honest, none of what she'd said bothered me or caused any form of shock.

"We all know too much. If one of us spoke, Jackson's career would be dead in the water. How do you think the media would perceive the Winters family if they knew Beau, the most beloved vice president in the history of ever knew where is grandson was and left him to rot? That he called upon the Mafia for help not once, not twice, but three times and then stiffed us on the bill?"

"True. Did any of them know Warren or Noah Lessor? Did they stage Nick's or your abduction?"

"That's the beauty of all of this—none of them knew a damn thing about the Lessors'. When Nick returned home, you received a threatening letter from an unknown party. That was Sarah Davis. How do I know? Handwriting analysis. Nick was reluctant to turn the letter over to Ally Newman, but eventually he did. It happened to come across my desk after the fact, and I did my job, but I was already safe at home, and Nick's sweet little boy had been placed in your custody. Plus, Sarah was dead, so it didn't matter anymore. Everyone was back where they were supposed to be, alive and well. Now the note that my husband received was penned by a different hand—a masculine one. Over the course of a few weeks, Marco and I took a ride to Jackson, Tag, and Beau's homes and did a little dumpster diving. We were able to collect a sample of their penmanship from random bits of trash, but it wasn't enough. The highest match was only seventy percent from Tag. So how do you trap someone? Easy. He's a politician which means he has tons of enemies, and those enemies love to dish dirt to anyone who is willing to listen. When we had even the tiniest nugget of information, I picked whatever the hell it was apart, until all of that picking led to a paper trail which led us to a crap ton of mismanaged illegal money. That's where Marco and I stopped, not because we wanted to, but because Jackson had other plans for us."

"How did you figure out it was Jackson and not Tag behind everything?"

"We never said Tag wasn't behind this. What we said was Jackson is the main suspect. What I realized just before Jackson snagged me was Jackson has been forging his father's signature on a multitude of documents. That's why Tag's handwriting only matched at seventy percent. The letter sent to my brother was meant to mimic Tag's handwriting, but if you looked at it close enough, Jackson's handwriting blended through a bit. Maybe Tag knew. Maybe he didn't. But if the press or the government ever got their hands on what we found with Tag's name on it—forged or not, well, your entire family would be fucked on every conceivable level, plain and simple," Marco said.

"What did you find from all of your digging?"

"The usual—high priced call girls, illegal fundraising, payoffs to criminals, hush money, misappropriated funds, offshore accounts…all the good stuff that would've caused a scandal and for Tag and Jackson to be dumped by their party. If we would've had more time it would've been worthy enough information for Luca to legally put them all away for a lifetime. Currently, with you and Liam gone, I'd bet my sweet ass Nick isn't safe. Jackson will want to put a stop to him as well out of sheer fear he's aware of more than he should be. With my family out of the picture no one will ever be made aware of Beau, Tag, and Jackson's shady ways. Jackson realized his threat to Luca was foolish because he's been experiencing serious clapback from it. He knows we're digging. He knows we're on to him. Now he's stuck in a real Catch-22 of sorts. He has to not only off me and Marco, but the entire Santino family. There's a ton of us. He'll never be able to accomplish that goal. For the moment, snagging me and Marco, the two most important people to my husband is a way to perhaps scare Luca into submission. It won't work. Luca is a bull. A real gun with no safety these days. Jackson should be running scared," Madison informed, currently walking in circles as her fingers vigorously rubbed her temples.

"Are you okay, Maddy?" Marco asked. His words were laced with deep concern. His loyalty and shared bond with his sister-in-law were unlike anything I'd ever witnessed, causing me to truly believe her little speech before was nothing more than bullshit. If anything, he was at least hot in the pants for her.

"I feel horribly nauseous, exhausted, and have a throbber of a headache."

"Why don't you go lay down for a little while? I'll rest with you. Okay?" Marco moved to where she stood and wrapped his muscular arms around her waist.

For a fleeting moment she rested her head against his broad chest. "Yeah, I think I will." With that, she and Marco disappeared into one of the back bedrooms. Once the sound of a door shutting and locking was heard, I walked to Liam's side.

"I don't have any answers, Jill," he said.

"Neither do I. It's a wait and see game right now. Eventually, someone will realize one of us is missing and will alert the authorities. I'm not shocked by the Santino tie-in though. Are you?"

"No, but we need those two on our side. All they see

is them versus us. That won't work if we want to survive this."

"Mafia mentality, but I applaud their thinking. Had this not have happened, they would've unearthed something solid and substantial, approached Jackson, and turned the table on him by either blackmailing him, or finding a way to slam his ass behind bars for life. I'm somewhat familiar with Madison's husband. Luca Santino is not only a product of Ally Newman's training, but he's *also* a product of his lifelong environment. Even though Madison says Luca would've pressed for prison, I wouldn't put it past any of them to have caused an accident which ended Jackson's pathetic life. They won't admit that, but I guarantee that was their plan all along." Over the years I'd done more than my fair share of research into their and other crime families. They were all cut from the same cloth. Brilliant bullies who lived like each day was their last.

"Don't underestimate their, especially *his*, intelligence."

"Who? Luca?"

"No. Marco. That guy is as crazy as a shit house rat, but in the same breath, as clever as a fox."

"I'm aware. There's more that they're not sharing."

"If we can get them on our team, they will. While they sleep it off, I propose we tear this place apart to see if we can locate a hidden door or something. Like I said before, legal basement apartments require two ways in and out. Let's hope this place has that."

Chapter Seven

Marco

As if this day could get any worse, here I was holding Maddy's hair back as she puked her guts up. Having known her fairly well, there was no way this was a reaction to fear. Something else was up. What? I had no freaking clue, but I prayed it wasn't anything too terribly serious.

"That's right. Get it all out, sweetheart," I said using my free hand to rub her back.

I knew that stupid bitch Jillian Winters thought I had a thing for Maddy. I could clearly see her immature assumptions in her accusatory, judgmental eyes. No. Never. Don't get me wrong. Maddy is an attractive, highly intelligent, firecracker of a woman, but she's my sister and a close friend. Viewing her otherwise was disgusting, but most people were these days. Not many understood the sanctity of family relationships, never mind knew what loyalty actually meant. Besides, my heart belonged to someone else. Though no one was aware of that little fact, it didn't matter. Perhaps I should've brought my girl into the fold. I'd thought about it, many times actually, but I could never pull the trigger. If I had, I'd have left her vulnerable and exposed to this murderous world—something I'd helped her escape from a long time ago.

Most individuals around me believe I'm a moron.

Yeah, okay. Furthest thing from it. A hothead, sure. Dumb? Nope. I may not have a fancy degree hanging on the wall from some overpriced university, but my wealth of knowledge is far superior to theirs. I can survive. They can't. I can walk through a shady neighborhood and come out untouched. They can't. Hell, it wasn't until recently that my own brother finally realized who I was and what I was capable of. It doesn't matter much though. Let whoever think whatever. I've got nothing to prove to anyone. All of the scars that decorate my body were earned. Some out of stupidity—a learning curve based off of a bad temper and immaturity, and others out of fierce protection based on allegiance. I may be a *'goodfella,'* but I'm a good man first and foremost.

After Maddy finished throwing up, she leaned her seated back against a cream tiled wall. Her head rested in her hands which were supported by her knees. Tears streamed down her flushed cheeks.

"Hey, Maddy. We're going to be okay. I promise. I'll get us out of here. It might take a hot second, but before you know it, you'll be back home with Luca and Frankie," I assured, crouching down beside her and softly touching her shoulder.

"I know you will, Marco. It's not that. I've been in a situation like this before, but the last time I was alone. With you here, I'm confident all will be well in short order."

"Then what is it? Are you sick?"

"Sort of. I think I might be pregnant," she said. Her quick, short bouts of hysterical sobbing resembled the sound of a muted machine gun.

Son of a bitch.

Granted, had she told me this yesterday or any other

day for that matter, the news would've been met with pure happiness. I loved my nieces and nephew—especially Frankie. That kid had a giant splash of me inside of him. Whenever someone would suggest we were two peas in a pod my heart would swell with pride over that. I was the first one at the hospital. The first one to hold him and feed him in the nursery. Hell, his first word was *Zio*, then he pointed his chubby finger at me. I was there the day he took his first steps, which were towards me, and was honored beyond all reason when Luca asked me to be his son's godfather. Frankie was smart and as sharp as a tack. One day he'd replace me and when that day came, I'd be more than happy to pass the torch. Let's be honest. I'm not too terribly old, but having a child at my age? By the time that child came into this world I'd already be well into my late fifties. Who the hell wants to be mistaken as their own kid's grandfather?

"That's awesome news. Isn't that what you wanted? Another baby? Haven't you been trying with Luca?"

"I've been. Luca not so much."

"Does Luca know?"

"No. I had a suspicion, but I wasn't going to say anything until I saw the doctor. I'm two months late."

"Okay. So time is of the essence with getting out of here."

Helping her off of the floor, I led her to the bed. The room she ran into only had one queen sized mattress in it, but it was fine. She could have it and I'd take the floor. It certainly wouldn't be the first time I slept in uncomfortable quarters. Curling onto her side she exhaled heavily.

"I'll be back in a second," I said before exiting.

Heading to the kitchen I saw Jillian and Liam investigating an area in the living room.

"Is Madison all right?" Liam asked.

"Yeah." I brushed his concern off.

"Hold on," Jillian said, pushing past me to rummage through the refrigerator and pantry. A moment later she handed me a can of ginger ale and a sleeve of Saltines. "This will help calm her stomach." She paused to examine my face. "I'm neither deaf, nor dumb. We could hear her vomiting and crying. That means she's either got some sort of stomach bug—let's hope that's not the case, is stressed out beyond belief, which is doubtful being she's been in a situation like this before and is a heavily trained investigator, *or* she's pregnant. I'm going to go out on a limb and say, congratulations, Uncle Marco. So again, take the drink and crackers. I'll see if I can find anything cinnamon around here. That helps with the nausea," she added, holding the items out in front of her.

"Thanks."

I found Maddy fast asleep when I returned. Placing the soda and crackers on her bedside table, I snatched a pillow from the bed. Moments later Liam knocked quietly.

"Clean blankets and a few extra pillows from the trunk in our room. I thought you could use them."

With a curt nod I accepted his gesture.

"Listen, Marco. I'm aware Jill can be, at times, a bit rough around the edges and that you three share an undesirable family history, but we're not the enemy—or at least, I'm not. My surname is Stevens *not* Winters. I've known and have worked with Jill for years. I've also gotten caught up in several of her schemes, my personal favorite being the Warren Lessor bullshit where I took a bullet to the leg. Nick isn't a bad person either. Misguided and entitled at times he, for the most part, is a good, solid, standup guy. Jill is like a daughter to me. The same way you side with your family—blood or not, is exactly how I operate, which is why I'm standing here attempting to call a truce. Madison is related to you by marriage, but I'd bet you'd throw yourself in front of a bus for her the same way you'd do for your brother. Love and loyalty are powerful forces."

"Good guy, huh?" I scoffed.

"He's more aware of his family's doings than you know, but for better or worse, family is family. If you knew something shady about your grandfather would you pick at it or choose to ignore it?"

"Depends on what it is."

"Would you turn your father into the authorities, Marco? You know what he does and exactly who he is. Come on now."

"I wouldn't. I'd rather die." No truer words had ever been spoken.

"Exactly. It doesn't matter which side your family fights for—good or evil, there's still a tie that binds you, an unbreakable bond. Nick is cognizant of Beau, Tag, and Jackson's shady shit. In all fairness, he stays away from his brother and father and their business dealings. His weakness is Beau, but he suspects Beau had his sticky fingers all over both Lessor incidents. Since then he's kept a distance. As for him running to his grandfather to clean up his messes when he was younger, haven't we all gone to someone we trust for assistance during times of crisis? It's not an excuse, but the man Nick was ten years ago is most certainly not the man he is today. I can assure you that I've personally witnessed his growing up stage." Liam paused for a breath. "I've got a wife I love to death—Kendra. We've been together for over forty years—hell and back. A real ride or die kind of setup. I've also got three kids. My oldest is a son, Liam Junior, L.J. for short—he's a chiropractor in the city. My middle and youngest are daughters—Sydney and Brianna. Both are elementary school teachers. They're all married. To date I have five grandchildren. One from L.J., two from Sydney—twins, and two from Brianna. All girls. I've been a producer/director for news programing my entire career. I've only worked for three networks. I only left the previous two because another network offered either better hours or a higher salary. I'm a family guy, Marco, but I'm getting too old for all of this shit. More than anything I'd love to get the hell out of New York and retire somewhere up north. Just me and Kendra, free to do whatever we please with no clocks to punch or any added, unnecessary stress. Anyway, try to get some rest. Tomorrow we'll attempt to figure something out. Personally, I plan on barricading the door to my room. I advise you to do similar. If Madison should require any sort of assistance, let me know. I was a medic in the United States Army for eight years. I'm not even sure if Jill knows that. Good night," he said with a shrug.

Liam's impromptu chat provided me with a bit of comfort. On the surface he appeared to be a decent guy. The kind of person I'd possibly grab a drink with. Jillian? I still didn't trust her, and I doubted I ever would.

"Marco?" Madison stirred.

"What's up, sweetheart?" I replied.

"I want Luca," she mumbled half-awake, half-asleep.

"I know. I'm going to fix this," I reassured her.

Taking hold of one end of the dresser I dragged it in front of the door. Once I was confident the room was secure enough, I sat beside Madison's restless body and held her close until she finally fell asleep again, silently praying I could live up to my promise to her.

Chapter Eight

Luca

"Where the hell is she?" I hissed, pacing my parents' living room.

For the past four hours Madison's phone kept going to voicemail. My gut strongly urged me that she found herself smack in the middle of trouble. Unless I was aware of exactly what said trouble was, I couldn't help or do a damn thing other than wait. The setup felt all too familiar as PTSD flashbacks from the Noah Lessor nightmare flooded my every thought. I foolishly assumed that by changing jobs and becoming 'made,' shit like this wouldn't be an issue anymore. I guess I was wrong.

"Frankie is asleep in your old bedroom," my mother said. "Why don't you take a ride with your father over to your house. Maybe she's there. Maybe her phone died. Maybe she's stuck in traffic on the Belt. Maybe a lot of things, but freaking out isn't going to figure this out any quicker. Have you tried Marco?"

"Several times. Same thing—voicemail."

"Frank," she called.

"Right behind you, Gina. What's up, *bella donna*?"

"Go with Luca back to his house. See if Marco or Maddy are there. I'll watch Frankie."

"I already sent Jimmy and Tony. The house is empty. They've been told to stay there until I tell them to leave. If they see or hear anything they will call me immediately. I have Salvatore and a few others checking out police stations and hospitals. Aside from randomly driving around, everything that could be done is being done," my father said calmly. "*Figliolo*—basement. *Andiamo*."

Once the lock clicked shut, my father spoke. "Shots were fired by the Winters. It's doubtful Beau pulled the trigger because the old shit is laid up in the hospital, which means one of the others are behind this. There's Tag, Miranda, Jackson, Keira, Savannah, Stanton, Morgan, Ashton, Nick, and Jillian—those are the key players here. Talk to me. Reduce the list."

"Shots? What shots?" I barked.

"I had Rocco track Marco and Madison's phones. Their last pings came from Saint Charles Cemetery in front of our family's mausoleum. Rocco called for backup before he went to investigate. He found two cells lying on the front steps of the crypt, but no Marco or Madison. However, Madison's SUV was close by in the main office lot. The LoJack had been turned off three days prior, so he couldn't get a hit off of that. He doesn't believe she parked it there or was at that location in general because the driver's seat was pushed back pretty far and Madison isn't that tall. Someone drove it to the cemetery and abandoned it. He didn't want to touch the SUV, but he and about two dozen of our men scoured every inch of the grounds. They didn't find anything, and evidently the cemetery's security cameras were being upgraded, meaning they were all conveniently offline. Marco's vehicle was found at a gas station on the Long Island/Queens border with four slashed tires. Rocco was able to get the location off of the LoJack. When he asked the clerk if he'd seen Marco, he said he did several hours ago. He purchased a pack of cigarettes and left the building. The one security camera they have is a fake to deter people from robbing them. A couple of minutes later, I get a call from Joey. He said he and Sammy overheard on a police scanner that a missing person's report on Liam Stevens came through. It was filed by Kendra Stevens, his wife. Apparently, he went to work and never returned home. Same bullshit. His Subaru was left abandoned in the staff lot at his job, and all calls to him go straight to voicemail because the device was found on the passenger seat of his car. He's tied to the Winters on many levels. Stevens works with and is friendly with Nick and Jillian. If I had to make an educated guess, whoever is behind this isn't done collecting bodies yet. They're going to attempt to pin this on one of us. Either you or me. I realize you're ready to storm out of here and knock some heads off of shoulders, but you cannot do that. We're in the Winters crosshairs. Be smart. I'll find Madison and Marco. Nailing the Winters in the process will be an added bonus, but we have to remain focused."

A deep, anger-fueled sound caught somewhere between a grunt and a scream spilled out of my mouth. Pivoting, my left fist smashed into a brick wall. Had I not been operating from a place of fear and rage, I would've directed my emotions at a somewhat softer object such as the sheet rock on the opposite side of the basement. With a crack and a crunch, my eyes saw stars. Calmly my father climbed the stairs and opened the door.

"I've got to take Luca to the ER, Gina. He broke his hand. He might need some stitches too," he called.

"How the hell did he do that? Is he all right?" My

mother's voice oozed with concern.

"He went to war with a brick wall. Santino temper. He'll be fine. We'll be back soon."

"Call if you need anything. I've got Frankie."

"She doesn't know?" I asked through gritted teeth.

"Not yet. I'll tell her when I tell her. Now get your ass in the car."

Twenty-two sutures, a cast, and a sling later, I sat on a gurney waiting for my father to return. He disappeared when the doctor arrived to stitch me up. Evidently, the notorious '*Don*' couldn't stand being in hospitals.

"We've got to go, *Figliolo*," he ordered, shoving the curtain open.

"What's going on? They haven't released me," I said on high alert, jumping off the bed.

"Screw the nurse. I'm telling you your good to leave. Jillian Winters was just reported missing by her husband. Seemingly, he spent the night at Beau's bedside. The nanny called him inquiring about their whereabouts because she couldn't reach Jillian, who allegedly went home earlier, but never made it there. Her car was located in the Manhasset Hospital parking garage and her parking ticket was found on the ground outside of the Emergency Room exit. Playtime is over. They're coming for us—the Winters *and* the cops. Whichever Winters is behind this is now going after their own family. Granted Jillian isn't their blood, but they've begun to attack from within their fold. This isn't good," he explained, grabbing my hoodie and yanking me by my good wrist.

Sprinting out of the building I hopped in his car. My brain was working in overdrive.

"Sally is meeting us at the house to triage this shit

show. Jimmy, Tony, Sammy, Rocco—all our men are scouring Long Island and the Five Boroughs for Marco, Madison, Liam Stevens, and now this bitch Jillian. We can't get near Beau at the moment, but we can lean on the others," my father said.

"Did you know this was coming?" I asked with a sigh.

"I had a feeling, but not like this," he admitted. "If I thought anyone of us were in danger I would've jumped out in front of whatever to stop it. By them doing whatever with one of their own, that means they're attempting to draw attention away from them as suspects and onto someone else. Us."

"It's Tag or Jackson pulling the strings. Beau wouldn't dare cross you. He's too afraid. He's got too much to lose. If he tells anyone we threatened him, their next question would be why. He'd have to admit to knowing us personally. Tag and Jackson, well, they're stupid enough to pull a move like this," I said. If I didn't like what Salvatore had to say, I'd pay the Winters family a visit. I'd wake their slimy asses up, drag them out of bed, and beat the truth out of them—bum hand and all.

"What's your gut say?"

"Jackson. He's young, dumb, and has a lot of skin in the game. There are a lot of skeletons in his closet that he wouldn't want splattered across the front pages. He'd lose the Presidential race and his career would be over with no chance of a comeback." The theory shot out of my mouth because it was the only scenario that made any sense. My logic behind why he would do this calmed my edgy nerves a bit. Jackson would threaten but not kill. If he had Marco and Madison they'd realize this and find a way to overtake or trick him. With Beau—the scandal cleanup master, down for the count, Jackson wouldn't know how to handle the disposal of bodies. If he contacted another Crime Family, they'd call my father immediately when Marco or Madison's names or faces came up. People thought the different families were often at war with each other, but truthfully we weren't. That doesn't mean it didn't occur—look at what happened to my grandfather and Salvatore's father, but since then, and even more so within recent years, we've all stayed on our own turf conducting our own business. The Santino Family didn't deal drugs, pimp hookers, or commit racist/homophobic attacks. We had our hands in other activities conducted through legitimate businesses. My father let the other families get screwed up with the tremendously illegal crap.

"Have you alerted the other four families?" I inquired.

"Yes. They're aware. The bosses are on alert and offered support should we require it. Do I trust them fully? Hell no, but none of them can stomach the Winters, and it's a hit against family. It's close to home for them as well, especially for Antonio and Carlo. Remember what happened to their children some years back? However, I one hundred percent agree with your Jackson theory."

Exiting the car and entering my parents' house through the basement door, we found Salvatore dressed in one of his classic jogging suits sitting arched forward behind my father's desk, cradling the phone against his thick neck while smoking a cigar. "Yeah, Frankie just walked in with Luca. I want eyes and ears everywhere, Tony, *capisci?*" He waited for his son's response. "*Stai attento. Ti amo.*"

"What's this shit?" Salvatore asked, pointing at my cast the second he hung up.

"Santino temper. The brick wall behind you won. What's doing on your end?" my father asked.

"Tony said the cops took Liam Stevens and Jillian Winters vehicles to an impound yard on Long Island—he texted me the address. Marco and Maddy's cars are currently where they left them. I'm guessing that's because the cops don't know they're missing yet. Give it until the morning and the cemetery will have Maddy's SUV towed. Who the hell knows how long it will take the gas station to pay attention to Marco's. Normally, I'd say let's go check out the impound yard, but that'll be too risky. The police are swarming the place and Tony heard a rumor that the Feds might get involved because of the high-profile nature of the people involved due to the Warren Lessor fiasco. Once Maddy and Marco are reported missing? Forget about it. The mob and politicians? It'll be damn near impossible to keep the media out of this. Then you have all of those damn freaking web sleuth pains in the asses who couldn't solve a crime if we told them who did it, with what weapon, and why, to contend with. Jimmy ran quick surveillance of Tag's daughters and their husbands. They've both been vacationing on Martha's Vineyard at the family compound for the past three weeks. Prior to the heart attack Beau was lying low. From what I hear he's been cut off by Tag and Jackson due to our little visit to them after Lessor snagged Maddy. That leaves Tag and Jackson. My vote and the boys' votes are for Jackson. All we need is some credible evidence. We cannot go in guns blazing this time. There will be too many eyes on us once the news breaks that Maddy and Marco have vanished as well. Someone has to report them missing, and soon. Then, give it an hour and this street will be crawling with pigs and the press. By the end of this week, one of us will be making toilet wine in a jail cell. Personally, I believe they're going to go after Luca—sorry kid."

"Damn it," I hissed, preparing to shove my good fist into something.

"Take it easy, *nipote*. Be cool," Salvatore warned, reaching for and grasping my wrist tightly.

"Take it easy? Be cool? This is the second time in less than three years my wife has been abducted. I thought being a part of this family meant protection. All I've done is put her life at risk. We have a child together. That child needs his mother more than his dirtbag, piece of shit father. I'm supposed to sit here and wait for Jimmy or Tony to call with news? There is no news," I shouted, grabbing the phone off the desk.

"Who are you calling?" my father asked.

"The police. We have to report Madison and Marco missing. Liam Steven's wife and Nick Winters already have open cases on their spouses. If I don't file something I'll definitely be the one wearing the orange jumpsuit."

"Your boy is right, Frankie." Salvatore nodded in agreement, not that I needed or required his approval, but it was nice to know he and I were at least on the same page.

Dialing the local precinct, I waited for someone to answer. Finally, twelve rings later, a desk sergeant did. As another PTSD flashback gripped every ounce of my being I began speaking.

"My name is Luca Santino and I need to report two missing people—my wife and brother."

Chapter Nine

Salvatore

Four days passed with no word from anyone about anything. I watched as big Frankie attempted to hold his shit together while Luca slipped farther and farther into a deep, dark abyss. That boy was filled with untapped potential, but more so, intense rage. He reminded me of the pressure cooker my wife, Donatella, often used. For hours all you'd hear was ticking until finally she'd remove the pot from the stove and unscrew the lid. The sound and steam that filled the air was powerful and consuming. This kid was about the crack, and who knew what that crack would entail. Without Marco or Madison around to diffuse the timebomb, we'd all be royally screwed when he eventually let go of reality.

As expected, the cops were everywhere. I couldn't take a damn leak without one of them snooping around the Santino property. The media and thousands of stupid web sleuths were picking at everything, desperate to make some kind of connection between the missing. Not a one was even remotely close. All they were doing was fueling the press, who in turn concocted stories more ridiculous than the last. Every damn front page was plastered with nonsensical pun catchlines on top of photos. The funny thing was the snapshots of Jillian and Liam were classy, whereas Marco and Madison were labeled as low lives. Marco was dubbed 'The Bully of

Brooklyn,' while Madison was 'The Mafia Princess.' Their pictures revealed an out-of-control Marco yelling at someone on the streets, and a spoiled Madison walking out of a wedding dressed to the nines. Apparently, Beau remained hospitalized with Tag and his wife by his side. The sisters flew up from Martha's Vineyard to join them. Nick remained in the shadows not speaking to the media or giving interviews. Kendra Stevens did the same. We also hung back, but for far different reasons. We knew, well, at least I knew, that the Feds were coming for one of us. This prophecy came to fruition earlier today when a wrap at the front door cut through the rock solid tension inside of Frankie's house.

"Can I help you?" I asked, opening the door. Frankie and Luca were in the basement. They'd spent the better part of the day prior disposing of anything incriminating lying around here and at Luca's home. I'd done the same at my place.

"Who is it?" Gina asked.

"The police," I replied.

Rushing to the door, Gina pushed me out of the way. "Have you found my Marco and Madison?" she practically yelled out of motherly terror.

"No. That's not why we're here. We have a warrant to search this house, Madison Santino's home, and one for Luca Santino's arrest. Please, if you'd step aside," the cop informed.

"Hold on," I said blocking the doorframe. "I have a right to see the warrants and have them explained to me before you enter."

"Fine. Here," he said shoving a blue envelope at me. The paperwork boldly suggested DNA evidence proved Luca had been with each victim prior to their disappearance.

Shit.

Frankie and Luca were now standing close behind me.

With a nod, Luca stepped forward. "Whenever you're ready." His tone was void of all emotion.

"Read him his rights and cuff him," the lead pig said to a slight, nervous, young man behind him.

"How, sir? He's got a sling and a cast on?" the newbie inquired.

"Figure it out," jerkoff number one barked.

"Uh, you have the right to remain silent. Anything you say can and will be used against you in a court of law. You have a right to an attorney. If you cannot afford an attorney one will be appointed for you. Do you understand these rights as I have read to you?" the young cop asked.

"Yeah. There's no way you're going to cuff me because if you remove my broken, stitched hand from this cast and sling I'll have your job faster than you can say sorry. You will also not be using a flex cuff, waist shackle, a belt, or any other type of tool to restrain me with. I'm not resisting arrest. I'm willingly going with you. So, let's take a nice and easy walk to the curb," Luca responded. His reactions remained vapid.

Frankie leaned over and whispered something quickly in Luca's ear before he was escorted out of the house. Hot on his heels, I followed him attempting to shield him from the freaking reporters who had been camped out on the street since this nightmare began. Using my body to protect him, I shoved the media out of the way. Luca ambled calm and cool with his head held high. I had to give it to the kid. He was amazing under pressure. Not a bead of sweat.

"Pop knows what to do. I'm sure I'll see you later at my arraignment," Luca said before the door closed.

Heading back inside, I found Gina crying on the sofa and Frankie on the phone.

"Ally Newman, the woman Luca used to work for, is meeting him down at the station. She said he'll be arraigned tonight or tomorrow, but depending on who the judge is or who she can wake up, it will more than likely be tonight. He'll have to be processed, but since he'll plead not guilty they can't take away his law license. It might get temporarily suspended, but who cares? She's going to try to get him out on bail, but it's going to be a hefty amount. Get as much money liquid as possible. Ally will sort through everything when she's at the precinct." Much like Luca, Frankie had turned off emotionally and was now operating from a mechanical position. We've all been there, me included. My sons have both been arrested at least a dozen times. There was no space for feelings during these moments.

"Don't worry about cash on hand. Between the both of us, I'm sure we have the bail covered and then some. Do you trust this Ally Newman woman?"

"I don't have a choice. It was Luca's call anyway. He insisted that if he were to get arrested for me to call her. She'll reach out when she has more details. For now, go home, grab the cash, and wait for my text."

"You got it, boss," I answered leaving.

The hours dragged by. I was currently lying in bed, unable to sleep, clutching my phone like my life depended on it.

"What's going on, sweetheart? I know something is up. I realize you might not be able to tell me everything, and that's okay, but tell me something," Donatella urged, turning a nightstand light on, then rolling onto her side.

"It's Luca. The kid got arrested. They think he's the mastermind behind all of the abductions," I admitted. After fifty years of marriage there were no secrets between her and I. That woman stole my heart the moment I laid eyes on her and has had it exclusively ever since. I never stepped out on her like Frankie had on Gina. I never even thought about it. She was my life, my world, my everything. Two beautiful sons later, I'd die for her, no questions asked. We never fought. She never pushed. We each understood the other inside and out.

"Did he do it?" One of her well-manicured eyebrows rose.

"Do you really think he's capable of murdering his brother and wife?" I scoffed.

"He's certainly not the sweet, funny, kind, charming, albeit womanizing man he used to be a few years ago. I look at him and can barely recognize him anymore."

"Yeah, he's changed for sure, but he's still a good boy. I'd bet the farm it wasn't him and we both know I'm not a gambler."

"Then who did it?"

"I have a strong feeling I know, but I would rather not tell you anymore. God forbid this shit gets any crazier, you're the last person I want being hauled in for questioning."

"Fair enough. I love you, Sal. You know that, right?"

"Of course I do and I love you too, *cara mia*," I said, leaning forward to kiss her sweet lips.

As if Frankie had a sixth sense about ruining tender

moments between my wife and I, the phone rang. Rattling off figures and locations in code in case the line was being tapped, I jotted everything down. Rolling off of the bed, I grabbed the cash stuffed duffle bag I had packed earlier, said goodbye to Donatella, and drove to the police station. From there I followed Frankie to a nearby courthouse where a prison transport van had just dropped off Luca. Once inside we sat in the gallery awaiting his turn.

"How do you plead, Mr. Santino?" a middle-aged, black, female judge asked.

"Not guilty, Your Honor."

"Your Honor, if I may," Ally Newman requested. A harsh looking blonde woman stood beside her to the left.

"Yes?"

"Mr. Santino is a reputable attorney for the state of New York. His personal and professional records are clean and clear of any wrongdoings. He doesn't even have a parking ticket. He's been wrongfully accused in this case and we intend to prove that. I'm still digging through the alleged DNA evidence, but this is a witch hunt against the Santino Family if I've ever seen one. They've searched Mr. Santino and his family's homes and came up empty. Madison Santino and Marco Santino are missing as well—*not* just Jillian Winters and Liam Stevens, whom might I add have been painted as saints by the media while my client, his missing wife, *and* brother have all been vilified. Mr. Santino is an upstanding, law-abiding citizen, a loving and caring husband and father. We humbly request that you set aside any prior knowledge of the Santino Family and take into account Mr. Santino's stellar reputation not only as an attorney, but as a community member and family man as well. Additionally, we accept and will not challenge bail or bond because Mr. Santino does not pose a flight risk as he has deep ties to the community, wishes to shelter in place in case his missing brother or wife return, and has a minor child whose mother is currently missing."

"Prosecution?"

"We seek no bail or bond. We urge due to the violent nature of these heinous crimes, Mr. Santino remain in jail until he stands trial."

"Heinous crimes? Violent nature? All the prosecution has is a few strands of Mr. Santino's hair on the car seats of the missing individuals. Two of those people he's related to and is with frequently. He's also worked with Jillian Winters in the past on a case when he was employed by me, and Jillian Winters is friends with and is a colleague of Liam Stevens. It's not out of the realm of possibility Mr. Santino was providing legal counsel to either one of them through an introduction via Jillian Winters. The court can now hold people on mere speculatory claims? I guess I didn't receive that memo—the one that says your guilty because we have weak evidence and have an axe to grind with the defendant's family."

"All right. All right. I've heard enough," the judge said, waving her hands as if by doing this she could reset the energy of the room. "I'm ordering five million dollars cash, eight million bond, or ten million partially secured bond. Mr. Santino is to surrender his passport and will be given an ankle monitor to wear, which he may not take off until the court orders its removal. He may leave his set five-mile radius *only* to go to work or to seek medical treatment for himself or his minor child. He may go grocery shopping and provide for the needs of his child within the radius without consequence. When he's sized for the device he must provide the names and addresses of all employers, physicians, and so on. Should he need to leave the radius to travel to an unlisted location, he must first obtain approval from his local police department. In light of everything going on, and the fact that there are many moving parts, pretrial will be scheduled for five months from today. Court is adjourned."

A tremendous sigh of relief escaped my lungs. One problem solved, six million more to go.

Chapter Ten

Luca

"I'm gonna ask one more time before this gets ugly. Where did you stash the bodies, Santino?" Detective Moran yelled in my face. One would imagine a seasoned man in his position would've obtained a better shakedown tactic over the years, but apparently he hadn't. Moran appeared to be in his late fifties with a body which suggested he'd given up ten years into his watch.

The jackass thought his strategies were intimidating, but in reality all he was doing was abusing his authority, something I easily could've reported him for, especially since our interrogation was being filmed. Would anyone *actually* do anything about it? No, but he was still a bully and asshole in my eyes. The more I dug my heels in and showed him no fear or negative effect towards his boorish ways was present, the more he turned up the volume. I was waiting for him to crack me or threaten to.

"And I'm going to tell you for the last time, I have no idea where my brother and wife are," I replied calmly.

"What about Winters and Stevens? Where did you bury them?"

"I didn't bury anyone. I have an alibi for every second of every day since my wife and brother went missing."

"You're nothing but a bullshit liar," Moran scoffed.

"Well I don't know about that, but as a New York State licensed attorney I can say I've been more than generous with my time, extremely patient with your verbally abusive interrogation, and I am sure my lawyer should be around here somewhere. I'd like to speak with her, now."

"If you have nothing to hide, why request a lawyer?"

"Because it's my right as a citizen of this country. The arresting officer clearly stated when he read me my rights that one of them is the right to an attorney. It's not a request at this point. I am legally entitled to speak with counsel and have verbalized this desire to you, twice. If you deny me this basic civil liberty, you—an officer of the law, will be held in violation. Ally Newman and Jennifer Glick were called two hours ago. I am beyond confident either one or both of them are in this building. Go do something useful and find them or else I'll have the Attorney General down here so fast firing you, you won't know what hit you."

With an evil grimace Moran exited the room, making sure to slam the door behind him. For two frigging hours, this moron threw everything at me to force me to admit to a crime I didn't commit. Though, some interesting information was obtained. Evidently, strands of my hair were found in Jillian and Liam's vehicles. Being I hadn't ever been in either's car and having never met Liam before, someone had to have planted it. My brain worked in overdrive attempting to connect all the dots, hoping this would reveal the true culprit.

"Walk me through this, Santino," Ally instructed the second she entered the room. Slamming her white, designer briefcase on the table, she opened it, extracting a legal pad and a gold pen.

"For starters, I had nothing to do with any of this," I snapped.

"Do you really believe that's what I think?" she shot back. "Because if you do you'd be sorely mistaken and I wouldn't be here. This isn't the time for ire or pity pony riding. Start spilling your guts."

An hour later, I had explained everything from receiving the photograph and letter to that moment. Somewhere in between Jennifer joined us and took copious notes.

"They have two strands of your hair from Jillian's SUV and one strand from Liam's. Any idea how it got there?" Ally questioned.

"No."

"Dumb question. Do you have or does your family have any enemies who'd want to see something like this happen to you?"

"Yeah. The Winters."

"I'm familiar with the connection," Jennifer piped up. "When Luca was representing Nick and Jillian Winters and Madison went missing, Luca disclosed everything to me under attorney/client privilege. For time's sake I can fill you in on it later. If we want him arraigned by Judge Johnson we have to get a move on. If not, Judge Crawford presides and you two aren't exactly on good terms which means I'd have to declare first chair as well as heavily suggest you not be in the room when he's being arraigned."

"Fair enough. I'm going to get you out of here, okay?" Ally assured.

"That's why I had my father call you." I produced the fakest of smiles.

"You look like shit, Santino. What's with the hand?"

"I wasn't aware that staring down the barrel of hard time was a reason to put my tux on."

"Still have that butterknife sharp wit, I see. The hand?"

"I hit a brick wall."

"When?"

"The night Madison and Marco went missing, after my father shared his thoughts on how the Winters were behind it."

"That could pose speculation from the plaintiff," Jennifer suggested. "They'll say the injury was a result of him attacking his brother, Madison, Liam, or Jillian. It's too late for anyone to swipe for DNA traces as I'm confident the hospital thoroughly cleaned the wound."

"There are a lot of factors that aren't looking good for us here, but first things first. Let's spring you from this joint. We'll work on our defense later." Lifting her cell phone she rapidly fired off an email. "I'll go speak with whoever is in charge here. You stay with Santino, Glick."

"I've cleared my calendar. My interns and associates already hate me so the extra work I dumped on them will just strengthen that sentiment for them. I'll be exclusively by your side through all of this—day, night, whenever. As will Ally. You're top priority," Jennifer comforted in her own unique way once we were alone.

"I appreciate that."

"It's going to get ugly, Luca."

"I'm aware. However, I could give a rat's ass about my name being the target of a smear campaign. All I want is for Madison and Marco to be all right and back home where they belong." Emotions I'd shut off hours ago returned with a vengeance.

"And they will," she stated boldly, leaning closer and placing her arm around my shoulder. "If anyone can get you out of here it's Ally. That email she sent was to Satan himself. I believe they have some sort of mutual understanding. She's summoning him right now in the lady's room, probably using the blood from the cop who interrogated you earlier."

"Funny." Her personal views of Ally broke some of my internal tension.

"I've been known to be entertaining, just not at work." She grinned.

A few hours later, after being fit for a tracker anklet, I was back at my parents' house, sitting on the couch, and staring out of the window. Desperately my mind endeavored to fit all of the puzzle pieces together, but my hands were tied. I'd never be stupid enough to test the limitations of the damn anklet, and anyone associated with my family was more than likely under tremendous surveillance. Even members who'd been kept under deep cover couldn't be sure the Feds weren't aware of their presence. I'd bet my ass it was Jackson Winters behind this with Tag's help, but how to prove this remained a mystery. Then there was my hair in Winters and Steven's cars. Obviously someone planted it, but who? Why? Why target me? Pinning this on my father would prove more difficult, but why not place the blame on Marco? He knew just as much, possibly more. And that's the reason…whatever information I'd been privileged to was nothing compared to what he'd been aware of. Why take Madison? She and Marco must've been on to something. Maybe they had the proof to accuse Jackson or Tag? With my brother and wife gone and me behind bars, dead men don't talk and convicted murderers aren't believed, especially ones who are tied to the Mafia. Jillian and Liam know something too, but again, what? There's a chance they don't know shit and are simply a loose end to tie up in case they were cognizant of something, but why not take Nick out as well? Surely he has to be acquainted with the ins and outs, comings and goings of the Winters clan. Is he next? A staged accident? An idea struck me causing me to grab my cell phone and dial Jennifer.

"You up?" I said quickly.

"I'm always awake. It's part of the pack I made with the Devil when I began working for Ally. I guess you weren't offered that deal. What's up?"

"This has to be face to face—in private. Being I'm a bit tied up on a government leash, I need you to come here."

"What time is it?"

"Three fifteen."

"I'm on my way. There shouldn't be too much traffic on the Belt. Give me an hour."

Snatching a pad and pen from the kitchen junk drawer I created copious notes based off of my working theory. Nowhere in that mess did I figure out where Marco and Madison were, but I did create a list of possible locations based off the old Sarah Davis/Noah Lessor file I retained on my laptop's hard drive and through public records searches. Nick was in danger. If we could play a rousing game of chicken using him as bait, which if he loved his wife and wanted her back he'd do, I would without a second thought, Jackson would hand us everything we required to find my brother and wife, clear my name, and destroy the Winters family all in one fell swoop.

In record time Jennifer made her way from Long Island to Brooklyn. Visually cueing her to remain quiet because the entire house was asleep, she joined me in the basement.

"What's going on?" she questioned. Her eyes surveyed the space around us as her nose crinkled. "It stinks down here. Could you open a window or the door? Perhaps you might want to consider investing in an air deodorizer for down here."

"My uncle smokes cigars. Sorry," I replied, cracking three windows on the opposite side of the room. "Sit, please."

Doing as instructed, she sat on my father's recliner, leaned over, and extracted a notebook and pen from her bag.

"Thank you for coming out here so quickly. My gut says Jackson Winters is behind all of this with the help of his father, Tag. I don't have any evidence, *yet*, but it makes sense. You know the story about the Santinos and Winters. The only update since then is the photograph I received when Madison was about five months pregnant with Frankie," I explained, reaching into one of the desk drawers, extracting the picture and handwritten note, and handing both documents over.

With careful consideration she examined them. "Since you've had this for over a year there probably won't be any DNA on it aside from yours, mine, and whoever else has touched it recently, *but* I'll have my contact over at Metrix Data give it a sweep. We might get lucky. I doubt it, but it's worth a shot. Have you compared Jackson or Tag's handwriting to this letter?"

"No." Why hadn't I thought of that?

"Do you have copier or scanner down here?"

"Yeah." Taking the papers back, I made a quick duplicate of both.

"Why would someone send you a crime scene photo?" she inquired.

"That's the Davis/Lessor murder/suicide aftermath."

"We can continue to beat around the bush, but I'd rather we didn't. Obviously based off this new information and being I'm not a moron, what really went down the day Madison was found? Something did because right after that you went all squirrely and quit your job, sold your house, and joined *The Apple Dumpling Gang*, while Madison, a few months later, did the same. Since then, the two of you have been as thick as thieves, avoiding any and all questions about pretty much anything more than surface crap. I'm confident you've been *made* and are a full-fledged member of whatever all of this is. However, since none of that matters to me and because you're protected under attorney/client privilege, tell me the entire story this time, please. Truth and all, no matter how bad you believe it might make you look."

"I didn't kill anyone. There's no blood of any kind on my hands. There never has been, and there never will be."

"I never thought there was, Luca. I'm not the enemy here. You might believe everyone who's not attached to this family is out to screw you over, but I swear I'm not going to do that. I will bust my ass to figure this out as soon as humanly possible. You're aware of my resume and have seen me in action. Though we might have butted heads while working together for Ally, I've always respected your abilities and talent for law. Three of the strongest, greatest legal minds are working on this case—you, me, and Ally. However, if you don't trust fall into my arms this isn't going to work." She paused. "Ally isn't charging you for her services. Neither am I. If we truly thought you were the guilty party here that wouldn't be the case."

"*Might* have butted heads?" A slight laugh rolled off my tongue.

"Fine. We couldn't stand the other's existence, but it wasn't because we didn't value and realize the other's skill at the job. If pressed to be completely transparent, I enjoyed working beside you."

"Same. I was an asshole who loved to press your buttons and drive you insane. I was also a womanizer who treated your best friend like crap for no good reason."

"You were immature and cocky—like most men."

"I suppose."

"Luca, in order to make this nightmare go away, I need you to share every last detail you can recall about what happened the day Maddy was found," she requested for a second time.

"I don't know who took out Sarah Davis, but I do know her death was the result of self-defense by either my father or uncle's hands. Noah Lessor died by suicide. I was there when he did it. So was Madison, Marco, Jimmy D'Angelo, and Tony D'Angelo. Jillian Winters came by the office the day after I was questioned by the police. She kept pressing to know what the connection between our families was. It was obvious she had no idea and was attempting to figure it out. She and Nick had suspicions, but no rock-solid proof. Though she suggested they planned to let things lie, a woman like her, an undercover journalist, doesn't know the meaning of that action. I'd bet she kept digging."

"How did she come to be aware of the family tie in?"

"When Madison went missing my uncle paid Nick a visit. My brother and cousins went to speak with Beau, Tag, and Jackson around that time as well. After that, Beau was shoved aside by Tag and Jackson. I suppose they deemed him too much of a liability to Jackson's campaign. That action leads me to believe either Beau is behind this to get back into their good graces, or he's got absolutely nothing to do with it, and Tag and Jackson are working together to clean up Beau's mess."

"Walk me through Noah Lessor's suicide. How did you know where to find him?"

"I'll be breaking confidentiality with Jillian Winters."

"Off the record, between us, break it."

"That same day when she was at the office, before she left she wrote down two addresses. One was for the house her husband had been held in—that's where we found Davis. We, meaning my father, Salvatore, Marco, Jimmy, Tony, and myself. The other location was for some shack in the woods not too terribly far from the Davis house. Both were owned by Lessor. My father and Salvatore stayed behind with Davis while the rest of us went to see what was going on at the shack. Madison and Noah were there. We broke in. I grabbed Madison as the others confirmed Lessor's identity. While Jimmy had him pinned to the wall, Lessor grabbed Tony's gun, quoted some passage from the Bible, and shot himself in the head. My father and uncle arrived at the scene several minutes later with Davis's body and her son. They took Madison and the child to safety and left the rest of us to clean shit up, which we did by staging the murder suicide scene. A story was spun and that's how it ended. I'd never done anything like that before. I'd never witnessed anything like that before, but it had to happen or else Madison wouldn't have survived. For a while after the incident I struggled to pull myself together, hence me selling my home and quitting my job. To be honest, a part of me has never been the same. I doubt I'll ever be 'me' again, but I'd rather that than be without Madison."

Admitting I'd mentally lost the plot felt like a sign of weakness, but now wasn't the time to lament over my unavoidable actions. Emotions were tricky little pains in the ass. Learning to control them wasn't as easy as people would lead you to believe, especially quack therapists like Nick Winters.

"Have you, personally, had any contact with any member of the Winters family since Madison's abduction? Any communication after Madison came home, aside from speculation over the photograph and note?"

My warning eyes locked on hers.

"I'll take that as an undesirable yes. Who?"

"Beau."

"When? Why?"

"A few of us went to have a chat with Beau. We followed him to a coffee shop on Long Island. He was alone. We approached him, took him to an alley behind the café, and talked."

"Was this the day Beau had his heart attack?"

"Yes."

"You chatted about what? Did you threaten him?

Cause any bodily harm? Did he know it was you or were you masked?"

"We wanted to discuss what he knew about the picture. He swore he had nothing to do with it, and honestly, I believed him. He was visibly shaken when we left, but he wasn't in any kind of medical distress. Had he been, one of us would've called nine-one-one. We wouldn't have left him dying on the streets, in spite of the fact he's a lying piece of shit. Did I threaten him? That depends on your version of a threat." I shrugged, happy I had been able to shift out of a place of feebleness and back into one of strength.

"You're a tough guy. I get it. No one bullies you. Duly noted. Did you strike or use excessive force? Did you verbally suggest physical abuse to him or others?"

"A bit of both. And yes, he saw me, Marco, and the others. Beau knows who we are. No weapons of any kind were used or shown to Beau. Everyone except me was carrying, but no one pulled a gun. I left mine at home in the safe. I'm not a fan of firearms. If necessary I'll use one, but I'd prefer not to."

"Are you or any of the others involved licensed to carry firearms?"

"We all are."

"Where there any surveillance cameras on the street or in the alley?"

"No. We checked."

"Take me through your Beau/Tag/Jackson theory."

"It's a hunch based off of them wanting and needing to eliminate anyone and everyone who knows anything about them that they wouldn't want leaked to the press or public. Get rid of Jillian, Liam, Madison, and Marco, who's left? Me and *The Apple Dumpling Gang*. Who in their right mind is going to believe a gangster? No one. With me behind bars for a crime I didn't commit, they have confidence that they've crippled my father, but since all eyes will be on him, he wouldn't dare strike back. They'd be safe. However, here's the fly in the ointment—Nick Winters. They haven't abducted or killed him, *yet*. He's next, Jennifer. I can't get eyes on him because I'm on a Federal leash, neither can anyone in my family, but you and Ally can. Use him as bait. Tell him about it or don't. It doesn't matter. Either way, he needs a tail. They're coming for him. That's how I'd play it. Also," I stated, opening my laptop. "Before you freak out, yes the cops seized all of the electronic devices in this house, but they were all cleaned professionally prior; no one will find anything on them other than online shopping and general search engine shit. This one is new and was carefully hidden from prying eyes. There's also a signal jammer on the Wi-Fi. As far as anyone is concerned there's no internet usage going on in this home. My personal cell phone is in lockup. This is my professional one, which again was cleverly concealed. Moving along. Here is a list of all of the properties owned by the Winters. Aside from Nick and Jillian, only Beau and Tag live in New York on Long Island. They're up in Sands Point. The rest of their holdings are out of state—Connecticut, Maryland, and Massachusetts. None of these locations are too terribly far from here, but it's doubtful Tag or Jackson moved Madison, Marco, Liam, and Jillian across state lines. If either did they'd be the worst lawyers in the history of law. Kidnapping is usually prosecuted on the state level. Moving them to another state would provoke the federal authorities to get involved—which the Feds already have their hands all over this, but now it would be considered a serious felony offense with a twenty or more year prison sentence attached to it. My wife and brother are still here in this area. Again, with my gut, but I'd bet my life they're at Tag's house. With Tag and Jackson staying away from Beau, they might use his property to stash the abducted, but it's doubtful. With everyone on Tag's property they call and control the shots. Besides, when Beau gets released from the hospital, his block will be crawling with the press. Having had to deal with that myself these days, it's a nightmare with no privacy. They see and hear everything. Tomorrow's headlines will have some ridiculous Mafia pun about me, with a story and picture about you because you entered the house at an ungodly hour. Somehow you'll turn into my mistress or I'll be labeled your pimp. A few days later they'll write and publish the tiniest retraction statement correcting their egregious error on a page in a location that no one ever reads."

"I've been accused of worse. I'm sure I'll find a way to carry on and cope. Okay. So you're suggesting we search Tag's house, which I get. Your logic is solid, but Luca, we don't have any evidence necessitating an inspection of the property. No judge in their right mind will sign off on a search warrant," Jennifer rationalized.

"We don't need a search warrant. We need a fire. A small, controlled one. The fire department will be dispatched and can legally enter the house without consent. According to county records they have an alarm permit. That alarm is linked to their smoke and carbon dioxide detectors. The second one of those trip, police, fire, and emergency services will be dispatched."

"I'm sure I'm going to regret going down this rabbit

hole with you, but how do you propose starting a fire?"

"That's for us to worry about."

"No, Luca. As your attorney in a criminal case where you're being charged on the federal level, it's for me to worry about."

"You have your ways, I have mine, but you have to trust me. In twenty-four hours you'll be contacted by a man named Arthur Lawrence. He's the Chief Fire Marshal for Nassau County. If he finds anything at all he will share whatever it is with you. We'll regroup from there."

"And if he doesn't find anything?"

"We have to at least try."

With a nod of agreement, she spoke again. "We didn't have this part of our discussion. Got it?"

"No idea what you're talking about."

"How's the hand?"

"Hurts like hell, but Madison and Marco's needs far surpass whatever crap I'm going through. Head in the game. You know?"

"Are you scared of going to jail?"

"No. As long as my wife and brother are alive, safe, and well I don't care what happens to me. They have to be, Jennifer. My son needs his mother. I don't know what I'd do if I lost any of them." The thought caused a catch in my throat.

"You've changed. I was wrong about you," she commented.

"Thanks?"

"I used to think you were this narcissistic jerk who was involved in a torrid love affair with himself. Always a different woman. Always with a smug attitude. You're a family man now who loves his wife and son. They're your everything. Most husbands wouldn't go to such extremes on their own in a situation like this. They'd bitch and moan, cry and carry on, and would expect their lawyers and the police to figure it all out. They'd give up. Not you. Never you. You're one of the good guys, and it's a shame this is happening to someone like you. For the record—never once did I ever judge you based off of your last name. I judged you because of the type of person you portrayed. That man is long gone. We'll be in touch. If you need anything, anything at all, or there's an update or change, call me. I'll be there in a flash."

Escorting her to the door, I watched as she skillfully navigated the sea of reporters. Once her car pulled away from the curb, I went to the kitchen. Pouring a cup of coffee, I heard Frankie stirring upstairs. Not wanting to wake my parents, I scaled the steps and helped him down the stairs.

"Daddy hand?" Frankie said touching my cast.

"It's feeling much better."

"Mommy?" he inquired, shrugging shoulders.

"She's still on a work trip, *miniatura io*."

"Mommy come home."

"Soon." I forced a smile. "We're going to stay here with Nonno and Nonna until she does. But, right now what do you want for breakfast?"

"Nonna cookies."

"Mommy will be mad if I gave you cookies for breakfast. Let's see what we can come up with. How about …," I started.

"How about Nonna does the cooking and Daddy gets out of my clean kitchen," my mother said, entering in her bathrobe. Immediately she picked up Frankie and proceeded to smother him with kisses. "He's the spitting image of you when you were his age. So handsome and smart."

The truth was, aside from Madison's green eyes he was a carbon copy of me, complete with temper and all. After flipping the kitchen television on, she went to work cooking.

"Daddy. Nonno," Frankie said excitedly, pointing his chubby finger at the screen.

My head whipped to the right to see what he was talking about. There on the screen was a photograph of my father set to the upper left of the frame, while a video of me doing the perp walk outside of the house played on a loop.

"Notorious Boss of the Santino Crime Family, Frank Santino's son, attorney Luca Santino was arrested last night in connection to the disappearances of *This Just In* host Jillian Winters, her producer Liam Stevens, the younger Santino's wife, Madison, and older brother, Marco. We were told by the prosecution DNA evidence links Santino to the crimes making him their prime suspect. Santino was released on five million dollars bail and was placed on house arrest. Ally Newman of Newman and Associates LLP, who also happens to be Santino's former employer, will be representing him. When asked if she had a statement, Newman replied with 'no comment.' Our reporters also made note Newman's second chair, attorney Jennifer Glick, was at the Santino compound early this morning. She too remains silent on the matter," a middle-aged female anchor stated.

"Wow," her male partner anchor replied. "Does anyone know how Vice President Winters is handling the disappearance of Jillian? How is he doing?"

"The Winters camp has been pretty quiet these past few days sheltering close to the Vice President while he remains hospitalized."

"Here at the station, we wish Vice President Winters a speedy recovery and pray for the safe return of Jillian Winters and Liam Stevens." A picture of each flashed across the screen. "How about this unseasonable weather we've been having?" he segued.

"What about the safe return of my wife and brother? You know the two scum pieces of shit that no one cares about because they're mobbed up?" I seethed.

"Your son is sitting right there. Stop it. Control yourself, Luca," my mother warned.

"Hold on. We've got something coming through from the wire. Developing—Underboss of the Santino Crime Family, Salvatore D'Angelo's vehicle was found abandoned on West Shore Road by the North Hempstead Beach Park. Police say blood was found at the scene. Rush tests on the samples are being run to positively identify the person or persons involved. We'll keep you posted on the latest as this story unfolds," the male anchor said.

"Pop," I shouted, charging up the steps.

I found him fully dressed, his hands supporting his head, as he sat on the foot of his bed. "I know, *Figliolo*." He sighed heavily. I'd never seen him appear as small, weak, disgusted, and done as I did in that moment.

Sitting beside him I placed my right hand on his back. "This is the plan. I need you to reach out to Arthur Lawrence. A small, not fatal, easily contained electrical fire needs to be set at Tag's home in Sands Point. Some of his men have to be there to put it out. While doing so they're to look for any signs of Madison or Marco or anything that may appear off. By doing this we gain legal access into the Winters' home without a search warrant, which we won't get. Have Lawrence report back to Jennifer Glick. She'll collect all of the information and share it with us. It's too dangerous for him to contact you directly right now. As for *Zio* you have to go to his house and dig a bit. Get Tony and Jimmy's help. You can come and go as you please, whereas I cannot. My ass is tethered here. The press will think you're going to your partner's house to console his wife and children. However, this happening does bode well for us. I was seen being arrested, transported to jail, then to the courthouse for arraignment, and driven home. I have a tracker anklet on and Jennifer came by a few hours after we got home. The press has been camping out outside, watching our every move. They would've seen me leaving. So what does this mean? Either the authorities will believe I'm working with someone but won't know who because we're all being hawked by the cops, or someone else did it. Whether they think Salvatore's abduction was committed by a copycat, an outlying associate, or an unrelated incident, it doesn't matter. It takes the heat off of me and us while the Feds attempt to figure out who else is involved. *Zio* disappearing was premeditated. He's crafty and sly like that. He'd also put his own life at risk to save those he loves. Lastly, when speaking with Lawrence see if he can get you updated blueprints from the town or an architect who did any kind of work on Tag's home. Maybe have him contact the alarm company. Their home surveillance system could be linked to that account. If we can get our hands on the videos that would be tremendously helpful. If not, we'll see who we can bribe to get what we need. Also, have him provide Jennifer with a copy of the report and pictures of the damage. They're in that house, Pop. I can feel it."

"You remind me so much of Nonno. Do you know that?" He smiled and gently slapped the side of my face.

"Aside from you and Marco, I can't think of a better person to resemble. Come on. We've got work to do," I said, standing.

Chapter Eleven

Salvatore

"What happened with Luca, Papa?" my oldest son, Tony, asked.

"They let him go. Five million big ones and an ankle bracelet later, but he's home with Frankie."

Tony let out a low whistle which echoed through the receiver.

"Yeah. Tell me about it," I said. "Where are you and Jimmy?"

"Just walked through the door. And yes, we're being quiet so we don't wake Mom."

"That's my good boy."

"Are you coming home?"

"Yeah, but I have to check something out first."

"Want company?"

"Nah. Your old man has it under control."

"Jimmy is making sandwiches. Do you want him to make you one? We'll leave it in the fridge with some iced coffee?"

"That would be great. Remember to clean up your mess so Mom doesn't find a surprise in the kitchen later. She works hard to keep us alive, healthy, and fed. She deserves respect."

"We know."

"Listen, Tone, do me a favor."

"What's that?"

"Should for some reason I not return to the house later, alert the cops, *immediately*. Have them come look for me. They'll be able to find my car because I've turned the LoJack on. There shouldn't be any issues with locating it. Remind them about the LoJack tracker because they won't ask. Then, I want you to leak it to the press. Start with Jillian Winters' station."

"What are you up to, Papa?" Tony's tone was serious but filled with concern.

"Sometimes when you need to solve a complicated problem you have to draw the bear out of its cave. That's what I'm doing. Don't worry about me, please. I'm a lot heartier than you think. I'm also exceptionally handsome and brilliant, if I don't say so myself." I chuckled attempting to lighten the mood.

"Yeah Papa, you're a real Miss America. Anything else?" The sound of his easy, light laugh put a smile on my face. My greatest wish was for him and his brother to find wives and make babies. Sure they dated, a lot, but with the lifestyle we lived it was difficult to get close to someone who truly understood. I'd hoped after watching Luca marry Maddy, then have a baby, they'd feel inspired to follow suit. Jimmy sort of did. He met a real pretty Italian girl and was talking about a possible future with her to Donatella, but something held him back. When I pressed him about it he suggested our loved ones were often targets for enemies. Now with all of this bullshit and Madison being kidnapped for a second time, the kid's point was proven. I doubted I'd ever be a Nonno and those boys would never settle down. At least they had each other.

"When you call Frankie to tell him I'm gone, tell him Luca was right when he said earlier that our family vacation to Sandy Shores many years ago was the best trip we'd ever taken. Those pointed sandcastles we made were spot on. However the trip we took to see the Jacksonville Jaguars was my personal favorite. Write that down so you don't forget."

"Luca right about Sandy Shores vacation. Pointed sandcastles were spot on. Jacksonville game trip was your favorite," Tony replied. The sound of a pen scratching against paper set my soul at ease. Frankie would know what all that meant. If not, Luca would.

"Be careful, Papa. I love you. Me, Jimmy, and Mom—we need you. Okay? Come home soon."

"I love you, Jimmy, and Mom too. I'll be back before you can miss me," I said, and hung up.

"Come out come out wherever you are, you filthy, slimy, piece of shit," I sang to myself as I turned onto West Shore Road.

The plan was to drive around the area drawing attention to myself. Though it was fairly late, if my hunch was correct, Jackson Winters would be targeting me next. I was the last piece to the puzzle. Surrendering myself would protect Jimmy, Tony, and Donatella. If I were handled, Jackson knew Frankie wouldn't and couldn't strike. He'd be missing his second and third in command. With Luca behind bars he'd be down three strong men. Granted, my kids would step up to the plate, but under Frankie's order, they wouldn't go after the Winters. The three men would know, but would be defenseless, thusly placing the Winters in a strong position of control and power. God forbid Frankie did attempt to pull shit with the Winters, the Feds would know and nab him. He wouldn't do that to Gina, the girls, and his grandchildren. Frankie and my boys would be sad and angry, but they'd be safe. That was all that mattered.

An hour and a half later, after driving past the Winters' mansion numerous times, I glanced in the rearview mirror. The front gates were now open. After casually cruising through side streets then back to West Shore Road, I was one hundred and ten percent confident Jackson was driving the car behind me, and was without a doubt tailing me.

"I got you, you bastard," I hissed.

Finding a fairly out in the open area right near North Hempstead Beach Park, I slowed down pulling onto the shoulder of the road. Grabbing a Swiss Army Knife from the glovebox, I carefully made a decent sized cut, but not too big to require stitches, on my left palm. Smearing some of the blood on the steering wheel and passenger seat so when the Feds finally arrived they'd be able to say with certainty I was the person in question, I yanked a few of my hairs out, disposing of them on the floor just to be sure. Balling my fist, I exited the car to find Jackson right there waiting.

"Jackson Winters. How the hell are you?" I said with a big smile on my face. Luca was right. That kid was as smart as a fox. If he could only keep his attitude and temper in check, he could rule the damn world if he ever endeavored to.

"Shut up and get into my car. Now," he warned. He looked exhausted and stressed out. Deep, dark bags hung from under his watery, bloodshot eyes. His country club chic clothing was wrinkled, while his tresses were horribly disheveled. A small handgun hung loosely from his right hand fingertips. "I'm not fooling around, tubby. Get your ass in the car or else I'll put one through your skull, *capisce paisan*?"

"I like what you did there. Excellent pot shot at my weight and heritage. Don't let anyone ever tell you that you're not as sharp as Beau and Tag," I drawled sarcastically. I made sure that my hands were up by my waist for his clear viewing pleasure while I walked to his vehicle.

"There's not a chance in hell that this *tubby* is going to fit in the back of this car. You've got two choices here. Either I ride shotgun or you tell me where to follow you to," I said, leaning over the roof of his vehicle on the passenger side.

"Try anything funny and you're dead. Got it?" he hissed while patting me down. I wasn't dumb. I'd left my gun at Frankie's place earlier.

He drove for about twenty minutes before returning to Tag's house. Entering the property, I noticed that there were no guards in the security booth. He parked around back by what appeared to be a pool house. Ordering I exit the vehicle, he escorted me inside of the home and pushed me into the kitchen area. From there he opened a hidden door which resembled the wall it was on. To the naked eye it appeared the sheetrock was solid. However, scratch and scuff marks in the shape of a semi-circle were on the light gray, wooden floor in front of the passageway. Heaving me down the stairs to the basement, I found myself face to face with Marco who was ready to pounce.

"*Zio*?" he asked.

"Hey, kid. Is Maddy here with you?"

"Yeah, hold on," Marco said. "Hey, shitbag. We've got a problem," he called to Jackson who was almost back up the steps.

"What?" he barked.

"Get your ass down here so we can talk about it face-to-face, man-to-whatever the hell you are."

With a huff Jackson did as told.

"My sister-in-law needs a doctor."

"Why? Is she sick?"

"She's pregnant."

"So? What do you want me to do about it?"

"You have children which means at one point your wife allowed you to bounce up and down on top of her. Is that what you told her when she shared the news that she was knocked up?"

"How is this my problem?"

"When a woman is pregnant they need to be seen by a doctor. Said doctor will examine mom and baby, plus run tests to make sure everyone is healthy. If something is wrong with either person, the situation needs to be dealt with immediately. Since you're obviously still collecting bodies to dispose of, and I'd bet my ass you're waiting to make sure whatever your plan of attack is sticks, if she dies, you're screwed. You won't be able to blame a Santino for the murder," Marco explained obnoxiously.

Jackson remained still. One could clearly see he was trying to process this new unexpected development while plotting his next move.

"Where is she?" He finally spoke.

"Sleeping. Your sister-in-law is watching her because she's been puking her guts up."

"I'll send for someone," he answered, scaling the stairs two by two.

"Maddy is pregnant?" I asked in disbelief. What shitty timing, but Frankie and Gina were going to be thrilled by this news.

"She suggests she probably is. I have no idea how any of that works. If she's not, she's got one hell of a stomach virus, or the stress of everything going on is crushing her," Marco said with a shrug, but being that I knew him his entire life, I saw intense worry dancing around in those dark eyes of his.

"I've got some good news."

"Oh yeah? Does it have something to do with Luca being arrested? Or maybe it has to do with you getting caught like the rest of us? No wait, I know. Did Jackson take the lead in the polls?" Marco scoffed.

"How do you know about Luca?"

"We have a working television down here. Maddy doesn't know yet, so don't say anything to her about it. She's got enough going on."

"Jackson is letting you watch TV?" That notion seemed odd to me.

"If I had to guess I'd say it's a form of torture for Maddy and I. Perhaps it's to show us how fantastically his plan is working. I haven't a clue, and I don't care either. I'm waiting to see how he strikes at Jillian and Liam. So what's this *good news*?"

"Luca is onto Jackson. He's collecting evidence to end all of this. Your brother is smart and works quickly with insane accuracy. Give him a little more time. Between him and your father, they'll figure this out soon and you'll all be able to go home where you belong." Raising my right hand to stop Marco from speaking, I continued. "I deliberately allowed Jackson to catch me, but I left plenty of clues behind for Luca and your father. Hopefully, it will be enough and all they'll need to nail this bastard."

"Back to waiting," Marco said, tossing himself on the sofa.

"Ah, we've got a new roommate I see," a black man said, walking into the living room area. I assumed this was Jillian's producer. "Liam Stevens." He extended his left hand, and I shook it.

"Salvatore D'Angelo. I'm Marco and Maddy's uncle. How is Maddy feeling?"

"Pregnant. I've been through it enough to realize the telltale signs."

"When she's up to it, all of us need to sit down, regroup, and figure something out. Luca, Maddy's husband, Marco's brother, and my nephew, is digging up shit on Jackson and the rest of the Winters. He's aware of what's going on, but until he receives my message—the one I left with my son before I got nabbed, he won't have one hundred percent confirmation his thought process is spot on. Currently, Luca is under house arrest. His trial is set to begin in five months, but with Maddy being pregnant, time is of the essence."

"Jillian and I have been concocting a few plans as well. Between what Luca's got up his sleeve and what we've been scheming it should be enough to end this nightmare shortly," Liam stated confidently. "We got this."

"Yeah. I'm sure we do." I smiled patting his left shoulder.

Maybe.

Chapter Twelve

Nick

Enough was enough. Despite all of my training and personal experience, my emotions would always run deep. Days had passed since Jillian went missing. Aside from Luca Santino—that mobbed up, low life, loser, being arrested no strides to find my wife had been made. Ally Newman somehow pulled a fast one with the court and was able to negotiate a deal where Santino was now out on bail and under house arrest. How could any judge allow that? Obviously the greasy thug was involved in one way, shape, or form, and the state of New York had freed him. They let him walk out the doors and back into society without a care in the damn world. My wife was out there, somewhere, possibly dead. That thought sent me straight back to the dark places my mind had been traveling to recently.

"I have a few errands I have to run, Linda. I might be late," I said to the nanny.

"Of course, Doctor Winters. The children will be fine. Should anything come up, I'll reach out." She smiled.

"Thank you."

Grabbing my keys, I took off. I wanted answers and I planned to get them now. Another day would not go by without knowing where Jillian was. Hauling ass I weaved in and out of traffic on the Belt Parkway, which was a feat because it was pouring. Within record time I made it to my desired location. Not caring about the swarm of press up and down the block, I aggressively bullied the car through the crowd, to the curb, and parked. The second my shoes hit the rain-soaked pavement, I charged for the front door, pounding on it to the point my white knuckled fists stung. The media had a field day snapping pictures, practically blinding me with the flash. A crash of thunder struck as a thicker framed, middle-aged woman with olive skin, a mess of bushy, curly, black hair, dark makeup, exceptionally long red fake nails, more jewelry on than anyone should ever accessorize with, wearing a short grey skirt, a pink blouse, and snow leopard spiked heels answered the door.

"Can I help you," she asked through the small crack in the door that she created.

"I'm Nick Winters." Keeping calm was an accomplishment. I wanted to yell and scream my head off, but this woman had nothing to do with it. Luca Santino did.

"All right. How can I help you?"

"I'd like to come in to speak with Luca Santino."

"I'm sorry, but that's not possible. If you need to talk to him you'll have to contact his attorneys—Ally Newman or Jennifer Glick at Newman and Associates LLP. Have a nice day," she replied sweetly, closing the door.

Pounding on the door again, I waited for her to return, except this time, Luca himself answered.

"What?" he spat.

"Where's *my* wife?" I demanded, jaw clenched.

"Where's *mine*?" he fired back. His one arm was

outstretched by his side while his fingers fanned open. With this gesture, he took a step back and pivoted slightly. His other arm was in a cast supported by a sling. I'd seen this stance before. He was preparing to physically strike me.

"I wasn't the one who was arrested, and I'm certainly not the one under house arrest for the abduction of four, now possibly five people," I stated boldly.

The clicking of cameras and the uproar of reporters amped up.

"Get the hell off of this property," Luca shouted at the press. "The street is public space, nothing else. You've been told several times to screw off. Take the suggestion and go fuck yourselves."

"Hey, *Fratello*. It's not worth it," the woman said as she gently squeezed his good shoulder. "Listen, Doctor Winters, we're all tremendously sorry about the disappearance of your wife. We too are struggling to wrap our heads around the absence of our other brother, sister, and now uncle. I understand that tension runs high during stressful times like these, but I can assure you, we are not the enemy. If you'd like to *calmly* discuss this situation or anything else with us, we'd love for you to come in. If you need some time to take a breath before that can happen, I can appreciate that. You tell us what you'd like. However, I'd be remiss if I didn't warn you; if you enter this house and cannot control yourself, we are not responsible for the outcome. By the way, I'm Gia Santino-Russo, Luca's oldest sister," she explained rationally, extending her hand, which I accepted.

Luca turned and faced her. The two exchanged a heated, but brief conversation in rapid Italian that ended with Gia roughly slapping the back of his head.

"What the hell?" he hissed, rubbing the spot she clocked.

She didn't speak a word. The most threatening glare I'd ever witnessed spread across her face acting as a warning. Shit, even I took a step back out of fear she'd smack me next.

"Please, come into our home," Luca said as if he were reading from a script. He moved mechanically out of the doorframe. "Sit," he added once we were all inside of the kitchen.

The sister went to work pulling things from the refrigerator and started a pot of coffee.

"It's been a while since we chatted last," Luca began. "I'm happy my wife's sacrifice was able to provide you with a larger family."

The son of a bitch couldn't stop himself from taking a pot shot.

"Your former employer was compensated handsomely—a large portion of that I imagine went directly into your pocket." Game, set, match, bitch.

"Nah. I quit long before your bill was rectified."

"Stop it, Luca," Gia said, turning away from whatever she was doing on the stovetop to face him.

"My apologies. I didn't take your wife. I have no idea where she is. Additionally, I'm going to venture a guess and suggest that she's somewhere with my wife, brother, uncle, and Liam Stevens."

"What happened to your hand?" I asked.

"A brick wall when I realized Madison was missing and your family was involved, *again*."

His tone of voice sent up an immediate red flag. He knew something he wasn't sharing. Before I could reply, a small toddler strongly resembling Luca raced into the room.

"Daddy, up," the little boy requested, raising his arms and grabbing at Luca's shirt. Casually, he lifted the child. His face, but especially his eyes, filled with paternal love. Pressing his forehead to his son's, Luca closed his eyes.

"Are you sad?" the boy asked.

"How could I possibly be sad when I'm holding you?"

"I miss Mommy."

"So do I, *miniatura io*, but she'll be home soon," Luca assured.

The child turned and faced me. "Hi."

"Hello," I replied. "I have a son a little older than you. His name is Ethan. Do you like superheroes, because Ethan loves them."

"I do. I like Thor, and Iron Man, and Loki, and Spiderman," the little boy said.

"Ethan likes Iron Man too."

"Where is Vallie?" Luca cut in, blocking his son from conversing with me.

"I'm so sorry, *Zio*," a teenage girl said hurriedly, sprinting in to collect the child.

"It's fine, Vallie. This is Doctor Nicholas Winters. Doctor Winters, this is my niece and God Daughter, Valentina," Luca said as he looked adoringly at the teen.

"It's nice to meet you, Doctor Winters," Valentina responded and smiled. Even the blind could see the robust Santino family resemblance which existed between each member. Dark hair, deep, threatening eyes, olive complexions, mannerisms—their traits bellowed Italian.

"Same here," I said with a nod.

"Could you do your favorite *Zio* a favor, *cara mia*?"

"Of course."

"Would you mind entertaining Frankie upstairs for a bit more so I can finish speaking with Doctor Winters? Frankie should be getting ready to crash within the next half hour or so."

"Of course. Again, I'm sorry. He slipped away from me."

"Hey, *cara—te amo fino alla luna e indietro e poi per sempre.*"

Valentina beamed with love for her uncle. Embracing him tightly from behind, she kissed his cheek while whispering the same Italian sentiment in his ear.

"Valentina seems like a mature, polite, and helpful young woman," I commented after she exited the space. Luca's attachment to his family was pure and honest, revealing a softness I doubted he ever showed the public. Having witnessed this encounter, it was blatantly obvious he wasn't the true culprit, but he was one hundred percent concealing something important.

"Thank you. I'm grateful she's the way she is especially since most teenagers these days lack respect for everything, themselves included. We just celebrated her sweet sixteen the weekend before all of this happened," Gia answered, placing a large platter of food, plates, silverware, and cups at the center of the table. "Please, have something to eat."

"Thank you, but I just ate."

"It's not poisoned," Luca snapped, taking a piece of focaccia bread.

"I never said it was. Look Luca, I understand I showed up here guns blazing, but like your sister said, we're all running off of high emotions. However, if I show you the cards I'm holding, would you be willing to do the same? Perhaps if we pool our resources we could find our wives, family members, and friends a hell of a lot faster."

He and Gia exchanged an intense look before Gia sat beside her brother and spoke. "What do you know, and what do you need answered, beside where Jillian is, because that we don't know—*yet*?"

"First, how are our families connected?" Part of me wished to be made aware of this, but the other part didn't. However, finding Jill was my top priority so whatever uncomfortable shit they had to share, I had no other choice but to hear it.

For an hour Gia explained how the Santinos were screwed over by Beau several times, how Beau made Kelly disappear, how he knew exactly where I was during the Warren Lessor ordeal because Marco Santino had been hired to find me, and how they believed I was the next target. Though Luca didn't speak a word and Gia was guarded with hers, it was clear they both suspected my family was behind this.

"I don't think there's much for me to add. It appears you two already know the whole story and are aware of far more than me. Would I put it past my father and brother to do this? To be honest? No. I wish I could say I'm shocked over what I just learned about my grandfather, but I'm not. What's your plan?" I asked.

"What's yours?" Luca finally spoke up. His dark eyes were full of anger.

"To go to my father's house, find my brother, and persuade him into believing that I'm weak willed and desperate to find Jill. I'll beg him to hold a family press conference where the Winters family will firmly place the blame on the Santino family. Then, I'll ask for all of the help he can possibly provide. Once I have full access to the inside of the house and my family thinks I'm with them and not against them, I'll snoop around and see what I can dig up. If Jill and the others are there, I'll alert the authorities and you." He paused. "I'm a highly decorated psychotherapist. If any one of them are lying I'll know. Their tells are easy to pick up on."

"Sounds like that will take a bit of time and time isn't something I have a lot of," Luca said.

"Fair enough. Where are you going from here?"

Before he or Gia could respond, my cell phone rang. "I'm sorry. Excuse me for one moment." Getting up, I went into the next room. "Nick Winters."

"Nicky, there's been a fire at Tag's house." My grandmother's voice shook.

"Is everyone okay? Are you all right?" I asked tensely.

Seriously? What the hell now?

"We weren't there. I was up at the hospital with Tag and Miranda when it happened. The alarm company called Tag. The fire chief said it had something to do with faulty wiring in the kitchen."

"As long as no one was hurt, that's all that matters. The kitchen can be repaired."

"Oh Nicky, I don't think I can take much more of this. With your grandfather being so ill and Jillian missing—my heart just can't endure anything else." Her tears were clearly heard.

"I know, Grandma. Listen, I need you to take a few slow deep breaths. Ones where when you inhale through your nose your stomach pops out. Then, exhale through your mouth with a sigh. I want you to do this circle breathing six times, okay? Let's do that together."

Once we completed the exercise she sounded considerably calmer, and even more so when I told her I'd swing by my father's home in a bit to check on the house and that I'd contact a contractor to assess and fix the damage so they could remain focused on Beau.

"I have to get going," I said to Luca and Gia.

"Is everything all right?" Gia's voice oozed genuine concern.

"There was an electrical fire at my father's house. My grandmother called to tell me. She's elderly and going through a lot at the moment with her husband's health. We're not all bad people."

"Go, be with your grandmother. I'm sure we'll all talk again soon. And please, be careful. Watch yourself and your surroundings. Don't let your two babies be without both of their parents," Gia said and smiled warmly.

Thanking her for her hospitality and shaking hands with Luca—who I still didn't trust, but had no choice but to at this point, I took off for Sands Point. It had been a while since I'd been out there for a visit. Part of me mused over the idea if the Santinos had anything to do with the fire, but it was doubtful. The house was older and, though well maintained, the electrical system was probably in need of an upgrade. I punched in the code, and the gates opened. My right foot froze over the gas pedal. Each and every single time I'd be here horrible PTSD flashbacks would consume me causing a panic attack to rage. Practicing what I preached earlier to my grandmother, I drew several soothing breaths. Jackson's sports car came into view once I pulled up the driveway a bit more. My parents and grandmother's vehicles were noticeably absent. Ringing the bell to the pool house because typically that's where Jackson and Keira stayed when they visited, I forced my focus on the matter at hand.

"What are you doing here?" Jackson asked appearing taken back by my presence.

"Grandma called. She said there was a fire in the kitchen. She was upset, so I decided to come over to check up on her. I know she's been staying here since grandpa's been in the hospital," I explained.

"Everything is fine," he brushed me off.

"Do you need any help with getting a contractor over here? Was there much damage?"

"The kitchen is a bit toasty, but it's fine. Mom hardly ever cooks anymore so they won't miss it. Dad said he'd call a repairman and the insurance company in the morning."

"Can I come in? There's something I need to discuss with you—in private. Please."

"All right," he said, walking into the foyer.

I followed him inside. "Where are Keira and the kids?"

"Home. She didn't come for this trip. What do you want?"

"Help." I made sure to lower my tone and have my facial expression fall.

"With?"

"Finding Jill. Now I'm aware you two don't get on well, but Jackson, she's my wife and I love her."

"How do you want me to help?"

"I thought we could hold a press conference as a family here at the house. Perhaps if we stand in solidarity and show a united front, the prosecutor will dig harder into Santino. Maybe they'll lean on him and apply pressure on his Mafia family, possibly sending his ass to jail—where he truly belongs, instead of being set free, giving his father time to bribe the trial judge or threaten the jury. I went to pay Luca Santino a visit before I got here."

"What happened?" Jackson asked.

"Yelling, screaming, intimidations—all on his part, of course. You know me. I didn't fight back. That's not my style. All of his ranting proved was he's guilty as sin, verifying my point that they're up to something."

"Why bother going over there?"

"I thought he might be stashing Jill somewhere in that big house his father owns, the one he's been staying at," I answered as warm tears streaming down my cheeks. "I just want her to come home. Not even for me, but for Jordyn and Ethan. I've made mistakes, Jackson, we all have, but you have the ability to help get her back. I need you." As I sobbed I kept a close eye on his body language and expressions. The faux display of emotions was meant to show him how wonderful a presser would be received by the public. How that purge of deep sentiment would make the public, even those who disliked him, side with him. The ego stroking was to soften his skepticism being I never went to him for anything. Hell, this was probably the most in-depth conversation we'd ever shared.

"I'm not like you, Jackson. I doubt I ever will be. How you can remain calm and carry on with Grandpa lying in a hospital bed, with Jill missing, and now with this house fire is a true testament as to why you need to become the next President of this country," I added, amping up the weeping.

"All right, Nick. Deep breaths and all that crap you peddle while treating patients. Do you really think Luca Santino is behind all of this?" His question was direct. However, his body went rigid, his pupils dilated, and his expression drew tense. That one moment, that singular query revealed he was the true mastermind behind all of the disappearances. In his mind he felt if he could trick me, an average, typical person, he could continue to fool the entire world.

"Of course. If not him or his family, who else would do something like this? They all need to be convicted and sent to prison for life. If anyone of them hurt my Jill," I started, but I forced another bout of bawling out of my mouth stopping the thought. All he saw was how wonderful this would look for the cameras. Curiously, after my declaration of Santino guilt, his entire being relaxed enough for him to finally take the seat across from me.

"It's going to be all right," he soothed in the fakest tone possibly. He was trying out ways to provide comfort that would come off as natural for the cameras. "I'll set up a press conference for either later today or tomorrow morning. We'll do it at Grandpa's house. Mom and Dad will be there. I'll see if Savannah and Morgan can make it here to be a part of it as well. We'll get Jill back. Don't worry."

"Thank you," I whispered with inflection filled with gratitude.

Dumb ass. You just walked right into my trap.

Chapter Thirteen

Frank

"Your father said Luca was right about our trip to Sandy Shores. The sandcastles were spot on, but he enjoyed the time we went to watch the Jacksonville Jaguars play more?" I questioned Tony, making sure he conveyed Salvatore's final message accurately.

"Yes, *Zio*."

"And he suspected he wouldn't be returning home?"

"Yes, *Zio*."

"About what time was that?"

"Pretty late. After Luca was sprung," he answered scrolling through something on his phone. "Quarter to midnight. We talked for four minutes and twelve seconds."

"Did he have anything else to say aside from what you've already told me?"

"No, *Zio*."

"What did you tell your mother?"

"Nothing, *Zio*."

"What are your thoughts?" This kid had always responded to anything—good or bad, like a robotic soldier. Jimmy did the same. Salvatore and Donatella certainly raised obedient, respectful men, but at times it would've been nice if they weren't so stoic.

"He knew. In fact, I believe he allowed himself to get caught. His hint about Luca being right means

Jackson took them to Tag's home in Sands Point. Whatever you deem necessary to get my father, Marco, and Madison back will be done with speed and accuracy. All I need is for you to order the hit," he responded. His feet were perfectly centered at a shoulder lengths distance apart, his hands were behind his back, and his face was blank. The last time I saw this kid smile or laugh seemed like ages ago.

"They'll be home soon. You have my word," I assured. "For now, I'd prefer if you didn't share any of this with your mother. There's no sense worrying her over this."

With a nod he took his leave up the stairs.

Gina sat in the living room consoling Donatella who, rightfully so, was tragically upset and full of anxiety. Unsure of what to say to provide any comfort whatsoever, I went to Salvatore's home office. Perhaps he'd left something lying around. Though we all swept our homes prior to Luca's arrest, Salvatore was infamous for leaving behind little breadcrumb clues. His workspace was considerably neater and far more organized than mine. It was decorated with several family photographs amassed over the years. A picture of his and my father sat front and center beside a shot of him, Donatella, and his sons at Luca's wedding. Tucked behind that was an old picture of him and I as teenagers. Nothing stood out immediately so I sat, carefully rifling through drawers. A ping from my cell phone caused me to jump slightly. These days whenever that damn thing went off it meant something bad was going down. Glancing at the screen I saw a text from Gia.

'Nick Winters showed up. He's at the door.' She wrote.

'What does he want?'

'Luca.'

'No.'

A few minutes passed before she replied. 'He's not going away. The press is going crazy over this.'

'Handle it. Mediate. Record him. Erase anyone else's voice.'

'On it.'

'Text me when he leaves.'

'Of course. Love you.'

'Love you too, *Bellissima*.'

Flipping on the flat screen beside the desk, I turned on a local news station I was sure was covering this nightmare. There, live in living color, was Nick Winters being ushered into my house by Gia. She'd take care of this. She always did. Many, Gina included, didn't realize Gia played a fairly sizable role in our *family business.* She knew more than most, but never got her hands dirty. Vicious, ruthless, and fearless my oldest daughter handled all of the money going in and out, took care of the payoff roster, purchased unmarked/untraceable items, collected debts, oversaw properties, applied for whatever licenses we required, rectified taxes, and made sure everyone got paid weekly. Aside from Salvatore, Marco, Luca, and Salvatore's kids—maybe her husband had knowledge though he never spoke a word of it, her identity remained as a former real-estate broker, housewife, and mother. A healthy dose of her mother's personality seamlessly blended with mine, along with her grandfather's savviness and her own sense of self made her a valuable key player. Thankfully, she lacked the Santino temper.

Salvatore's office turned up empty. Not a scrap of

new information was found. Keeping an eye on the television I saw Nick exit the house. Seconds later Gia texted.

'He's gone. He's going to go rogue which might bode well for us, but it might not. We'll talk when you get home.'

Before I could reply the phone rang.

"How are you, my friend?" I asked Arthur Lawrence.

"Well. Won't ask how you are because I'm pretty sure I know. Anyway, I wanted to tell you that I ran into Carmine the other day. I always find it strange—an Italian with flaming red hair. He's an electrician now you know. He's going to do work on my daughter's fuse box at no charge. Said family takes care of family. I tried to fight him over it, but he said it's a done deal."

"That's rather generous. I'm sure you'll tip him and he *won't* say shit about it." After everything I'd done for him over the years Lawrence doing one favor for me was refreshing. "How's the rat problem?" I inquired.

"Not a one. The wife and I checked the entire house."

Damn it. Luca was wrong.

"Interesting."

"That's not to say they're not in the walls or some crap like that, but we couldn't find a single one."

His suggestion that Marco, Madison, and Salvatore might still be there provided me with a small amount of hope.

"Listen, I have to get going. I've got to pick up a few things from the market. Thanks for calling."

"We'll be in touch. Oh, I haven't forgotten that you wanted to see those pictures from the trip to Myrtle

Beach the wife and I took. I'm having them printed up as we speak. Let's grab dinner soon so I can show you."

"Sounds like a plan," I responded, then hung up.

Struggling to maintain composure I wasn't sure what to do. Without proof Luca was screwed. Marco, Maddy, and Salvatore were as well. Not to mention the loss and blow my grandson would sustain. Yanking at my hair I forced my brain to focus. Maybe the blueprints would show something Lawrence wasn't able to inspect when he was there. Internally I felt as if I was fighting a battle I'd never win. Externally I had to hold my shit together.

"Gina, I need to get home. There are a few things I have to handle there. Plus, I don't want to leave Luca with Gia alone for too long. When they're together for a stretch of time only trouble comes from it," I said, attempting to come across considerably cooler than I felt. What I'd said wasn't a lie. I did have to get back to the house, and Luca and Gia were infamous for their thick as thieves bond. Don't get me wrong—the fact they were close was great. They'd always been. To spite the sizable age difference, my oldest constantly looked after my youngest. It wasn't abnormal for him to turn to her before anyone else. Recently he and Marco had become attached at the hip, but for different reasons.

"I can drive *Zia* home," Jimmy offered.

Gina opted to stay and have Jimmy drop her back at the house. Grateful for the ability to take off alone, I spent the five-minute ride preparing to be accosted by the media. As expected, the brief walk from the driveway to the porch was a fiasco.

The second I stepped foot through the door, Gia grabbed my elbow, yanking me through the kitchen and into the basement.

"Luca is pissed. Like fuming pissed Nick was here. The second he left we had one of our knockdown, drag 'em out fights. Nick wanted to know about how our families are connected so I gave him a condensed, watered-down version which seemed to sate his curiosity. In turn he shared his plans—to appeal to Jackson, convincing him to hold a press conference," Gia informed.

"Where's Luca now?"

"Upstairs, probably sleeping. After our argument ended he said he was exhausted, that he hadn't been sleeping. I suggested he continue to stay here this way we can help out with Frankie. I'm around every day so it's not a big deal. His house arrest bracelet is set for him to be here for work. I'm sure Ally can speak with the judge if he wants to temporarily move back in, but he's obsessed Maddy will call or show up and what would happen if he wasn't at his house?"

"I'll talk to him and see if I can get through to him. Sheltering in place for the time being isn't a bad idea," I agreed.

"He's a bomb with a short fuse, Dad. Luca is going to go off and the blast produced from that explosion is going to be catastrophic. You and I know him better than anyone. He's obsessed with Maddy and Frankie. His fixation borderlines on insane when it comes to the two of them. The second he brought her into this house he was visibly possessive. I cannot tell you how many calls we shared where he took deep digs at the dentist she was dating after he dumped her. If I was fearful for, as Luca refers to him as 'Doctor No Nuts,' you can only imagine how terrified I am if he gets within a ten-foot radius of any Winters family member. The funny thing is, everyone has always perceived Marco as the lunatic, when in reality it's always been Luca. Now that he's a 'made man' his rage has grown and his sanity has vanished. I'm trying really hard to keep his ass in check, but he's making it damn near impossible." Gia paced the basement, anxiously chewing on her right thumb nail.

"*Bellissima*, calm down," I urged, feeling the strength of her uneasy energy. "I'm aware that you and Luca have always been confidants—that you always felt the responsibility to protect him, but he's a grown man —"

"Who one day will become the Don," she snapped, cutting me off. "I'm aware of the plan. When you retire Marco is up. Marco's first order of business will be promoting Luca to Underboss, shoving Salvatore aside and keeping Tony and Jimmy as Capos. When Marco's time is up, Luca is in, then Frankie, because we both know Marco is never going to settle down and create a legitimate son. I haven't slept in years, Dad—freaking years. I worry endlessly about my brothers. When can I take a breath? When can I put my head on the damn pillow at night and sleep the sleep of the just? Oh, and let's not forget about my Vallie. She's one hundred percent her '*Zio Luca's girl*.' I'm a wreck over the day she comes to me to take over my role in this nightmare." Tears streamed without shame from her beautiful, dark brown eyes.

"Gia, sweetheart —"

"Don't sweetheart or *Bellissima* me. My brother is missing. My sister-in-law and uncle have vanished as well. But the absolute worst is my perfect, handsome, brilliant Luca is being accused of kidnapping, possible murder, and a slew of other trumped up charges, and the District Attorney won't be happy until a Santino is behind bars. Now Nick Winters is going to host a press conference with his shit family, further driving the nail in Luca's coffin. The media and public are going to hang him without even knowing a scrap of truth. They're going to ruin him. Luca isn't sleeping or eating. He's just losing it and that will not happen as long as I'm around," she shouted, full on hysterically crying.

"What's with all the screaming? I heard you from upstairs, G," Luca questioned, entering the basement.

Without speaking she threw herself into his wounded embrace. His good arm held her close and tight, while the casted one attempted to provide the same protection.

"What's going on, G?" he whispered.

Their closeness was beyond evident in that moment. Gia had always been his second mother and partner-in-crime so-to-speak. In lieu of speaking, she simply continued to cry, heavily. Looking at me, Luca wanted answers.

"She's upset over all of this. We all are, but I swear to God we will clear your name and bring Marco, Maddy, and Salvatore home—all alive and well," I attested, unsure of how realistic that statement was. "Look, we're down, but not out. I have to take care of a few things. I'll see you both later. Jimmy is going to drive Mom home in a bit," I added, taking off up the steps, out of the house, through the mess of reporters, and into my car. With not a clue in the world as to how to proceed, I thought it best to return to the scene of the crime—where the cops found Salvatore, Maddy, and Marco's abandoned vehicles. Someone had to have seen something. A camera had to have picked something up, and I'd be damned if I didn't find it.

Chapter Fourteen

Madison

I'd forgotten how horrible pregnancy was, *especially* the first trimester. In the end all of the throwing up, food/smell aversions, mood swings, and whatnot were worth it, but nevertheless, the journey to holding your beautiful miracle in your arms blows ass. It was awful with Frankie when I was home with Luca and had my family's support, but here, trapped in Tag Winters' basement magnified everything by a million. Marco, Liam, and Salvatore were all constant sources of comfort. However, Jillian had become a friend of sorts. She'd lie in bed beside me or on the couch sharing her own pregnancy story while providing whatever was required so I'd feel safe. There were plenty of ups and downs particularly on days when I'd watch the news. Jillian suggested Jackson allowing us to watch the television was his way of torturing me, Marco, and Salvatore. We'd view reports in silence as updates on Luca came in. Each clip left me an emotional wreck. Marco, however, refused to allow me to see my husband perp walk from his parents' home. Knowing he didn't do anything wrong proved murderous. This pent-up anger surged inside of me. I felt like a rat trapped in a cage— like a prisoner who knew they were in the slammer for life.

A glimmer of happiness did occur the day after

Salvatore joined us. Jackson charged down the stairs demanding I go to the main floor with him, warning me not to try anything funny or else he'd shoot me. Initially, I didn't believe him until I saw the outline of a handgun tucked into the back waist of his slacks. Thankfully, after a tremendous verbal altercation with Marco and Salvatore, he allowed Jillian to join me. Jackson shoved us up two flights of stairs to what appeared to be a guest room. Inside were two people—one male and one female, both dressed in hospital scrubs. Neither wore name tags or identification badges. I was told to lie on the bed and the female proceeded to ask me a ton of routine questions about my health. After drawing at least a dozen vials of blood, the female followed me to a bathroom where I had to provide a urine sample. Once we were back in the room, the male set up a portable ultrasound machine. I held my breath until I saw and heard my baby's heartbeat.

"That's your baby, Maddy." Jillian's eyes were moist and her smile bright while she squeezed my hand.

"It's too early to detect the sex, but you're roughly three months pregnant. Your baby is completely healthy, developing normally, and has a strong heartbeat. I'll have the blood and urine run at the lab, but for now rest, eat healthy, drink plenty of water, and take prenatal vitamins. You've done this before so if anything feels odd or off, reach out to us or head to the Emergency Room," the male stated.

"Thank you," I replied, desperately wanting to scream out that I was being held against my will by Jackson, but I held the urge inside because I had no idea if these two were in on it.

Jackson hung back by the door waiting for the exam

to be over. Once the male and female had packed up, they spoke briefly with him and left. Jillian and I were ordered to return to the basement.

"Are you okay, Maddy?" Marco questioned, practically jumping on me the second he saw my feet appear on the top step.

"I'm good. I'm about three months pregnant, but the baby is totally fine."

"Best news I've heard in a long time," Liam added.

"Thanks." I smiled weakly, unsure of why he'd care. "Where's Salvatore?"

"In the bathroom checking something out," Liam said. "If all goes well and our hunch is right, we've got a plan. You being pregnant sweetens the pot."

"How so?" And there it was. His true motive for happiness over my current condition. Granted, Liam seemed like a nice enough man, but he remained a perfect stranger. Though Jillian trusted him immensely, I still harbored doubts.

"While you were upstairs I came across an old dial up router and an ancient computer from prehistoric times in a box in the bedroom closet. Marco and Salvatore have been popping open random ceiling tiles to see if they can find anything up there that we might able to use," Liam explained.

"You need a phone jack to use dial up," I said.

"One step ahead of you. There's one behind the television cabinet. Added bonus, the phone cords were still attached to the router."

"Is the jack still attached to an active landline?"

"I can't say for sure."

"Does the computer fire up?" Jillian chimed in. You could see the wheels turning inside of her head.

"No, *but* I used to work on these models early on in my career. I've spent enough time watching IT techs fix them. With some luck, I'll be able to figure out what the problem is. The downside is, it's going to take time. After it loads, we'll be able to test the phone line. If that's a go, which the box appears to be intact, we can send an email to everyone and anyone with our location that can be confirmed by the IP address attached to it. That bit of information will lead them to this address."

"You're brilliant, Liam," Jillian exclaimed.

"It's a great course of action, but only *if* all of that can happen. The computer might need parts we can't readily purchase or the phone line might be a dud," Marco said.

"We won't know until we try." Liam encouraged.

"All right, boys and girls. I found a bunch of discarded wires inside of the drop ceiling. I highly doubt anyone even knows they're there. When technology becomes obsolete, the old crap that went along with it is usually left to die. Installers don't want to haul it away, so they leave it behind. Plus, there was this eyeglass screwdriver in the bathroom. We'll have to create tools, but it's a start," Salvatore said, entering the room. Sweat dripped from his brow. "If we need to solder something we've got paperclips and a gas stove. We'll improvise. Let's get cracking."

With that, Liam and Salvatore began their work.

****

"Breaking news. The home of Mister Speaker of the House Tag Winters has caught fire. We're told local fire and police are on the scene," a male anchor reported. Aerial footage showed at least a dozen cop cars, three ambulances, and six fire trucks swarming the house.

Marco, who was in the kitchen preparing dinner, stopped what he was doing, let out a sharp whistle which caused Salvatore and Liam to appear, and joined me on the couch.

"That's the main house. It looks like attention was concentrated on the kitchen." Jillian spoke up, moving closer to the screen. "Do you hear anything?"

The room fell silent with everyone straining an ear in an attempt to catch a sound clip of sirens or something, anything at this point.

"Are we in a soundproof room, or are we too far away and too underground from the outside world?" Liam asked himself, walking to the wall near the steps and knocking on the surface. "Son of a bitch," he hissed.

"What?" Salvatore asked.

"Sound proofed. We're in a sound proofed prison."

"That's not a bad thing," Marco interjected. "If we can't hear them, they can't hear us, just like in Pop's basement. Are you sure you didn't see any camera wires in the ceiling, *Zio*?"

"Nothing and I promise, I did a *deep* dive. There's electrical, phone, cable lines—shit like that up there, but no cameras. Not even a pinhole or nanny cam is around here. I checked every room."

"Good, good," Marco mused, rubbing his goatee. Usually, he was clean shaven. Due to his lack of grooming, with facial hair he resembled an older version of Luca. "Let's all do one more intense sweep before we start anything."

"It appears nobody was in the house at the time of the fire, which we're being told is being considered an electrical one originating from the kitchen. Firemen were able to contain and stop the fire before it became a blaze," the reporter added.

A tremendous expression of relief spread over Jillian's concerned face. Falling back onto the couch she took several long, slow, deep breaths. Out of the corner of my eye I spotted Marco and Salvatore exchange a brief, but somewhat telling look. This transaction caused me to take pause. What did they know or suspect? Did one of the Santinos start the fire? Did Luca have something to do with it? Before I could process the extent of my thoughts, the newscaster returned to the screen.

"Further breaking news. Doctor Nicholas Winters, husband of missing journalist and talk show host Jillian Winters, was just spotted entering the house of known Mafia Crime Boss Frank Santino. We have word Luca Santino, who's awaiting trial for the abduction of not only Winters' wife, but of his own, along with his brother, Marco Santino, Liam Stevens, and now notorious Underboss for the Santino Crime Family, Salvatore D'Angelo, is currently staying at the Brooklyn home. Brandy, what can you tell us about what's happening at the Santino home?" a news reporter said catching my attention and causing me to walk over to the television. I stood inches away from the screen. Marco joined me, equally captivated. He placed his hand on my shoulder.

"About five minutes ago Doctor Winters SUV slammed to a halt right over here on the curb where's its currently parked. He stormed out of the unproperly parked vehicle and proceeded to bang on the door. Sources have confirmed Gia Santino-Russo answered the door, with Santino close behind. You can see here in this clip how Santino aggressively addressed the press."

A clip played of Luca with one arm in a cast which was slinged against his chest, screaming, 'Get the hell off of this property. The street is public space, nothing else. You've been told several times to screw off. Take the suggestion and go fuck yourselves,' while being pulled back by Gia. He looked horrible as exhaustion hung heavily from the bags under his dark brown eyes.

"What happened to his arm?" I shot at Salvatore.

"Santino temper. He's fine. I promise," he replied while his pupils remained fixated on the screen.

"Winters then entered the house, surfacing about an hour later. Though he refused to provide any comments, his demeaner was considerably calmer. Winters got into his SUV and took off. We're told he's with his brother, Presidential hopeful Jackson Winters at Mister Speaker of the House Tag Winters' home. Stay with us for the latest developments on this story."

"Nick is here." Jillian sprang to life.

"That's great, lady, but how do you propose you get to him?" Marco questioned. There was something about her that rubbed him the wrong way. Perhaps it was because you had two Type A personalities locked away together in close quarters, or maybe he knew something about her that he wasn't willing to share. Whatever the case, he needed to take a breath. We needed her and Liam to get out of here alive.

"I don't, but it means he's still out there alive and well, actively searching for me. If he's here, I'd bet you anything it's because he's snooping around and is on to something," Jillian defended.

"That still doesn't save any of our sorry asses," Marco scoffed. He turned on his heel and headed back into the kitchen area.

Jillian, ready to pounce, was stopped when I held my hand up and shook my head. Following Marco, I approached him and whispered, "Hey. You've got to stop attacking her. We're all in this together *for the moment*. When everything is over, you can tell whoever you'd like where to go, how to get there, and what to do once there. As for Nick Winters being in the general vicinity, that might be a good thing. Maybe he's nosing around, maybe he's not. If Jillian always suspected Beau and the other Winters of concealing information about the Lessor abduction and the Lesser/Davis disaster, that sentiment could ring true with Nick as well. Husbands and wives talk—a lot. There have been many times when Luca has shared his take on a situation with me which caused me to view whatever the issue differently. Don't forget, his wife is missing too. If Luca is on the case, why wouldn't Nick? He was just at your house. Why would he be there?"

"Liam has to start tooling around with that damn computer," he replied, brushing me off.

"Don't dismiss me, Marco."

"I'm not, Madison." His voice rose as his expression twisted with annoyance.

"You're hiding something about Jillian and I demand to know exactly what it is. I realize and acknowledge all of the crap that exists between her family and ours, but you've been on the attack with her since day one. Why?"

"Her being a Winters isn't enough?"

"No, this time it's not. There's more."

Shaking his head, then running his right hand through his hair, he sighed heavily. "I adore you, Maddy. There's nothing in this world that I wouldn't do for you, no questions asked, but stay out of my business."

In all the time that I knew Marco he had never spoken to me like that before. His threat caused me to take a step back. "Were you one of her affairs?" I asked. If he could act like a jerk so could I.

"Excuse me?"

"I guess I just got my answer."

"You'd do best to learn your place in this family, Madison," he said, then exited the kitchen.

Chapter Fifteen

Liam

Weeks, I imagine, passed with me tinkering around with that Smithsonian relic of a computer. Had I had access to the tools required to fix the damn thing the process would've gone considerably faster and a hell of a lot smoother, perhaps I might even have been done by now. Using a butter knife, coins, my nails, thumbtacks, hair and safety pins, and a paperclip as a solder iron, all while improvising parts with random shit lying around this damn prison cell, I'd made progress, but not enough. The system finally booted up, but it remained glitchy. Without one hundred percent assurances, there was no way I'd present a 'let's see what happens' approach to the others. Jillian would give it a go because she trusted me. She'd be able to get Madison on board, but Salvatore and Marco—not a chance in Hell. Salvatore mainly hung back with me. He proved to be a tremendous help and pretty solid, calming company. Shockingly enough he seemed to know quite a bit about network systems and computers. The ideal that this man was an illiterate bully was judgmental and wrong. In fact, many times we'd sit and chat while working. Salvatore was a passionate family-oriented person, who enjoyed cigars, golfing, and crossword puzzles. Truthfully, if I'd met him on the job we'd probably be friends. Not only was he kind, he was funny and a reassuring presence. He thought before speaking and acting, unlike his nephew.

Worry remained not only on the task at hand, but with Madison and her pregnancy and with Marco's nonexistent fuse. For a short while it seemed that Madison and Marco were engaging in some sort of spat, but it didn't last too terribly long. With each passing day Madison's baby was growing. In roughly five-ish months she'd pop, unless the moment occurred earlier. Then what? We'd still be stuck down here, but now with an infant to contend with. The goal was to get out of here as soon as humanly possible.

"I got the monitor to stop showing static," Salvatore informed.

"Excellent. Only, what? Six hundred other things left to do?" I replied.

"Hey, we've made strides. A few weeks ago, this thing wouldn't even turn on. It's a process, and the only option available. We take what we can get and deal with the cards we're holding."

"Too true, my friend," I said, slapping the large man on his shoulder.

When Salvatore joined us we all thought it best to change up our sleeping arrangements. Currently, he and I were sharing the room with the twin beds, while Madison and Jillian shared the room with the queen sized bed. Marco rode the couch, which didn't seem to bother him one bit.

"*Zio*," Madison called.

"What's up, *bella*?" he shouted back.

"Come see this," she said, through audible tears.

Sprinting down the short hallway, I followed him into the living room. Madison, Marco, and Jillian all sat on the couch watching the television. 'Winters Family

Speaks Out,' scrolled across the bottom of the screen. Jackson, acting as the spokesman for the group spoke while Nick and the rest of the family—grandmother, sisters, and spouses, sans Beau, stood in solidarity beside him. Their heads all down and their faces were filled with faux concern.

"We ask you, the public, to assist us in bringing home our dear Jill. We miss and love her. Without Jill's presence we're lost. She's always been our pillar of strength and our rock during trying times. As many of you may have noticed, our grandfather, Vice President Beau Winters is absent. He remains hospitalized. We're hopeful his return home will be soon. We have faith his doctors and nurses will release him when they're confident he's better. Between his heart attack and the news of Jill's abduction, he's beside himself with grief and pain. We all are. Whoever has taken our beloved Jill, we beg of you, please return her to us, healthy and whole. She's not only a sister, daughter, and granddaughter, but my brother's wife, and my niece and nephew's mother. If you have any information about her whereabouts, or have information pertaining to her abduction, we humbly ask that you come forward and alert the authorities. FBI Special Agent Timothy Wilder, as well as Nassau County Police Commissioner Dan Lindsey are working tirelessly in conjunction with surrounding law enforcement to locate not only our sweet Jill, but also Liam Stevens, her producer. The Winters family is offering a ten-million-dollar reward for any information that leads to the safe return of my sister-in-law. Before turning things over to Special Agent Wilder and Commissioner Lindsey, I'll answer a few questions on behalf of our family."

"Why is Luca Santino out on bail?" one reporter shouted.

"That's a very good question, sir. I encourage you to ask it again to Commissioner Lindsey," Jackson responded.

"Do you believe the Santino Family is behind this?" another yelled.

"We're all innocent until proven guilty. Mr. Santino will have his day in court to plead his case. I have tremendous faith in our justice system, as should you."

"Why was Nick at the Santino home?" an older female questioned.

"During a moment of intense anguish, my brother went to the home of Frank and Marco Santino searching for answers—answers we're all seeking. Unfortunately, he was met with nothing but a volatile outburst from Luca Santino. Thankfully, Nick wasn't harmed during the altercation. I cannot imagine what Nick is enduring. If it were me and my wonderful wife, Keira, went missing…" He paused looking down and shaking his head. "I don't know what I'd do. Family is everything."

"What about Liam Stevens, Madison Santino, Marco Santino, and Salvatore D'Angelo? Does your reward apply to them as well? Do you think they're with Jillian?" a short, chubby reporter queried.

"Our thoughts are with the Stevens, Santino, and D'Angelo families. We continue to pray for their safe return as well. Should any of them be with our Jillian, please know, we're searching high and low for you. We will do whatever necessary to find you too," Jackson said, side stepping the reward question. "I'm going to turn this press conference over to Special Agent Wilder."

Moving forward Wilder took the microphone.

"Good afternoon. I'm FBI Special Agent Timothy Wilder. The FBI has been working closely with local law enforcement to locate Jillian Winters, Liam Stevens, Marco Santino, Madison Santino, and Salvatore D'Angelo. We've also been in contact with Ms. Santino's family—the Langmores, the Stevens family, Mr. Santino's family, and the D'Angelo family. All angles are being explored. A tip line and email address have been set up for anyone with information pertaining to this case. All tips will remain anonymous. To date, Luca Santino has been charged with the abduction of the five individuals, but their whereabouts remain unknown. As to why Mr. Santino has been released on bail, that's for the criminal justice system to explain, not the FBI or Commissioner Lindsey. For the moment we are not going to entertain any questions from the press. Thank you for your time and help."

"They're throwing my husband under the bus," Madison spat, standing. Her body revealed a sizable pregnant belly.

"It's a ploy, Maddy," Jillian said. "You're a private investigator. Put it together. Nick realizes something is up with his family. I'd bet anything he knows they're behind this. He went to them *after* speaking with your husband, which tells me Luca is just as cognizant as Nick. My husband then ran to Jackson, whose kryptonite is good press and his name in the headlines pushing his political agenda. A move like this will have his likeability rating shoot through the roof. While Jackson is basking in all the fake glory, Nick will be digging, and I promise, deep."

"This is all speculation, Jill," Madison replied, rubbing her temples. "Shortly Luca will stand trial for crimes he didn't commit. There's a strong chance the jury will not rule in his favor. I have a son and another kid on the way. They need their mother *and* their father. You don't know Luca the way that I do. He's an incredible husband, loving father, and brilliant lawyer. If Nick's unconfirmed plan doesn't work, or Liam can't fix the damn computer we're screwed—me especially."

"Maddy." Jillian attempted to comfort her, but Madison walked away.

Throwing his hands up in the air, Marco went after Maddy.

"We've got work to do," I said to Salvatore.

His nod in response suggested he felt the same. This basement had become a powder keg of sorts. The pressure had built so much, the situation was bound to explode.

Chapter Sixteen

Luca

The nightmare titled 'my life' continued at the same frigging pace—slow and with no updates. Ally and Jennifer were busting their asses day and night creating an iron clad defense, but Madison, Marco, and Salvatore still remained missing. True to his word, Nick did run with his tail between his legs to Jackson, who in turn held a press conference. It didn't matter though. Nothing came of it. Well, maybe it had for him and his family, but not for me and mine. To date, my wife, brother, and uncle had been gone for nearly five months. Having knowledge of how abductions worked, typically the longer the person was missing, the higher the chance they weren't alive. Whenever this thought crept inside of me—usually late at night, I'd shove it away by remembering Madison, Marco, and Salvatore were smart and sharp—especially Marco.

Not being able to handle the triggering effects of the crowded space in my parents' house anymore I returned home with Frankie. I needed room to breathe. Besides, I was confident my brother and wife would come here first. What blew my mind was not only were local police and the FBI working the case, but all of the major crime families in New York and surrounding areas were as well. Granted, the authorities were merely putting on a show—they already considered this open and shut business with me as the culprit, but my colleagues hadn't. Lawrence suggested no one was present in the main house during the fire, but something wasn't sitting right. Dragging his ass on providing the requested blueprints of Tag's Sands Point home—his excuse was he had to make one hundred percent sure no one was aware of his ties to my father, I was certain something was there that he missed.

Now today, after demanding I be present at Voir Dire, the trial was imminent. The only bit of evidence the prosecutor had was my hair in Jillian and Liam's vehicles. Ally assured me that wasn't enough to convince a jury, but I'd seen juries lock people's asses up for far less. The trial was expected to last one week, possibly a touch longer. Pretty much every member of the Winters family was scheduled to testify for the prosecution, as well as the Langmores, and Stevens. My family was also on the hit list. The usual lineup of suspects such as DNA analysts, the arresting officers, and so on were also on the docket. Items recovered during discovery were, in fact, terribly weak, but who knew what the Winters or Langmores would say? Who knew if the prosecution had a surprise up their sleeve? This trial wasn't only about the issue at hand, but about the Santino Crime Family—a group the authorities have been trying to toss in the slammer for decades, as well. The judge might use this case as an example for the other crime families in the country.

"We were able to secure Doctor Kensington," Jennifer whispered with a smile.

Newman and Associates had often called upon Kensington in the past. Earning his reputation as one of the top trial scientists in the country, a slight sense of relief was experienced on my part. If anyone could stack the jury in my favor it was him. Hours later, eight men and eight women were carefully selected. While I flipped through random paperwork lying on the defense table, Ally approached me and sat.

"Listen Santino, I'm confident we *will* win this, but in light of some new evidence I just received a few moments ago, I've decided it's best that you don't testify," she explained.

"What's the evidence?" I replied, attempting to come across as calm. Leaning back in my chair, I braced myself for the worst.

"For starters the Winters—Beau, Tag, and Jackson, intend to discuss your family and how they were bullied by them over the years. Tag is saying that some years ago your father and Mr. D'Angelo approached him about a gambling license. He suggests they offered him a large sum of money to obtain the license, but he declined and informed them of the proper channels and paperwork required to legally get said license. They're also going to bring up how you were there before Beau had his heart attack. Other mentions will include a video of your brother speaking to Beau before a presser which was held when Nick Winters went missing which will be spun as Marco having involvement in that abduction, testimony from Richard and Donna Langmore over your relationship with their daughter, Noel Wasserman will be commenting on your aggressive temper, your reasons for leaving my firm will be under a white hot spotlight, you being named a suspect in Madison's previous abduction, how your family broke into the Winters' home to shake down Beau, Tag, and Jackson and a crap ton of what I already know to be lies. They want to get under your skin, place focus on the Santinos *not* the Winters."

"Interesting, but I'm still testifying. I'm guilty of none of that. Well, some yes, but most no. I'm telling you Ally, Jackson Winters is behind all of this. I can't prove it, but I know he is. When that little shit Nick came to my home I warned him he was Jackson's next target. Evidently he agreed with that sentiment because he's been up his brother's ass, which is completely untypical behavior being the two of them can't stomach each other. Isn't there some way to search Tag's property—the entire plot of land, not just the main house? I've been racking my brain, but I can't come up with anything legal." There was no way in hell I was sitting this one out. The jury had to hear my side of the story regardless of how black the prosecution planned on painting me.

"On what grounds? Unless we have solid probable cause, there's no way any judge would willingly sign a search warrant of that magnitude, especially when it involves the Winters. And I highly recommend that you refrain from having any more fires started there either."

I went to speak, but no words came out. Frustration, defeat, as well as an entire host of emotions swarmed my head like bees around a honey hive.

"There's one more thing."

"Oh yeah? What's that?"

"The District Attorney requested cameras, meaning this will be televised. It's a high-profile case. You've got the prestigious, elite, political Winters family verses, well, the Mafia." She paused, holding her hand up to stop me from responding while taking a sip of coffee. "I'm certain the Winters are going to petition the court to keep it private, but after doing this for as long as I have, the motion will be denied. You're going into this with pretty much everyone thinking you're guilty as sin and the Winters are the innocents."

"If I don't take the stand they'll think we're hiding something," I countered, not giving a damn if the trial would be center stage for the entire world to see.

"If you do take the stand they'll know you are, Santino. You might not be the one behind these abductions, but you're certainly behind other crimes. Luca, you were there when Beau had his heart attack," she warned sternly, but I wasn't about to give in.

"No, I was not. The old shitbag was totally fine when we left him. Don't you think the public should be made aware of the fact Beau Winters has had several dealings with my family—all at *his* request?"

"He'll deny it and spin a tale over how your family targeted and bullied him. He already is. It will all end up being hearsay anyway. Who do you think the jury will believe while deliberating? Winters—that's who. Unless you've got some proof stashed away that can be authenticated within the next few days pinning Jackson to crimes thusly showing how Beau was involved with the Santino Crime Family, you've got nothing."

"I might, Ally," I replied, standing. "Give me a few hours. I'll call you."

A look of confusion hung from her face. "Don't make this situation any worse than it already is. That means stay away from all of the Winters. Under no circumstances are you to be anywhere near them. What Nick did by going to your home was wrong and now poses another problem for us. His version of what happened inside your home will be vastly different than yours and your sister's. And don't forget—you're on that anklet. Let's not give the prosecution anymore fuel for the fire."

"I'm not going anywhere, nor do I plan on doing anything I shouldn't. I'll be going home with my father," I said smiling as I patted her shoulder. "Talk soon."

With a quick glance and cue of the eye, my father followed me to the car. Dodging reporters had become second nature. You just keep walking with your mouth firmly shut.

"Hey, Pop. All those times when Beau reached out to you, did you keep any of that correspondence or record any of those calls?" I inquired once we reached the highway.

"Salvatore probably did. He's calculated like that; always wanting to have blackmail at the ready. I have no idea where he hid all of that. I didn't find a scrap of anything useful in the house, but I can certainly give it another sweep, this time with his sons. They might know where he concealed the good stuff. Why?"

"If you can dig something up and it can be authenticated, Ally can present that as evidence showing Beau came to us and he knew you."

"I'll look," he said. His eyes never left the road, making me believe that he was aware of something more than what he was willing to share.

"Listen Pop," I began.

"When I get you home I'll handle it, Luca. When the time is right you'll know everything I do. Until then, I'm the father *and* the boss of this shit show."

"Why would you want to share anything with me? I'm just the spare to the missing heir of what did you call it? This shit show?" I scoffed, instantly regretting my blatant display of disrespect.

"What do you want to know?" he snapped.

"Whatever the hell you do."

"All I can tell you is you're right about Jackson."

"So what's the problem? Why am I still standing trial?"

"Because all I have is the cryptic message Salvatore gave Tony before he vanished. Lawrence and his men couldn't find anything inside of the damn house and he's been dragging his ass on the latest copies of the Winters compound blueprints. He says he's trying not to draw any attention to himself or us. There was nothing in Salvatore's office and nothing notable at the site where the police found his car. His LoJack was turned on about an hour or so before the car parked. He was circling Jackson's block trying to draw him out. The cops found some of Salvatore's blood and hairs in the car, but nothing else. Since there's no way you could've been there, the police are now speculating you're working in conjunction with someone—me. We're all at a stalemate. They can't prove it was either of us and we can't prove it was Jackson."

There were many things that I wanted to express, but instead I leaned back in the seat in silence. The trial was right around the corner and with nothing solid, I was screwed. It was time to face fact. I had to get my shit in order so Frankie would be well cared for in my and Madison's absence.

"Your house or mine?" my father inquired.

"Yours. I have some work to do, papers to draft."

"For whom?"

"Me. Let's be honest. I'm going to prison, and for a long time. I need to make sure everything of mine and Madison's transfers to Gia so she can care for Frankie."

"Frankie will be fine. *You'll* be fine."

"I'm as good as screwed. This is going to come down to whether the jury believes the Winters or us. Guess what, Pop? We don't have a snowball's chance in Hell of anyone seeing us as upstanding citizens."

"It's not over until *I* say it's over. Cut the crap."

Fully aware that whatever I said next would earn me a crack to the back of my head, I opted to remain quiet, silently praying for a miracle.

Chapter Seventeen

Luca

The weeks leading to the trial flew by. Comfort in knowing that Frankie would be with Gia in her more than capable hands, soothed me, but the night before opening arguments I was too amped up to focus on anything else. Every free second up until then I spent with my son. I feared once he was old enough he'd view me as a loser dirtbag responsible for his mother's absence. Though he probably wouldn't remember her much, he'd harbor a deep hatred for me over stealing his childhood and his mother's affections away from him. Having to lie to him whenever he'd question where Madison was broke my heart. Every night when I'd tuck him into his bed, I'd lay on the floor until he knocked out. His little fingers squeezing my hand so tightly caused tears to fall freely without shame from my eyes. The profoundness of missing my wife weighed heavily on my soul. Instead of being out there actively searching for her, I was stuck under the Winters' thumb—right where they wanted me. If I'd only thought of Madison first and not persuaded her to take me back, none of this would've happened. Everything since then was completely and totally my fault.

As predicted, the Winters attempted to block the cameras but lost. A win in my book. Another triumph arose when my father, with the help of Tony and Jimmy, located recordings Salvatore had taken. Being New York State was a one-party consent state the evidence was legal and admissible. However, Salvatore, in his infinite wisdom, coyly worked into each and every chat that Beau was being taped. After my father anonymously turned the tapes over, Ally had them authenticated. The bottom line was, the recordings clearly revealed Beau Winters had exchanged phone calls with my father and Salvatore. The prosecution attempted to discredit the evidence, but when all was said and done, the judge allowed it. The last victory came when Gia agreed to turn over a portion of her books and would testify that our family had collected money from Beau. My father would also be called to the stand, as would Tony and Jimmy to corroborate the story. A side investigation was being done by Tony who collected the blueprints from Arthur Lawrence. After comparing them to an ariel view of the compound, he immediately spotted inconsistencies. To the back of the house there was a guest home which hadn't been picked through by Lawrence during the fire. Why that particular structure hadn't been logged by the county for tax purposes was beyond me, but that was another problem for another time. Jimmy and Tony took turns scoping the place out which was a difficult task with Tag's intense security. To spite these strong points, my anxiety remained clear and present.

"The prosecution rests," Joshua Lyman said, taking a seat.

"Is the defense ready to call their first witness?" the judge questioned.

"Yes, Your Honor. We call Luca Santino to the stand." Ally's bold declaration was met with gasps not only from Lyman and his team, but from the jury and the gallery viewers as well. Typically, the accused was called last.

"Please raise your right hand. Do you swear or affirm the testimony you're about to give will be the truth, the whole truth, and nothing but the truth, so help you God?" Judge Stone asked.

"I do," I said.

"Have a seat," he instructed.

Doing as told, I calmly walked to the witness box and sat.

"You may proceed."

"Could you please state your full name for the record?" Ally began.

"Luca Santino."

"Would you tell the court your credentials starting with your college education?"

"I attended Harvard University where I obtained two undergraduate degrees, one in psychology and one in criminology. I graduated four years later, Summa Cum Laude. After that I went to Yale Law School where I was the editor of the *Yale Law Journal*. Again, I graduated at the top of my class, and I earned a perfect score on the Bar Exam. After leaving Yale, I was sought out by you, Ally Newman, who hired me as an Associate for your law firm, Newman and Associates LLP. Under your guidance I worked on many cases mostly dealing with criminal and constitutional law, but I also handled several civil rights violation cases. My litigation record remains undefeated. After several years, you promoted me to non-equity partner where my central focus was more research based. Some years after that you offered me an equity partnership with my name on the wall, but I declined because I wished to branch out on my own.

Today I own and operate a small, private, family law business."

"Why did you turn down my offer to become an equity partner with your name being added to my firm's letterhead?"

"At that time my then girlfriend now wife, Madison, had been abducted by Noah Lessor. The stress of the entire situation took its toll on me. When the dust settled down, I decided to make a change."

"Where is your law firm located?"

"In my parents' home in Brooklyn. After resigning from Newman and Associates I sold my house and moved back in with my mother and father. Seeing as their house is fairly large and empty, I set up shop in one of the vacant upstairs rooms. Out of sheer laziness and the desire to not have to drop several thousand dollars a month on rent, I continue to work there. I am a one man show, meaning I don't have any employees."

"Weren't you initially accused of abducting Madison Langmore-Santino by the police?"

"Yes."

"But you didn't have anything to do with the situation?"

"No."

"Why *do you* believe you were the authorities prime suspect?"

"Objection. Calls for speculation," Lyman spoke.

"Overruled. Ms. Newman is clearly asking for Mr. Santino's opinion. Please answer the question, Mr. Santino," the judge replied.

"Because of my last name. Because of whom they believe my family to be. Because the Langmore family and Doctor Wasserman didn't care for me. Because of many reasons, none good, I suspect."

"What does your surname and family have to do with any of this?"

"Whenever anyone hears the last name 'Santino' you're immediately associated with the Mafia."

"So your family is in the Mafia?"

"Yes. All United States citizens are afforded the right to have freedom of assembly. The First Amendment in The Bill of Rights clearly states that Congress cannot prohibit people from peaceably assembling. The '*Mafia*' is a group, an organization, who gathers to discuss various issues and topics. My family, the Santino Family, has never engaged in any illegal activity. Aside from me being arrested over the abductions and possible murders of five people—my brother, wife, and uncle included in that mix, no one has ever spent a night in prison. Some have been detained by the police, and many of us have been wrongfully accused of committing crimes we did not, but ultimately our innocence was beyond a shadow of a doubt proven. My father, sisters, brother, uncle, cousins, and myself, we all have jobs, and we all pay our fair share of taxes. For example, I'm an attorney. My sisters are real estate agents. Being a part of the Mafia is one small part of who we are. We help our community and the surrounding communities. We've even assisted the Winters Family several times."

"Objection. Hearsay," the prosecution shouted.

"Overruled, but I will pull the plug on this if I don't like where it's going, Ms. Newman."

"Of course, Your Honor. Can you explain your last statement further, Mr. Santino?" Ally continued flawlessly.

For the better part of thirty minutes, I detailed the many times Beau Winters had contacted my family. Then, Ally played Salvatore's tapes highlighting the one where Beau requested that my family look for Nick. As the recording was heard in the courtroom, she showed pictures of Marco whispering in Beau's ear at the 'Find Nick Winters' press conference to discredit what Beau had stated earlier in the trial about how he didn't know us personally. Many objections were made by Lyman, but all were struck down—thankfully.

"It's odd how Vice President Winters suggests he never had any relationship with your family." Ally mused.

"Objection. Not a question," Lyman chimed in.

"Sustained. You know better, Ms. Newman. Play nice or else you'll be held in contempt."

"Apologies. What is your relationship with Jillian and Nick Winters?" Ally asked.

"It's always been in a professional capacity."

"Can you elaborate?"

"Of course. While employed by Newman and Associates I was assigned the Winters case. Doctor and Mrs. Winters retained the firm to represent them. Due to my position as first chair, I interacted with both Winters on separate occasions. However, because of attorney/client confidentiality I cannot discuss the particulars of the case, not unless the court compels me to."

"Were you aware of your family's involvement with the Winters family while representing Doctor and Mrs. Winters?"

"At the time of hire, no."

"When did you become cognizant?"

"After my wife went missing."

"Did this knowledge effect anything?"

"No. The Winters case settled in their favor and thankfully my wife was able to escape her captors."

"Do you speak with either Winters today?"

"No."

"Then why was Doctor Winters at your home recently?"

"Objection. Calls for speculation," Lyman barked.

"Overruled. Answer the question, Mr. Santino," the judge ordered.

"He wanted to know what I knew about our wives' disappearance."

"Do you know anything about it?"

"No."

"Where were you the night of May twenty-seventh when your wife and brother went missing?"

"In my car driving to my parents' home for a family dinner. Madison and Marco were expected to arrive earlier than me. From what I was told by my father, Marco was at the house then left. Madison showed up a few minutes later with our son and left without any explanation. By the time I arrived, only two of my sisters, my mother, and my father were present. I waited a short time before reaching out to Madison. When I called her she said she was running a few last-minute errands and would be back shortly. That never happened. From there the police were informed and a missing person's report was filed for her and Marco."

"What about during the day?"

"During the day of May twenty-seventh, I was with my brother and two cousins on Long Island."

"What were you doing there?"

"We went to speak with Beau Winters."

"About?"

"The anonymous photograph and letter I received when my wife was pregnant with our son. Initially, I had no idea who sent the envelope, which is why it took so long for me to approach Beau. I considered taking the correspondence to the police, but decided against that, mainly because what were they going to do? They'd file a report and the threat to me and my family would still be an active and present one."

"We'd like to admit the photograph and letter received by Mr. Santino into evidence." Turning her attention back on me, she spoke again. "So to reiterate you, your brother, and two cousins drove out to Long Island to speak with Vice President Winters about a picture and note you received. Why?"

"Because we had reason to believe Beau knew who sent it."

"What was that reason?"

"Due to attorney/client privilege for Nick and Jillian Winters I cannot go into much detail, but while representing them, private, intimate details arose that my wife and I became privy to due to working on the case. Madison and I also signed a fairly airtight nondisclosure agreement you drafted once the case came to a close. I'm bound by law to keep my mouth shut, an agreement I will honor unless otherwise forced not to by a judge. Additionally, with the deep ties the Winters have with my family, and with Beau Winters owing my family quite a bit of money, we believed the picture and note were a not so subtle threat."

"Fair enough." She turned to Stone. "I'd like to enter the nondisclosure agreement Mr. and Mrs. Santino signed into evidence. Mrs. Santino's name will read Madison Langmore as she was not married at the time." Looking at me she continued. "Can you walk us through what happened that day with Vice President Winters?"

"While driving through a town local to his home, we saw him enter a coffee shop. We followed him in. I approached him requesting an audience. He agreed and we left the café. Once we were outside, to avoid him being seen with a Santino, we walked to a somewhat secluded area where we chatted about the photograph and letter. He assured he knew nothing of the matter and we believed him. After that we said our goodbyes and left."

"Were any weapons used or pressed into the Vice President's back?"

"No. Absolutely not."

"How was he when you left?"

"Objection. Calls for speculation," Lyman said.

"I'll rephrase," Ally replied. "When you were finished with your conversation, was the Vice President on the ground, or showing any visible signs of being in medical distress, or verbalizing a need for help from a physician?"

"I'm not a medical professional, but he was standing in the upright position and appeared totally fine. He made no mention of requiring a doctor's support. Had he have not been feeling well we would've taken him to the hospital or called for help. We wouldn't leave an ill, elderly man on the streets alone."

"Thank you, Mr. Santino. No further questions."

"Mr. Lyman, are you ready?"

"Yes. Thank you, Your Honor." He stood, approaching the witness box. "Are you familiar with the terms *consigliere* and *il capo*?"

"Yes." I knew exactly where this jackass was taking this line of questioning. There was no way I'd let him win, smearing my family's name any more than he already had.

"Can you tell the court what those words mean?"

"*Consigliere* is Italian for advisor or counselor. *Il capo* is also an Italian word meaning boss, head, chief, or leader."

"How are you familiar with these words?"

"I speak fluent Sicilian. Additionally, anyone who's ever watched a movie about the Mafia would have heard those words and many more."

"Are you the Santino Family *consigliere*?"

"No."

"Have you ever represented them in court?"

"I have. It's public record."

"So you *have* acted as an advisor for the Santino Family then."

"That's not a question, but rather a statement. However, if we're to be truthful with one another, every single attorney in the world has acted as an advisor for their clients," I retorted before Ally could object. Granted, the response was tremendously disrespectful, but even if it were stricken from the record it didn't matter. The jury had already heard it. They'd be hard pressed to completely dismiss the stated fact.

"Mr. Santino, the court demands reverence. As an officer of it, you should already be aware of this. Do it again and I'll be forced to hold you in contempt," Stone stated.

"My apologies, Your Honor."

"Could you describe your relationship with your

wife, Mrs. Santino, during the time prior to the Noah Lessor/Sarah Davis abduction?"

"How so?" I asked, fully aware he was trying to make the jury see me as a bully and someone of low moral values. Doctor No Nuts as well as all of Madison's family had painted me with that brush a few days ago when they testified.

"During the period of time prior to and during her previous abduction, what was your relationship like? What would you classify it as?"

"Madison and I had dated for a year prior to the Lessor/Davis abduction. Newman and Associates was retained to handle Nick and Jillian Winters' sensitive case. Said case was given to me. Often when dealing with delicate matters the firm would hire Looking Glass Consultants—Richard and Donna Langmore's business. Madison, their daughter, was employed as a private investigator through Looking Glass. At the time she and I had been broken up for a little over a year. As we worked the case we realized how much we loved and missed the other and decided to get back together. Madison went missing an hour after I proposed marriage to her at my parents' house. When she returned home after escaping from Noah Lessor and Sarah Davis, I proposed again to which she said yes. Shortly after that we were married and some months later we found out she was pregnant with our son."

"Were you aware Mrs. Santino was involved with Doctor Noel Wasserman at the time of your reunification?"

"Yes."

"And that knowledge didn't stop you from pursuing another man's significant other?"

"I'm glad you asked me that, because in fact, it did. Very much so actually. Many times I told Madison the situation wasn't right to any party involved, but ultimately I left the decision as to when she planned to address the matter with Noel Wasserman up to her."

"Were you engaging in physical intimacies with her while she was with Doctor Wasserman?"

"Yes—consensually."

"Did you strike Doctor Wasserman in Mrs. Santino's home?"

"Yes—only *after* he attempted to strike me."

"Did you threaten him?"

"I cannot accurately recall what words were exchanged. It occurred some years ago."

"Do you own a firearm?"

"Yes."

"What kind?"

"A Glock Nineteen, nine-millimeter."

"Were you carrying the weapon the day of May twenty-seventh?"

"No."

"Where was it?"

"Locked in my home safe."

"Can you furnish the court with proof the weapon was where you say it was?"

The dick thought he had me because he knew I couldn't. He truly believed he proved beyond a shadow of a doubt to the jury that he was the dead to rights winner of this trial.

"No."

"So we're supposed to take your word?"

"Yes. I haven't lied on this stand once and have no plans to do so. If I openly admitted who and what my family and myself are, why would I start lying now? Additionally, if this court demands respect, being I'm an officer of it myself, I believe I should be afforded the same sentiment. I take severe umbrage to the fact you're attempting to cast doubt over my honesty to the jury—a group of *my* peers. I want my wife found. I want her returned safely to me and our son, where she belongs, which makes me question why anyone in here would believe I wasn't telling the truth?" I clapped back fully aware I was seconds away from being held in contempt.

"Mr. Santino, before I hold you in contempt, I'm going to give you two options. One, Ms. Newman can request a brief recess where you can take a breath and refocus the lens. Two, you can spend the night behind bars cooling off. Dealer's choice, but I highly recommend the first option," Stone spoke.

"I apologize, Your Honor. My wife, brother, and uncle, as well as two other people are out there and there's not a damn thing I can do to help them," I said, choking back emotions.

"Understandable, which is why I'm going to save everyone the time and trouble and call for a recess. Court is adjourned for thirty minutes," he said, slamming his gavel down.

Once session resumed, Lyman went on grilling me for the better part of an hour before he called it quits. He wasn't getting the response from the jury he'd been desperately seeking. My emotional outburst appeared to have touched the jury, convincing them that I had been speaking the truth. Ally quickly cleared up several of Lyman's insinuations during her redirect making sure the jury knew simple omitted facts such as the details pertaining to Doctor No Nuts provoking me, how my handgun was legal and being an officer of the court I had a right to carry one, and that the weapon had been tested and hadn't been fired recently.

"You did great, Santino," Ally said over lunch in one of the back rooms.

"Because I didn't lie, Ally," I replied, totally disinterested in the food that was in front of me.

"This afternoon we've got two expert witnesses and your sister on tap."

"You're one hundred and ten percent certain Gia won't get into any trouble for testifying?"

"Yes. She's done nothing wrong. She's a bookkeeper for your father's businesses which are all legal and in good standing. His corporation pays taxes and has donated thousands of dollars to various community charities and causes. This will show your father is above board and will confirm that Beau gave your father money in exchange for your family's services. Which, might I add, all of those funds collected from Beau were donated to several schools, libraries, churches, and hospitals."

"I have to go," Jennifer chimed in. Her eyes were wide as she clutched her cell phone so hard her knuckles were turning white. Jumping up, she dashed for the door.

"Whoa. Hold on. Are you okay?" I asked, swiftly rising and stopping her by blocking the exit.

"Yes. More than okay. If this lead is credible it will shift the juries focus away from you and onto Beau and his scummy family, where it belongs."

"What is it?" She'd piqued immense interest.

"I don't want to get your hopes up. Ally, if possible, persuade the judge into adjourning until tomorrow morning," she replied hurriedly.

"I think I can do that."

"Great. Thanks. Give me some time and I'll call you as soon as I know something solid."

"What was that about?" I asked once Jennifer had exited the room.

"Damned if I know, but one must never underestimate Jennifer Glick." She paused. "That woman has been working her ass off for you. Day and night, she hasn't come up for air once."

"We both love Madison and want her back."

"True, but she also staunchly believes in your innocence and cares for you tremendously."

"Five-minute warning," a bailiff informed, popping his head into the room.

Twenty minutes later, court adjourned and I was headed home praying whatever Jennifer was up to would pan out in my favor.

Chapter Eighteen

Luca

With no word from Ally or Jennifer all night, I entered the courtroom anxious as ever.

"We have to make a motion to add a new witness. I'm unsure if the judge will go for it because technically this witness plays no role in your case, *but* she can testify to Beau's involvement with your family, verifying everything you've said about his actions," Ally informed.

"Once Beau hears the name he's going to shit himself," Jennifer added, grinning from ear to ear, something not often seen.

Before I could speak, we were instructed to rise for the judge.

"Your Honor, I'd like to add a new witness to the list. We only located her yesterday evening. We believe she will be able to shed light on several key points surrounding my client's innocence," Ally said.

"Who is this witness?" the judge questioned. Every eye, mine included, in the room was firmly fixed on Ally.

"Courtney Blackstone. She used to go by the name Kelly Greenly before moving and legally changing it."

I couldn't hold my reaction inside. My body arched closer to Ally's as my pupils widened, and my mouth hung wide open. Holding my breath, I waited for the judge's final answer which after a half hour of back-and-forth debate with Lyman and Ally in chambers, he granted the request, giving the prosecution the rest of the day to prepare.

"How did you —" I stammered, unable to complete the thought.

"I'm Jennifer Glick, bitch." She smiled brightly. "Aren't you glad I'm on your side?"

And I was because the following day in front of the cameras and mass media this stunningly petite, curvaceous woman with long, straight, perfectly styled, expresso colored hair told the world about her affair with Nick Winters, and how Beau had hired my father to speak with her. She gushed over how nice my father and Salvatore treated her. She explained how they offered her an amazing deal to move to California—a true opportunity to change her life, in exchange for leaving Nick Winters alone and to never breathe a word of the affair to anyone, ever. All set to leave the following morning, she was attacked by a masked assailant. Luckily, another man who happened to be outside of her condo witnessed the event and rescued her. From there the knight in white shining armor drove her from New York to Maine, safely hiding her while creating an entirely new identity for her. Fortunately for her, her story was proved accurate beyond a shadow of a doubt because she'd recorded the conversation with my father and Salvatore on her cell phone and her former condo complex had security cameras, with sound. How Jennifer was able to get the condo property owners to search for the video feed, then find the time to authenticate it, blew my mind. There was a strong chance she still hadn't gone to bed yet.

"Who do you work for?" a pixilated man growled,

forcefully shoving a man wearing a black knit ski mask to the ground. At that point Kelly, or rather Courtney, was lying motionlessly on the grass a few feet away.

The attacker didn't speak.

"I can do this all day, *stronzo prepotente*. You think beating on a woman is okay? Try smacking around someone your own size," the grainy man hissed, but I knew exactly who it was. A sense of shock caused me to sit back in the chair to fully process what my eyes were viewing.

Finally, after several minutes of being aggressively handled, the masked man clearly spoke.

"Winters. Beau Winters hired me."

"To do what?"

"To kill her."

"Who's her?"

"Kelly Greenly."

"Tell Beau Winters his plan didn't work. Now get the hell out of here before I change my mind and pop a cap up your ass."

With that, the hitman for hire ran to a black hatchback and sped away. Courtney's savior helped her off the ground, grabbed her belongings, and walked out of the frame. The surveillance video ended.

"Do you know the name of the person who helped you?" Ally asked Courtney.

"Yes," Courtney said. A small, secret smile flashed across her lips.

"Could you tell the court?"

Her big, brown eyes darted from left to right. A severe hesitation filled her every movement causing her to resemble a deer caught in headlights.

"It's okay, Ms. Blackstone. They're not in any kind

of trouble for their heroic measures," Ally assured.

"Marco. Marco Santino," she whispered.

Glancing at the jury, they sat poised, hungrily waiting to see how the rest of this soap opera would play out.

"Marco Santino then placed you in hiding?"

"Yes. He made sure my cuts and injuries from being attacked were tended to, then he drove us to Maine. We stayed at a hotel for a week or so before he took me to a beautiful, gated townhouse community, handed me new identification—which is all legal paperwork, I know because I pay taxes using the provided social security number, and had a bank account set up with money in it. He also set me up with an amazing, new, stable job, and a car. Before he left, he made sure everything I needed and wanted was mine. I'd never been treated so warmly and kindly in my life. I felt safe with Marco. I still do."

"Still do? Does that mean you remain in communication?"

"Yes. Once a month he comes up for a long weekend to visit me to make sure I'm okay." She paused briefly. "I know everyone thinks the Santino Family are comprised of dangerous criminals and the Winters Family are perfect angels, but they have it wrong. It's the other way around."

"Objection. Speculation and opinion," Lyman barked.

"Sustained. Ms. Blackstone, I know this can be difficult and I can see you're visibly anxious, but please just answer the questions with facts only. If you're asked for your opinion you may provide it, but until then, refrain from stating personal sentiments," Stone instructed.

"Last question. What's your involvement in this case?" Ally said.

With a deep breath she spoke. "For a little while now, I can't exactly remember when it began, every time Marco came for a visit he seemed distracted. Usually, he jokes around a lot. He's always present and in the moment with whatever we're doing, but he wasn't. I asked him what was bothering him and after much persuasion he opened up. Historically, he's never told me about anything work wise. We'd chat about my career, but not his. He'd speak of his family and what they were up to, but never about his profession because I already knew what he did. Seeing me was his escape from the stress of the world. Our relationship was our secret. No one else's. When others get involved things typically go south, fast. Anyway, he broke down and told me about a letter and photograph his younger brother, Luca, received —"

"That letter and photograph have already been logged into evidence," Ally cut her off midsentence. "Exhibit B-32," she added, handing two pieces of paper to the judge who carefully considered them. With a curt nod, the documents appeared on the screens for the jury to view again. They'd already seen them but viewing them again couldn't hurt. "I'd also like to enter several pictures which have been authenticated taken on Ms. Blackstone's cell phone of her and Marco Santino to furnish the court and jury with proof of the relationship between Blackstone and Santino." The images of the Lessor/Davis crime scene and letter vanished from the screen and were replaced by a collage of pictures of Marco and Courtney. A side of Marco I hadn't seen since childhood reflected in his expression. He appeared happy, relaxed, and madly in love.

After several moments to allow the jury to soak the new information in, Ally continued. "My apologies for interrupting you. Please go on, Ms. Blackstone."

"Marco was worried. He had suspicions the Winters Family was behind it, but he couldn't find anything concrete to directly pin on them. I wanted to help him the same way he'd helped me. Watching someone you love and care about tremendously sit in a position of terrible stress is painful. I told him everything I knew about the Winters which wasn't much, but it appeared to be enough because the lost spark in his eyes returned. The last time I saw him was about six months ago. I called and texted him tons of times before seeing the news report stating he was missing along with the other people. I didn't come forward because Marco insisted and made me swear if anything ever happened to him I'd keep my mouth shut, especially if whatever it was involved anyone with the last name Winters. It wasn't until I got a call a few days ago from Jennifer Glick who explained what was going on that I spoke. She said she was going through all of the evidence the police had, and had some IT person investigate the private number I'd call Marco from. When she got the number she did a deep dive and I suppose put two and two together that I was Kelly Greenly. I imagine she had some kind of understanding of my identity because of Luca. For the record, until today I have never seen or met Luca or his wife. The only people involved in this I know, and vaguely at that, is Frank Santino and Salvatore D'Angelo, and that was for less than an hour years ago while they were doing Beau Winters' bidding. I'm here to hopefully shed light on whatever necessary—to help

Marco and his family."

"Thank you, Ms. Blackstone for your courage to speak and for your time. No further questions, Your Honor."

Instantly Lyman rose ready to attack.

"Ms. Blackstone, if Vice President Winters staged an attack on your life like you suggest he did in the past, why come here today to blow the carefully crafted cover Mr. Santino created?" The words shot out of his mouth faster than the judge could give him permission to speak.

"Like I said, I want to help Marco."

"So you're not afraid any of the Winters will come after you now?"

"They might. I don't know, but whatever may be will be worth it if Marco is found safe."

"Can you describe your relationship with Mr. Santino?"

"In what respect?" Courtney asked. To the unknowing soul she seemed confused, but to someone such as myself, she didn't want to purge the inner workings of her emotions for a man everyone saw as a gangster to people who wouldn't understand.

"Is Mr. Santino your boyfriend? A friend? A lover?" Lyman pressed, seemingly annoyed for having to clarify.

"I have no idea how to classify what Marco and I share. I suppose we're good friends."

"Do you sleep together?"

"I don't see how that's anyone's business but mine and Marco's," Courtney snapped.

"Ms. Blackstone, again I realize this is a stressful time for you, and though I commend your loyalty and bravery for revealing your new identity, I have to caution you. This courtroom is a place of respect. If you cannot respectfully answer questions, I'll be forced to hold you in contempt, which I'd hate to have to do," the judge chimed in.

"I'm sorry. I simply do not wish to answer such a personal question," Courtney replied.

"Then you may exercise your fifth amendment right," the judge informed.

"I exercise my fifth amendment right."

"Have you ever personally met Vice President Winters?" Lyman asked irritated.

He wanted her to admit that she and Marco were screwing around so he could discredit the relationship by suggesting Marco had been seen with numerous women over the years all of which weren't her. He was also hoping Marco's infidelity would make her livid. Even if that had been the case, this woman had clearly been schooled on the unspoken and fully understood the Santino code all of its members had to play by. Courtney revealed loyalty and unwavering love for Marco to spite his undesirable ways. The Winters, Lyman, whoever, would never break her.

"No."

"Then how do you know for sure he was the one who ordered the attack on you?"

"The man in the mask who attacked me said so."

"Perhaps it could've been a setup? Maybe the masked attacker was working for the Santino Family?"

"Objection. Calls for speculation," Ally said.

"Sustained."

"No further questions, Your Honor."

The jury sat with their mouths agape. If they looked like that I could only imagine how the rest of the world appeared as they stared at their television screens. This was good. Very good.

Chapter Nineteen

Courtney
Eleven Years Ago...

"Excuse me, miss. Might we have a word with you?" an older, well dressed, handsome man requested as I exited the nail salon. A much larger man wearing a heather gray tracksuit stood behind him.

"What can I help you with?" I asked cautiously. The world was a scary place and had gotten even more terrifying after Jillian Winters barged into Nick's room last week. According to everything Nick had shared with me about her, she was an awful woman with a horrible nasty streak. Of course, Nick hastily ended our affair, promptly firing me, but that was okay. For quite some time I'd been over what we'd been doing and was tired of being his personal assistant. There was no future with him or the job, but I kept sleeping with him because why not and I kept working for him because I needed the steady paycheck. With no prospects for a potential spouse in my future, Nick was always ready, willing, and able. The second I found someone to share my life with, I planned to quit anyway. Jillian just happened to beat me to the punch. Oh well. Shit happens. I suppose one could say she did me a favor and saved me from having to have an unavoidable, uncomfortable conversation with her husband.

"You're not in any kind of danger. We mean

absolutely no harm. We simply want to discuss your next steps post the Nick Winters affair," he explained.

"Okay," my voice trailed. My eyes darted from side to side as I endeavored to make sure I was in a somewhat populated area. For some reason both men's faces appeared familiar, but I couldn't put my finger on how I knew them. Thankfully, my cell phone was in my hand and I was able to hit the voice record button with neither of them realizing it.

"Would you like to get a cup of coffee or tea? If you're hungry, we could grab something to eat. We could also take a walk. You tell us what would make you feel most at ease, Miss Greenly." He paused and smiled. "By the way, I'm Frank. This is Salvatore." He extended his hand.

Accepting the gesture, I spoke. "There's a decent coffee place across the street, but I really don't have a ton of time. I've got several appointments I cannot miss. Is this going to take long?" The café, though not as busy as I would've liked it, was in a well-lit, open area. If they tried something I'd easily be able to draw attention to what was going on.

"We understand. We're busy too. This won't take long," he assured, leading the way.

After ordering, which Frank insisted on paying for my drink as well, Salvatore guided us to a table in the back, far away from everyone else. It was then it dawned on me where I knew them from. He was Frank Santino, known Mafia Crime Boss and Salvatore was his henchman. A fear I never experienced gripped the back of my neck.

"I see you figured out who we are," Salvatore said with a chuckle.

I couldn't speak. My brain, body—everything went blank.

"If we had a dollar for every time someone responded to us like you are right now we'd be made men." The once light chortle turned into a full-on belly laugh. "It's okay, honey. Again, we're here to help you, not hurt you. The world has tragic misconceptions about our family; misconceptions I hope will be squashed when this conversation is over."

"What can I do for you?" I inquired with an obscene amount of caution while fidgeting in my chair.

"Listen, we've all made mistakes at one point in our lives. For you, it was carrying on an affair with Nick Winters. Being he's part of a public, political family and is a celebrity in his own right, we're here to make you an offer. You're so young. You've got so much more of your life left to live. Do yourself a favor and accept our proposal. If you leave New York and agree to never speak to the press, or to reach out to Nick Winters again, we'll provide you with a strong foundation so you can be free from all of the ties that bind. That means you can forget about this error in judgement. I have a daughter just about your age, Kelly. I beg of you to carefully consider what we're saying. In this envelope," he explained, sliding a large, tan packet across the table, "you'll find a new beginning. A first-class plane ticket to California, a fully furnished condo, a new car, a new job as a legal secretary for a prestigious law firm, and a half a million dollars. It's more than enough to start over. If you should require additional support, give me a call. Whatever you need, it's yours."

Lifting the flap of the package, I surveyed the contents. Inside was a house key, a key fob for a

Volkswagen, a photograph of a condo which was paperclipped to a deed that had my name on it, two bank accounts with tremendous balances, cash, an airline ticket, and a letter from a law office stating my new job description, salary, and benefits package.

What do you really have here? Not much. No job, not many friends, little family. Why stay? Bills will start rolling in shortly and how do you plan on paying them? Unemployment? That won't last for too long. This offer is libel to be the best one you'll ever receive.

"If you were my daughter I'd strongly encourage you to accept the offer, Kelly," Frank urged. "You don't want to go up against a political giant like the Winters Family. That's not a threat, it's a reality. People like them will do whatever they deem necessary to dispose of their dirty little secrets, like you. Why do you think we're here? Another man might be threatening you, whereas we're trying to help you escape; providing you with a chance to hit the reset button."

"The flight takes off tomorrow morning from Kennedy Airport?"

"Yes. That should be enough time for you to pack some clothing and whatever personal items you'd like to take. Once you're settled, contact Gia Russo. Her card is in the envelope. She'll help you sell your condo in New York by proxy. Everything you'll need, aside from clothing, is already waiting for you."

"How do I know this isn't a setup—a trap of sorts set up by Nick or his family? How do I know I can trust you? That what you're saying and offering me is true, not a smoke and mirror show?"

"I like this one. She's smart. Honestly, sweetheart? You don't. You have to have blind faith in our words. If we wanted to hurt you we would've done it already. We're not interested in harming anyone, ever. That's always the absolute last option and it takes a long time to get us there. In my culture we revere our women. We never lay a finger on them or cause them distress of any kind. They're our most prized possessions and the one thing, aside from our children, that we love and protect the most. Perhaps once you're settled in California you should find yourself a nice Italian man to start a family with, then you'll understand what I'm saying," Salvatore said.

"Perhaps. Thank you for the coffee, honest conversation, and your kindness. I have to go," I replied, stuffing the papers into my purse and standing.

"Good luck, Kelly. Reach out if you need anything," Frank said. He flashed an easy smile, then turned his attention to Salvatore.

Sprinting to my car, I took off for home for the last time. Tossing everything from my closet and bathroom vanity into three bags, I sat on the couch and waited for dawn. Fear caused sleep to evade me. Obviously Nick shared some connection to the Mafia. He'd hired them to get rid of me. Thankfully, the notorious crime boss and his sidekick appeared to be nice, reasonable men, but I'd read stories about them. If I didn't do as told, they'd murder me regardless of their assurances that they wouldn't. Chances were they knew everything about me realizing if they did kill me no one would give a damn. I didn't have an employer, family, or friends to wonder over my whereabouts. Getting out of here was a necessity. It was doubtful they'd change their minds and renege on the offer, but never-the-less, what if it was a ruse? The moment the clock struck five in the morning, duffels in hand, I hurried to my car. However, before I got to the parking lot, out of nowhere someone seized me from behind. Struggling to free myself, I simply couldn't. The person was far too big and strong to take on alone. Screaming and praying that someone would hear me while I thrashed around proved useless. Finally, I felt the assailant's arms release their hold from my waist. A masculine voice roared threats to my attacker. Spinning around I saw the man who saved me beating the life out of the man who was trying to harm me. Stunned, I remained down on the grass unsure if I should run, jump in the car, go back in the house, or shelter in place. After a few minutes the accoster, who wore black clothing and a ski mask covering his entire face, bolted from the lot and the other man approached me. Crouching down beside me he spoke.

"Are you all right?" he asked.

"I think so," my voice shook.

"I'm Marco. I believe you spoke with my father and uncle yesterday. Let's get you the hell out of here, okay?"

"Who was that? Why were they attacking me? What do they want from me? What the hell is going on?" I stammered as he helped me to my feet.

"I have no idea who that was, but I can assure you that they won't be back anytime soon if they know what's good for them. As for why they attacked you, they were working on Beau Winters' orders. Evidently you slept with his married grandson and the wife found out. Nick cried to his grandfather, who in turn hired my family to clean up the mess. Beau didn't care for my father's solution to his problem, so he stiffed us on the payment and found whoever that was to perform a hit.

But don't worry. I have eyes and ears everywhere. When I find out his identity he'll be dealt with. Right now, we have to go."

"A hit?"

"Yeah, a hit. As in murder you. Listen, we can chat about whatever you'd like in as much detail as you wish when we're on the road, but we have to get out of here."

Collecting my bags from the pavement, then taking me by the hand, he led the way to a large, black SUV which I assumed was his. A choice presented. Either I got in the vehicle with him or made a run for it, but for some unknown reason, I didn't fear Marco. I probably should have. Tossing my personal belongings into the trunk, he took off. He must've driven for about an hour before he broke the ice.

"We've got a long ride ahead of us and personally I could use a cup of coffee. It's funny. Years ago, coffee used to wire my ass so I could stay awake or wake up for an early morning call. Now, I drink it just to avoid the soul crushing headache I get when I don't." He laughed lightly.

"Same," I replied, smiling slightly. "I'm Kelly by the way."

"I know, but not for long, honey."

"What's that supposed to mean?" I asked. My once calm nerves returned to an on-edge state.

"No, no. Not like that. Man, is that all anyone ever sees when they look at me? A thug? A goodfella?"

"Well, no, but when you say something like, '*not for long*' with respect to my identity, on top of me not knowing you from a hole in the wall, what kind of reaction do you expect? I met you a little over an hour ago when you were kicking the stuffing out of a masked man who was trying to attack me, and all of this is after having a meeting with your father and uncle yesterday where I was instructed to get lost. Shouldn't the years of crappy, unfulfilling sex with Nick Winters be punishment enough?"

"Kicking the stuffing out of? Cute." He chuckled, grinning.

"Okay, fine. *Beating the shit out of.* Better?"

"You're not a native New Yorker."

"I'm not. I'm originally from Tallahassee. How'd you know, or did someone give you a write-up on me?"

"You're too nice, too sweet to be from here."

Unsure of why, but his soft sentiment was touching. Snapping myself back to reality was difficult. Perhaps it was because I'd just been dumped or because I'd always been naive, but there was something about Marco that pulled me in aside from his good looks. Marco was a touch over six feet, had cropped neat salt and pepper hair, clean shaven, dark, brown eyes, olive skin, broad shoulders, and from what I could make out from under his tight, black t-shirt, a killer body. He was masculine in a way I wasn't familiar with.

"Why were you at my house, Marco?"

"Truth? Gut instinct. I knew about the Beau thing—how pissed he was because my father and uncle didn't whack you, so I played a hunch he'd find someone else to do it. I parked outside your house late last night and waited. All I planned on doing was following you to the airport and watching you get on the plane. I had someone in California who was going to keep an eye on you for a bit after you arrived. However, I guess my intuition was correct."

"Thank you. Thank you for giving a crap about me."

"I am a nice guy."

"Yes. Yes you are."

After stopping to grab something to eat and coffee, we were back on the road heading north.

"Where are we going?" I asked.

"Greenville, Maine. You'll be safe there. I have a contact in the area who is in the process of setting you up with all of the things you'll need. He'll keep watch over you. If something should go down, he'll handle it and call me."

"Why are you doing this for me?"

"Honestly? I don't know."

His answer, though truthful, irked me. I'm not quite sure what I expected him to say. I suppose he picked up on that and changed the topic of conversation.

"What's your story? Everyone has one and we have nothing but time to waste. Tell me yours and I'll share mine. Seems like a fair trade."

"Okay. Like I said before, I was born in Tallahassee. My mother was sixteen and my father was seventeen, but he took off shortly after finding out about the pregnancy. My maternal grandmother and grandfather raised me. My mother was young. She wanted a life and truthfully she should've terminated the pregnancy, but she thought by having me something awesome would happen to her. Spoiler alert—it didn't. After my grandfather passed away, my grandmother wanted to move to Manhattan to be closer to her sister. So, we packed up and left Florida, leaving my mother, her new husband, and two children from that marriage behind. They didn't want me around, and that's okay. After years of desperately trying to understand the inner workings of my mother, I gave up. It hurt too much, and I was tired of attempting to win her time, attention, and love. Once I was in New York and high school ended, I went to college, then got a Master's Degree. By that time my grandmother and my great aunt were getting on in years. Their memories were rapidly fading. Keeping them in the apartment we lived in when I wasn't there wasn't safe. I found a retirement home for them and they're very happy there—I think. Whenever I visit they have no idea who I am. It's sad actually, but I continue to make sure they're well cared for and have whatever they need. It's costly, but they're the only family I have. You do for family, right? Anyway, I worked a few office/secretarial jobs before getting the job as Nick Winters personal assistant. There's no need to dive into that chapter of my life because I'm confident you're aware of how that played out. To be frank, initially I was mesmerized by him and his fame. I thought he was such a powerful man, and I was flattered by the attention he showered me with. I kept the relationship going because I was craving something to anchor to. When I realized my interest had faded, the allure vanished. However, I needed a job and that particular one allowed me to travel, provided a clothing allowance, benefits, security, and so on. If I broke things off, I feared he'd fire me. What I did was wrong. I'm aware. My rationale behind it was misguided. Not a day goes by where I don't hate myself over all of this and regret everything. Look at where it got me."

"We all screw up. The trick is finding a way to forgive yourself. It took me some time to learn that life lesson. I'm sorry about how your mother and her new family treated you. I'm also sorry about your grandmother and great aunt's failing health. I know what it's like to put on airs and pretend all is well when you're slowly dying inside. Suffering in silence while shouldering all of the burdens can be weighty."

"Thank you, but it's okay. In a way one could say it was a good thing because it taught me how to stand on my own two feet. I am capable of caring for and providing for myself. Not a lot of people can do that."

"True, but you can't spend forever kicking the stuffing out of yourself for past mistakes," he added, nodding.

Slapping his shoulder I smiled. "Jerk. Your turn. What's your story?"

"I was born, raised, and still live in Brooklyn. Oldest of five—three sisters and one brother. We're a close-knit family. I graduated high school and went to work for my father."

"Wow. Five kids? That's a lot. What was that like?" Part of me felt envy over his family structure. The security of knowing someone would always be there was a concept I yearned for.

"Crowded. Loud. Little to no privacy. I'm pretty tight with Gia, Tina, and Marie—my sisters. They're all married with kids of their own. In fact, Tina's pregnant. She's due next month. Personally, I'm hoping for a boy this time because I already have eight nieces—which is great, I love and adore them, but we need to boost the masculinity a bit."

"Aw. Congratulations. What about your brother?"

"Luca?" He snorted. "I love him to death, but we've never been on the same page. I doubt we ever will be. He's a Harvard and Yale man who is a fancy attorney for a prestigious law firm. Don't get me wrong, I'm proud of him for going all of the way in school, but he's always had a chip on his shoulder. I can't remember the last time we did anything together aside from family meals and celebrating holidays. He made it clear he wanted nothing to do with the family business, and that's fine. It's not for everyone. I guess the ten-year age gap between us is why we've never been too terribly close."

Marco seemed caught somewhere between jealousy and great sadness over Luca. Involuntarily my hand reached for his knee and patted it gently. This simple gesture appeared to please him in a way I'd never seen a man delight in before. Wrapping his fingers around mine, he squeezed tightly.

"Listen, I'm going to make sure you're safe. I've got you, okay?"

"For some crazy reason I trust you."

After driving for what seemed like forever, he parked in a hotel garage. He checked us in and promptly ordered us room service. Stepping into the hallway to make a call he returned a bit later. He assured me that all was well and arrangements were being made, but it might take a few days to gather everything. I'm not going to lie. I panicked out of fear that he was going to leave me here in this strange, new state. I guess he realized this because he swore he wasn't going anywhere until I was settled in. By the end of the week, he had me moved into a beautiful townhouse, had taken me shopping for household items and furnishings, and had the cable, a landline, and the internet hooked up. A remote job was waiting for me whenever I was ready to start. A brand-new, white Subaru SUV was in the driveway. A new cell phone was purchased, and my clothing was upgraded to support the frigid weather. I'd never lived in such a beautiful home before. I also never had a brand new, reliable vehicle, nor had a man ever treated me so well, expecting nothing in return. He'd been a perfect gentleman the entire time. Never once did he attempt to touch me in a sexual fashion or raise his voice. He showed me nothing but total respect.

"One last thing. You're no longer Kelly Greenly, *dolcezza*. You're now Courtney Blackstone," Marco said over dinner, sliding a large folder across the table. "You'll be safer this way. I have a hair stylist coming over tomorrow to change your appearance. His name is Kris and he'll also help you switch up your makeup as well. He's already on the payroll. Whenever you need or want to see him, just give him a call. We need to make you look different enough on the surface so no one will ever put two and two together."

"New everything I suppose," I replied, looking down at my dinner plate. I wanted to thank him for his kindness so I'd spent all day cooking him a meal, which for me was a feat because I can't even boil water.

"Hey, you're still you, just with a different name and surface style," he assured softly. "By the way, dinner is fantastic."

"You're an amazing liar," I said with a slight laugh. "It's awful."

"You don't tell the girl who worked her ass off to prepare a meal that it's awful. Especially if you really liked her and would enjoy seeing her again in a few weeks—if she felt the same way, of course. No pressure. It would also be completely fine if she just wanted to be friends or acquaintances. If she wanted to think about it, then call or text him with her answer at a later date, that would be okay as well."

"She doesn't need any time to mull it over because she feels the exact same way. If that's all right with him."

"Oh *dolcezza*, its more than all right. I've been dying to do this since the moment I met you, Courtney," Marco said, calling me by my new name. He stood and approached me. Tugging me off of my chair, he pressed his body dangerously close to mine. Tenderly he brushed a whisp of hair out of my face and affectionately stroked my cheek with his thumb. Finally, he moved in for the kill shot allowing me to breathe again. The moment our lips collided, that was it. I had to have him. I had to be with him. He, Marco Santino, was not only my knight in white shining armor, but 'the one.'

****

Two Days Ago…

"We'll keep you up to date with the latest on the Luca Santino trial," a female reporter said outside the courthouse where Marco's brother was being tried.

"Damn it," I hissed, throwing the remote across the couch.

Nearly six months. Nearly six long months without a scrap of news. Marco was missing, his brother was being blamed for it, and to add insult to injury, the Winters Family was involved. Oh, how I loathed myself for being with Nick on any level. The thought of him, never mind what we did, disgusted me. It actually made me feel sick to my stomach, but had that not occurred, there would've been no Marco, and I loved that man with all that I was. Him not being around, possibly dead, crushed my heart. I couldn't eat or sleep, let alone work. All I did was sit on the couch with my nose pressed to the television, clutching my phone, praying he'd call. What could I do? Nothing. Reaching out to his family would've been useless. They had no idea who I was, and people like them would deem some random woman coming out of the woodwork during a time like this suspicious. Besides, Marco told me to shelter in place. The few people who knew Marco around here were just as clueless as I. Some of the neighbors made the connection as to who Marco truly was after seeing his face and family splashed all over the newspapers, nightly reports, and internet articles. There were several people who were once nice to me that were now spreading rumors that I was Marco's secret mistress, while others stayed far away. However, a handful of residents didn't seem bothered one bit. Small towns were great for many reasons but were terrible with gossip. The sound of my phone ringing caused panic, fear, and a sense of hope to fill my core.

"Hello?" I spoke without checking the caller ID.

"Hey, sweetie. It's Britt. How are you holding up?"

"I'm okay. Thanks for checking in," I replied with a slight smile. Britt had been my first real friend since moving to Maine. Though older than me, she had three boys that were all in college, we somehow bonded and socialized frequently. She was aware of who Marco was but was unaware of my true identity. I kept my romantic relationship with Marco rather surface with everyone, simply stating his job required frequent travel.

"I ran to the market and grabbed some things for you. I'm heading over now to drop them off. I won't stay, unless you want me to, but I need you to eat. Since you won't leave the house, this is the only way you'll do that."

"You don't have to keep doing this, Britt. I appreciate it, but it's unnecessary. I can order things through an app and have them delivered."

"But you won't. You're worried about Marco. I get

it. Let me be your friend and allow me to take care of you."

"I'm paying you this time," I insisted.

"You will do no such thing."

"I don't deserve your kindness."

"Oh sweetie, you of all people deserve far more. I'll see you in a bit," she replied before hanging up.

The truth was, I had friends over the years, but no one like Britt. She was beyond motherly and kind to me, always. Never once did she press for information about Marco or his family. Our conversations were uplifting and supportive.

Several minutes later, the phone rang again.

"Use your key to come in, Britt. I don't feel like getting off of the couch," I said into the receiver.

"Excuse me?" an unfamiliar voice spoke.

"I'm sorry. Can I help you?"

"I hope so. Are you, by chance, Kelly Greenly?"

My body froze. Fear flooded every cell of my being. Springing off of the sofa, I raced to the front window, peering out from behind the curtains. Not spotting anyone or anything, I ran up the stairs to my bedroom. My fingers wildly punched in the code to the safe in the closet. Retrieving Marco's gun, I had no idea what to do next. Did I get in the car and take off? But to where? Did I stay, sheltering in place like Marco advised? Did I call one of Marco's contacts here?

"Hello? Are you still there?"

"What do you want?" I shouted.

"It's okay. I'm a friend of Luca Santino's, Ms. Greenly. I'm actually one of his lawyers, Jennifer Glick. Marco Santino's phone was in evidence lockup. I found a reoccurring, private number on it, and had someone from our inhouse IT department look into it. Many rabbit holes later, I figured out the phone belonged to you. I assure you, Marco did an amazing job of hiding you. I'm just a skilled revealer of the truth. Your secret will remain safe, I promise. I care about Luca and Madison Santino far too much to do anything to cause harm to anyone in their family."

"Where's Marco?" My one hand clutched the phone, the other the Glock.

"I wish I knew, but I'm working on it."

"Why are you calling me?"

"I need your help."

"Help with what?"

"To testify for us—the defense."

"I don't know Luca. I have nothing to offer."

"You do, actually."

For an hour, Jennifer explained her strategy. To be honest, it was a pretty solid way to create doubt in the jurors' minds. She was looking to suggest that the Winters family had something to do with the disappearances based off of their business dealings with the Santinos, all of which screwed over Marco's family. In exchange, I shared my story with her.

"You don't have to do it, Kelly. I'm merely asking if you'd consider it. Unfortunately, time is of the essence, so I need an answer within the next twelve hours. You have my word that I'll make sure you're kept safe, with armed guards outside of your hotel room. Or, if you'd like, you can stay with me at my home. The same setup with regard to protection in place will be provided. If we can pin this on the Winters, which I'm confident we can, we can find Marco because I'd be willing to bet my life he's with Madison, Salvatore, and the others. I realize this bold move will out you, but Ally and I will do everything in our power, and then some, to help you disappear again."

"I'm in," I said.

"Excellent. I'll be on the next flight out. Is it possible for you to meet me at Greenville Municipal Airport? I'm chartering a private flight and obtaining security as we speak. I swear, I will keep you safe, Kelly."

"Please, call me Courtney, and I'm sure you will. Text me when you get on the plane and I'll head over to the airport."

Six hours later, without doubt or fear over what the Winters would do once they realized I was still very much alive, I was lying down in Jennifer's guest room ready for whatever would transpire next. If traveling into the deepest recesses of Hell meant I could help or save Marco, it was the least I could do for the man who'd done everything for me.

Chapter Twenty

Marco
Six Months Ago...
"I missed you, *dolcezza*," I moaned, taking hold of Courtney's slender waist, and squeezing her so hard I feared I might crack her ribs. I needed this. I wanted this. I craved her—only her, always her.

"Same," she replied, happily accepting my embrace, and pressing her warm, soft lips to mine. Pulling away after a few moments, she carefully studied my face. "Hey, what's going on?"

"Nothing."

"Something is up, honey."

"I'm tired. It was a long ride, especially since I missed the hell out of you these past few weeks. I couldn't get here fast enough," I answered while nuzzling her neck.

"Okay." She backed off of the topic and allowed me to worship her in ways only I was capable of.

"I'm liking you as a brunette by the way. It's a change from the red, but never-the-less, very sexy," I said, toying with a few loose strands of her hair.

"It's not too harsh? I had Kris add a few highlights to soften it up."

"You're perfect, Court. Inside and out." I wasn't selling her a line of crap either. She was an extremely attractive woman. Standing at a touch over five feet, she was petite, but full in all the right places. Even dressed down in sweats, she looked divine. Though her hair was a bit longer than I liked, it didn't matter. Hell, Courtney Blackstone could do anything she wanted to me and I'd happily accept whatever. Whenever she'd look up at me through those curled eyelashes with those big, brown eyes, I'd die. Never did I imagine I'd be lucky enough to find and be with someone like her.

This visit I planned to stay the entire week. A break from Luca and his crap was required. God love the guy, but he was a real pain in the ass. He wouldn't let the photograph and note rest. He had a beautiful wife, an adorable son—everything a man could ever hope and dream for, but yet he was stuck in this emotional constipation, and driving me insane. It was Beau Winters behind all of this, but instead of him watching and waiting to pounce, nope, we couldn't do that. We had to nail Beau's ass to the barnyard door right now this very moment. Shit didn't work that way. It never has. It never would. Usually when I'd take off for my once-a-month rendezvous with Courtney I'd lie and tell my father I was going hunting or fishing with some buddies. Surely he had to realize I wasn't doing either because I never brought home a fish or a dead animal. Hell, I didn't even own a fishing rod or a rifle. Unless he thought I was whipping out my Glock and picking off deer with a nine-millimeter he had to be aware I was seeing someone, in private, on the side. Of course I'd bring women around—real low-class bimbos from time to time as a means to get everyone off of my ass about being single, but the truth was, I wasn't single. I had Courtney. My sweet, perfect girl. On several occasions I'll admit that I screwed up and slept with someone other than Courtney.

I'd feel awful and hate myself when the deed was done. I wasn't exactly sure why I had sex with other women because Courtney satisfied all of my needs and wants in the bedroom. Honestly? I was scared to bring the woman I loved, the woman I'd die for, out of hiding, and back to New York to be a sitting duck for the Winters. And now with Beau going after Luca? No way. She had to remain here, where it was safe. Maybe when this was all wrapped up we'd talk about relocation, but for the unforeseeable future she had to stay tucked away in Maine.

"Thank you," I whispered, holding her in my arms while we lay in bed.

"For what?" Her long fingernails lightly scratched my left bicep.

"For knowing what I need and when I need it. For knowing all of me and my moods. For loving me without restriction. For putting up with this messed up setup. For never asking for anything more than I can provide. For being you. For everything, Court."

"I love you, Marco. I've loved you and you alone for the past eleven years. There's no one else I want to be with. I realize what we have isn't perfect, but it works for us. I'd like to be able to see you daily, or at the least celebrate a holiday with you on the actual holiday, but I do understand your fears over that. So, I'll take what I can get because when you're here with me, you give me more than any man ever has."

"It won't be like this forever, *dolcezza*."

"And if it is, it is. I'll always be around. How's work?"

"It sucks." I moaned and rolled onto my side.

"Is Luca still riding your ass?"

"Yeah. He's a stone's throw away from losing his damn mind. The guy has the world by the balls and yet he still can't seem to pull it together. I really don't want to talk about Brooklyn bullshit. I've already got enough on my plate as it is. To have to relive this past week might send me over the edge right behind Luca. The heartburn I've been having has been unreal."

"I'm sorry, honey. Is there anything I can do to help distract you? To make things better?"

"This, you and me, right here is what I need."

As always, Courtney provided me with the perfect environment. She did everything in her power to distract my troubled, exhausted mind. However, it was plain to see that she was painfully aware that the load on my back was far too heavy for me to support alone.

"We've been together for eleven years and during those eleven years I've prided myself on the fact that we've never once had a fight. We've bickered a bit here and there over silly things that mattered at the time, but not in the long run. Said disagreements were brief and always ended with amazing makeup sex. I accept the fact that I'm madly in love with you and that you can't give me any more than what you're already doing. That was a tough pill to swallow, but you're worth it. I've turned a blind eye over your infidelity while I remain faithful. And please, Marco, don't say you haven't been with other women. Lying cheapens us. We're better than that. I've given you a break from reality. I've distracted your mind. I've provided you with comfort, peace, rest, and held space for you to process your family drama. I've been your rock and have provided copious amounts of support over the years. So when I ask you what's going on, what's wrong, I damn well expect a freaking answer," Courtney snapped. "You're leaving tomorrow. I cannot send you home knowing that you're not okay. If you love me the way you suggest you do, if you respect me, you'll let me in. I refuse to spend the next month worried sick over you. That's not fair to me."

"I don't want to drag you into my work life, Court."

"If it's good enough for Luca to do with Madison, then it's good enough for me. I'm not a delicate flower who withers when conditions aren't perfect."

"I know you're not, but your mine to shield and to protect. It's my job to beat back your pain. Look at Luca and Madison. Not that long ago she went missing. I couldn't live with myself if something ever happened to you."

"Madison's abduction had nothing to do with your family ties."

I was tasked with a choice. Tell her the truth or keep her in the dark. She was right though. Courtney deserved to hear my reality, even if that reality was about Nick Winters. Part of me feared she might still be holding a torch for him. We never discussed him, what happened, how she felt about it, or anything pertaining to their relationship after that first day together. Insecurity scared me into remaining silent over what had transpired between them.

"*Dolcezza*," I began, but stopped myself. I sat up and ran my hands through my hair, like that would solve the problem.

"You can trust me, Marco," she said softly, sitting beside me.

"Winters," I hissed as if the word were some awful, unforgivable swear.

"Winters meaning the season or the Winters

Family?"

"Family."

For the next several hours I explained everything through gritted teeth. Distress that she would reveal unresolved, deep emotions for Nick fueled my harsh delivery.

"Nick is a weak bitch. Why don't you shake him down first? See what you can get out of him? The fear of physical harm to his over inflated ego or gym rat body will make for loose lips."

My shoulders instantly dropped upon her denouncement and derogatory statements over Nick. A sense of feeling foolish for even thinking she still harbored emotions for him settled in.

"Surely you're not worried that I still care about him? If you are, get over it, honey. Doctor Nicholas Winters is a fraud. It's all an act. He puts on this 'every man' bit to sell books and to get subscribers. He used to get weekly manicures, massages, haircuts, and shaves. Does John Q. Public do that? Hell no. He can't afford it. Nick dresses down to appear typical and relatable to his fans. Meanwhile, he wears five-thousand-dollar suits and shoes—which he gets shined nightly. For Christ's sake his wallet cost more than most people earn in a year. He would never stay in a modest hotel room. Oh, no. His ass was always in the best suite available. As a man who possesses exceptional street smarts you didn't pick up on that? Please," Courtney scoffed. "Nick is nothing like you. You're better in every way, shape, and form. You're a man. He's a scared little wimp. I never felt safe with him. Had we ever been in a situation where he had to protect me, he'd offer me up to save his own sorry hide. You'd never do that. You'd throw yourself in front of a bullet for me. That's why I love you and would do the same for you."

"I'm so sorry, *dolcezza*." To be honest, I felt like a giant ass for doubting her affections and loyalty.

"It's okay. I get jealous and possessive too when it comes to us, but I know you'll always come home to me which helps my brain and emotions get past the moments of doubt and fear. I'm going to ask again, what's going on? Let me help."

"Madison is following a dirty money trail and I've been locating the Winters enemies. If you're aware of anything, I beg of you to share it with me. Please, tell me everything you know."

And she did, for six hours. At the time I didn't realize she had provided me with key information; information which would lead me to the heart of the situation, to my own abduction. I also made a promise to myself that when this shit wrapped up, I'd propose. Obviously, she'd have to move back to New York, but with the Winters crap handled they wouldn't pose a threat any longer to her health, wellbeing, and safety. As for the other horrors she'd face—my job, family, and lifestyle, we'd find a way to manage.

"Listen Court, if for some reason you don't hear from me, if I go MIA, or don't answer your calls, texts, or emails do not come looking for me. Please, *dolcezza*. Shelter in place. When I can reach out, I will. I promise. Also, should I be killed, there's a ton of cash and two letters in the bedroom safe. One of them is for you. The other for either my father or Luca. Follow the instructions I've left. Do not off book anything. When you're safe and settled, contact my father, Gia, or Luca."

"You're scaring me, Marco," her voice trembled.

"There's nothing to be afraid of," I said.

With a curt shake of her head, she looked directly into my eyes. Courtney had this ability to push past pain and doubt and face situations with realism and strength. I'd never seen anyone conduct themselves as well as she. The future Mrs. Marco Santino would make the perfect wife for a future crime boss. "I love you. I'll miss you. This past week was amazing, as always. Please be careful and call me later. At a minimum, shoot me a text to let me know that you got back to Brooklyn in one piece. I'll see you next month." Leaning in, she pressed her lips to mine, kissing me with a bit more passion than usual.

"I love you," I said. I turned to get into my car but stopped abruptly. "When this nightmare with the Winters is over, we need to talk about the future. What our next steps together are going to look like."

"I look forward to that."

Chapter Twenty-One

Marco

With Salvatore and Liam still feverishly working to get the computer up and running, I paced the kitchen desperately attempting to craft a fallout plan. My faith that the two men would be able to restore such an old piece of equipment with crude instruments had dwindled. Had Madison not been pregnant she might've been able to crawl out of one of the windows. There was no chance in hell Salvatore or Liam could squeeze through anything that small with their full figures. If anything, they'd get stuck in a Winnie the Pooh and the honey pot situation. I was far too broad shouldered to clear the frame, and Jillian's wide ass and hips would hinder her from making it all of the way out. As an idea formed in my brain, the sound of the television caught my ear.

Jillian and Madison diligently watched Luca's trial daily. I caught a bit here and there, but what was the point? Chances were he'd be convicted. The only way to save all of us was to get the hell out of here. Our five statements to the authorities would force the truth out and Luca would go free. The police would have no other choice. Jackson would be locked up, and hopefully so would Tag and Beau.

"Please state your full name for the record," Luca's lawyer said.

"Courtney Blackstone, formally Kelly Greenly."
Court? No. What the hell?

Sprinting into the living room I caught a glimpse of Jillian's face. Her expression resembled that of seeing a ghost. Madison appeared confused. Slumping into a recliner I sat, watching in horror as Courtney spoke, revealing our shared secrets to the world. Years ago, after Beau demanded my father dispose of Courtney and he refused, I felt off about the entire situation. If one of my father's men didn't handle it I was one hundred percent sure Beau would find someone who would, and he did. At the time Courtney was Kelly Greenly, Nick Winters former personal assistant. Without orders from my father, I sat outside of Courtney's house to make sure she was okay. Thankfully I was there because the next morning, bags all packed ready to take off to California as per my father and Salvatore's agreement with her—the same agreement Beau insisted wasn't good enough, some jerkoff dressed in black with a ski mask covering his face assaulted her. After a brief beatdown, the guy told me everything I needed to know. Once I scared him off, I grabbed Courtney and took her to Maine—far enough away from New York, but not too far and placed her in a townhome in a remote area where I knew she'd be safe. Before I left, I installed cameras all around the property. I also paid off the guards at the front gates to ensure she received careful attention. Her new SUV was untraceable, a sealed legal name change had been created, she had a ton of cash, a cell phone, and a job she'd never be fired from. However, while getting from point A to point B there was something about her that captivated me. Sure she's a knockout, but Courtney was funny, sweet, caring, considerate, attentive, and smart.

So what that she made a poor choice by engaging in an affair with a married man. We've all suffered from moments of crap judgement. The night before I was scheduled to return to Brooklyn, we made love and I fell in love. I'm confident she did as well.

Unfortunately, due to the nature of my vocation, I couldn't commit to the type of relationship she desired. I wanted to, but I couldn't risk putting her in harm's way, especially after what happened to Luca with Madison. So, once a month I'd spend a long weekend with her. We'd speak and text daily, but that was all I was capable of providing. For some unknown reason, perhaps out of love, she accepted what I could offer, and never complained. But, recently I started feeling a bit differently. I had no idea why, maybe it was out of aging or loneliness, but I made a promise to her and myself that once the bullshit with Luca and the cryptic picture was settled, I'd open a dialogue about our next steps.

The last time I saw her I wasn't myself. She saw right through my false smiles and pressed until I came clean. No woman had ever done that. The way she provided companionship, loyalty, love, and an uncaringness for what I did for a living, accepting me for whom I really was, the son of a mobster, endeared her to me more. She did, however, provide information about the Winters that I was seeking, I just didn't realize it in that moment. I did several days later, which is what inspired me to check out Tag's Sands Point house. How anyone was able to locate Courtney was a mystery. Apparently, I failed to keep this perfect creature as shielded as I had intended.

She carefully skirted the details of our relationship, but did admit to caring for and loving me, which to spite where I currently was, meant everything to me. I couldn't help but crack a small smile. Courtney had that effect on me. Whenever I was in her company I was always grinning like a fool and laughing. As Jillian's physical demeanor revealed horror and anger, Madison shot a look of disbelief in my direction.

"You didn't think this was important information to share?" Jillian spat.

"No, Your Royal Highness. I did not because it's none of your damn business. Courtney is no longer your problem. She's mine, so back the hell off, lady. Had your family never put us here, we never would've met, and you never would've known anything about me or my family. This is your fault—*all of it*, not mine," I growled defensively.

"If this were truly all of my fault I wouldn't be locked in this basement with you," she fired back, moving closer. Her jaw was locked. Her eyes were wide, and her fists were balled tightly by her sides.

"Stop it," Madison barked, struggling to stand. Giving her a hand, she accepted my gesture. "It doesn't matter why we're here or who is screwing around with whoever's ex. The point is, we're here and to be honest, Jill, Kelly/Courtney's testimony helps my husband's case. I don't give a shit if Nick slept with someone else while he was married to you. We've all been cheated on whether we're aware of it or not, or we've all cheated at some point. I stepped out on Noel Wasserman with Luca. My husband admitted to our affair on live television. Sure, Noel is obviously still butt hurt over it, as that was clearly seen in his sworn testimony, but sometimes we have to build a bridge. Though I can't say for sure, but it appears Nick is working his ass off to find you. That's got to mean something. Since the Kelly/Courtney incident has he given you any reason to believe he'd willingly do it again?"

"Well, no."

"Then that's all you need to know. You and Marco sniping at one another isn't going to solve a damn thing. Let him be in love with Kelly/Courtney. Who cares? She's not your problem anymore and furthermore, she hasn't caused you any issues since you caught her and Nick. Additionally, cheating is a two-way street with many hairpin turns. I'd bet my life there are aspects of their relationship that you'll never know about, but who cares? It's long over and done with," Madison said. "When we finally bust out of here you never have to lay eyes on her or Marco ever again. Even you and I don't have to remain in contact, but for the moment, we need to band together, shoving all ill will and negative feelings aside. I have to go to the bathroom—again, for the millionth time today. When I return, you two better have kissed and made up. Period," Madison demanded before she waddled off down the hallway.

Jillian returned to her seat on the couch. Her eyes anxiously hawked the screen. A look of horror spread across her face when she realized Nick had taken the stand. I, myself, couldn't help but move closer to the television to watch the rest of this train wreck of a trial.

"Did you engage in an affair with Courtney Blackstone, who at the time was Kelly Greenly, Doctor Winters?" Ally Newman asked.

"Yes," Nick stated emotionlessly.

"How long did the affair last?"

"Five years? Give or take."

"How did it end?"

"My wife walked in on us in a hotel room." His eyes, then head dropped. Obviously, this man was filled with shame over his past transgressions.

"How did you handle that particular situation—being caught with another woman?"

With a great sigh, he spoke. "Not well."

"Can you elaborate?"

"I avoided discussing the matter with Jillian. As a psychotherapist I should've addressed what happened with my wife. I should've opened a meaningful dialogue no matter how hard or messy the conversation might've been, instead of remaining silent."

"Did you do anything else?"

He paused. It was his moment of truth. He could remain faithful to his wife or switch alliances and side with his family by lying. Jillian's breath caught in her throat. Her face grew pale. "I called my grandfather. I was scared over how Jillian would react, and I was worried that the press would get ahold of the story. My team and I were in the middle of a book tour and I couldn't be subjected to bad PR."

"Former Vice President Beau Winters is your grandfather?"

"Yes."

"What did you speak about with your grandfather?"

"Like I said, I was in a panicked state. When we're embroiled in a stressful situation often we don't think things through. We're looking to solve the problem as quickly as possible by any means or measures necessary. I explained to my grandfather what had occurred and requested he do something, anything to help me. He asked me to provide some information about Courtney such as her full name, address, etcetera, and said he'd handle it. He also requested that I speak with my wife and work on my marriage."

"Do you know what he did to *fix* the Courtney problem?"

"No."

"You never asked out of curiosity?"

"No."

"Did you ever hear from Courtney Blackstone after your grandfather became involved?"

"No. I had my new personal assistant pen Courtney a letter of employment termination under her old name Kelly Greenly. She was offered a severance package which she never collected, to which she's still more than entitled to accept. Until today, I had no idea where she was, what she was up to, or that she changed her name. I am, however, happy to see that she's doing well, and I am more than willing to have my assistant furnish the court with a copy of said letter or any other information that it may need."

"How do you feel about Ms. Blackstone?"

"Objection. Irrelevant," Lyman barked.

"Sustained."

"My apologies, Your Honor. I'll rephrase. During the course of your affair with Ms. Blackstone, what were your feelings for her?"

"To protect my wife, as well as Courtney's reputation, I invoke my fifth amendment right."

"Do you continue to maintain a relationship with your grandfather?"

"Yes. We speak regularly."

Newman and eventually Lyman continued to grill Nick for the better part of an hour before he was excused. It would've been obvious to even the blind that Jillian was crushed. Her heart and soul were destroyed. All of her dirty laundry as well as her husband's family's, had just exploded in her face. Her character and career were possibly ruined over Nick's admission of not only his affair, but over allegations of their previous desire to divorce, her explosive temper—even though he attempted to sugarcoat that fact, Jillian's former diva-like ways, details of how his family not only treated him, but her—which was unfairly and poorly, and the kill shot, the true reason of how Jillian and Nick came to know Luca—Ethan, the Winters' toddler son. All of this was old news to me, but incredibly shocking to the court of public opinion, who couldn't get enough of Nick and Jillian, America's sweethearts.

"I bet you're happy about this," Jillian hissed, holding back tears of rage.

"No, I'm really not. I'm actually quite sorry you had to endure that."

"I hate you," she screamed, charging at me. Her tightly balled fists smashed against my chest. I allowed her to punch me without restraint until her body finally gave out. She fell into my arms and sobbed uncontrollably.

"You don't hate me, and I don't hate you," I said softly, providing her with a firm, comforting embrace. If anything, hate wasn't a factor at the moment. Only pity and sympathy.

"My marriage, my life, my career, it's all gone," she cried into my neck.

"It's not, Jillian. Nick obviously loves you or else he would've sided with his crap family and thrown you to the wolves," I said.

"My children are going to hate us."

"They won't. What you did for Ethan was, and will always be, a pure act of unconditional love. Sarah Davis was a nutcase. We're both aware of that. If the kid had stayed with her, he would've ended up being one too. You provided him with a life filled with affection, stability, and means. That baby wasn't yours. He was the product of some odd ass, forced cult affair. You've never held his heritage against him. You made him *your* child, *your* son. If he holds any of what happened today against you, send him my way and I'll set him straight. The problem with people is they refuse to embrace the mess because it's too painful and ugly to face. We'd rather lie about who and what we truly are to save our precious reputations. It's not worth it. The moment I accepted who I was, a gangster, a mobster, a goodfella, the future Don of a crime family—whatever the hell anyone wants to label me, was the moment all of the bullshit, all of the name calling stopped bothering me. I'm okay with my life, with what I do. All the monkey chatter coming from people is just white noise. I know the type of man I am and the type of man I strive to be. When we get out of here, embrace your mess. Let people talk. Who cares? They're not living your life."

Jillian held onto me for a few moments before she released her grip and took a seat.

"Listen, I'm sorry your husband cheated on you. I can't imagine how horrible that experience must've made you feel, but I'm not going to apologize for helping Courtney out of a dangerous situation and for falling for her," I explained with a sigh. Madison was right. Plus, the second we busted free from this joint I'd never have to deal with Jillian Winters again.

"The heart wants what the heart wants," Jillian

replied, dabbing her eyes with her fingertips.

"I suppose so."

"Do you love her?"

"Yeah, I do," I admitted freely.

"Then that's all that matters. Love is an amazing force. Moving along. I have an idea." She cleared her throat as a means of regaining composure.

"Oh yeah? What's that?"

"We need to get Maddy out of here before she gives birth. She's not that far away from blowing, and sometimes women go into labor earlier than expected. I was thinking that we could stage some kind of pregnancy emergency which would force Jackson to take her to a hospital."

"I agree. Quick question. What's labor like?" I asked. Being made aware of how giving birth went down might inspire a plan of attack.

"Painful," Jillian answered with a snort.

"I gathered that—the whole squeezing a human out of your body doesn't exactly sound like a day at the beach, but what's it like? The stages? What happens blow by blow?"

"The experience is different for every woman, but for me, I started getting contractions which felt like period cramps. Over the course of an hour, the intensity of the contractions increased and I was having one every few minutes. When you're fully dilated, you start pushing unless you need a c-section, which is a different animal all together and something we cannot safely perform down here. Most times, but not always, your water breaks which is a telltale sign you're almost ready to deliver. Thankfully, my daughter's birth was short and sweet. I stood up from the kitchen table after dinner one night and my water broke. Nick rushed me to the hospital where two hours later, after minimal pushing, I was being handed a baby. There was no time for the doctors to give me an epidural so I went with a natural birth. When I was talking about this with Maddy, she said her labor spanned over the course of four days, but the delivery was natural and uneventful."

"What does it look like when your water breaks? Does it smell?"

"It looks like you're peeing yourself. You can't control it. It doesn't smell at all."

"Could regular tap water replicate it?"

"Yes, but sometimes the liquid is a pale yellow."

Heading to the kitchen she followed me. Grabbing a small Ziplock bag, I filled it with water. Pressing the seal shut, I handed the bag to Jillian. Snatching an apron from the counter I carefully tied it around her waist to create a makeshift skirt.

"Put this between your legs and try to waddle like Maddy does. Don't squeeze. The point of this game is to keep the baggie intact. If you pop the bag, you lose, and we have to start all over again," I instructed.

For once she didn't question my orders but rather complied without a word.

"Is it difficult?"

"A little, but it's doable," she said sitting.

"Excellent. Now pop the bag without it making a sound."

Upon standing, the bag burst without a noise causing water to run freely down her legs.

"Perfect. After Jackson sees that, I'll lay Madison down and you'll take a peek at whatever the hell happens down there before birth begins using the time to remove the bag. She can moan and groan in pain while we threaten Jackson with a potential problem if we have to deliver the baby down here ourselves. Our best bet is we bully him into sending her to the hospital with one of us. I vote for Salvatore to go as he's well versed in laying traps for people to find him. Then you, me, and Liam will figure out how to break out of this basement. Hopefully, the computer is up and running by that point."

"If it's not we could always have Salvatore leave last from the basement when he's with Jackson and Maddy. He can make sure the lock isn't locked from the other side."

"That's good—really good. Let's tell the others."

But before we could share our news, Liam and Salvatore burst into the kitchen.

"We did it," Liam announced.

Chapter Twenty-Two

Liam

"The computer works?" Jillian stammered in disbelief.

"Yup. It's all ready to go. We did a quick test run to Salvatore's email address and everything is there. The message went through—albeit slow as a snail, but once it hit the account, the IP address showed up, which will be traced back to here," I replied, thrilled and relieved that I was able to accomplish this not so tiny feat.

"We need more," Marco inputted.

"Like what?" Salvatore questioned.

"The email is a great way to draw attention to us here, but the cops might want to authenticate the email before they dispatch a SWAT team to the Winters' private property. Plus, we don't know if any of our men are actively checking your email account. In that timeframe, Jackson might realize what happened and kill all of us. With that in mind, Jillian and I came up with a plan to get Madison and Salvatore out of here. Madison is going to go into fake labor. While Jackson is delivering her and Salvatore to the hospital, the three of us will send another email to Luca's lawyer, sneak out because Salvatore is going to find a way to make sure that the door isn't locked, steal one of the cars, and head over to the nearest police station."

"There's a precinct not too far from here. As for a

vehicle, Tag has a collection of vintage cars in the garage. They're easy as hell to hotwire," Jillian replied.

"The door to get down here is covered by a hutch of sorts that's full of heavy crap like dishes and glasses. I can make sure the door isn't locked, but when you push out, you're going to have to proceed with tremendous caution so as to not dump the furniture, causing a racket," Salvatore said.

"One last thing," Marco added.

"What's that?" Jillian asked.

"We have to make sure that Jackson can't alert anyone. Can either one of you jump a car?"

"Yes. It's been a while, but I'm sure I'll be able to do it," I answered. If I could resurrect that dinosaur of a computer, I was fairly confident I could five finger a vehicle.

"Great. While you and Jillian do that, I will take care of Jackson. When he's handled, we'll leave. I won't take long. By the time you get the car running, I'll be right behind you."

"Handle how, Marco," Madison inquired. A look of warning spread across her worried face.

"I'm not going to kill him. Harm him, yes, but murder him, no. I plan to tie him up and keep him down here until the police find him."

"When do we do this?" Salvatore asked.

"As soon as we can successfully walk through the plan a few times," Jillian instructed, handing Madison a Ziplock bag filled with water and a touch of cooking oil.

A short while later, everyone knew their mark. We waited for hours for Jackson to show up, but he didn't. A certain frustration mounted causing everyone's nerves to be on edge. While stuck in the holding pattern we continued to watch the trial. Marco's father and sister testified beautifully, not breaking or stumbling over the prosecution's accusations. If this didn't work, Luca still stood a decent chance of beating the charges against him. Court adjourned for the day suggesting tomorrow would be the last day of witnesses before closing arguments began. Unfortunately, Jackson didn't appear for the next two days. We had plenty of food and water, but normally he showed up daily. Something was up for him not to be around. The media was buzzing over Courtney Blackstone and the Santinos' testimony, as well as a sign language expert's statements. Footage of Jillian outside of the hospital where Beau was the night she was taken clearly revealed Jillian's hand motions before disappearing off camera. Her fingers spelled the name Jackson. Perhaps this new bit of evidence sent him straight into hiding.

That evening, I climbed the stairs and pressed my ear to the door, praying to hear something and thankfully I did. However, it wasn't anything good.

"Now what, Dad?" Jackson screamed.

"You were sloppy," Tag shouted back.

"Great. I was sloppy. I admit it, but that doesn't fix the problem at hand. We're in the FBI's crosshairs."

"Our lawyers said they can't do anything, *yet*. We have time. Not a lot, but we have it."

"Should we bring Beau into this?" Jackson asked.

"No. Leave that old bastard out of it. He's done enough damage as it is."

"Does he know about what's in the basement?"

"Who do you think paid off the cops to plant Santino's hair in all of the vehicles? He's on a need-to-know basis. As long as he can hold audiences with the police and whoever else is in his pocket, we don't have to worry about any whistle blowers."

"What should we do about our *guests*?"

"What choice do we have? They've got to be eliminated, then disposed of somewhere secure." He paused. "Your perfect crime of pinning Santino to the abductions while tying up loose ends before the election didn't work, you moron."

"What do the polls say?"

"Nothing good. Chances are if Santino walks, which it looks like he will, you'll be booted from the race. We'll all be investigated, possibly arrested, and the Winters name will be destroyed forever."

"What about Nick?"

"What about him?"

"What should we do with him, Dad?"

"I don't know. He might have to disappear as well. Maybe we can spin a story to blame him for all of this. He found out Marco Santino was banging his former lover and became drunk with anger. That would at least explain why Jillian, Marco, and Madison are missing. As for Liam and Salvatore, perhaps they were collateral damage. We'll figure something out, but right now you need to handle the basement situation."

A door slammed and silence filled the space.

"Hey," I whispered. "There's no room for error with this play. The second Jackson gets down here we've got to act fast or else we're all on the chopping block. He and his father aren't too happy about what's been happening with the trial. We've seen the news. The Winters family is disgraced at the moment. The two sisters are already being pressed to resign, and it's suspected Tag will be asked to step down as well this week. They're hatching a plan to pin our murders on Nick, suggesting he saw red when he realized Marco was with Courtney. Tag also admitted he had Beau pay off the cops to plant Luca's hair in my and Jillian's vehicles."

"That son of a bitch," Jillian hissed.

"Good. Be angry. Use that rage because we're going to need it," I instructed.

Chapter Twenty-Three

Madison

"You don't have to do this, Maddy," Salvatore urged.

"I'm not giving birth in this place, especially not without my husband. If we don't take action now, we're screwed. Jackson will murder us. Another chance might not present itself for a while. The trial is ending tomorrow morning. I'll be damned if Luca takes the rap for Jackson Winters, causing my son to become temporarily orphaned, and for this new baby to be born into this freaking nightmare," I replied. Without telling the other three, Salvatore and I tweaked the plan a bit to make sure it was airtight. We should've shared the update, but we felt it was best to keep it between us.

"Over these past several months I've realized why Luca loves you so much. You've got some brass balls, *bella*." He chuckled.

"It's either that or I'm completely insane. Dealer's choice. Do you want to go over the plan again?"

"I got it. Don't worry."

"Are you ready?"

"I was born ready, *bella*."

A half-hour later Jackson clicked the exterior lock open and stomped down the stairs. We were ready to go, so no one moved from where they were sitting except for Marco, who always met him at the bottom of the steps, ready to attack should Jackson try anything funny. As Jackson placed bags of food on the kitchen table, I stood.

"Oh," I wailed clutching my swollen stomach and hunching over.

"Are you okay, Maddy?" Marco questioned me while the others' heads turned.

"Yeah," I started. "No. No, I'm not," I added, this time moaning louder.

Jillian rose moving beside me. "What are you feeling, sweetie?"

"Contractions," I answered through gritted teeth.

"Deep breaths. I'll time them," Liam said.

Squeezing his hand, I clenched my thighs together forcing the Ziplock bag filled with water and oil to burst.

"What the hell is that?" Marco asked horrified.

"Her water broke. She's in active labor. Jackson, you have to get her to a hospital immediately," Liam said.

"Can't you deliver it?" Jackson barked at Jillian.

"I'm a journalist, not a midwife," she snapped.

With Salvatore by my side, Marco holding my hand, and Liam timing contractions, Jillian helped me lie down.

"Let me take a quick peek, okay?" Jillian said, making sure my legs were positioned where Jackson couldn't see up my dress. Sliding the plastic bag under a couch cushion, she paused.

"She's gonna pop and soon," she declared.

Continuing to carry on as if I were in pain wasn't too difficult. The tears I shed were those of fear and necessity.

"Damn it," Jackson screamed, tugging on his hair.

"She needs to go to the Emergency Room now,"

Jillian hissed.

"I know," Jackson raged.

After a hot second, he began speaking. "This is how this is going to play out. I'm going to drive you to the hospital. You're to register under the name Becky Baker. You're here in New York visiting family and friends. Tell them in the heat of the moment you left your ID and insurance cards in your hotel room and you'll deal with it later. Shit the kid out and call me. I'll give you directions from there. Try anything funny and I'll kill your husband and son. Got it?"

After I nodded in agreement, he attempted to aggressively yank me to my feet.

"Watch it, asshole," Marco threatened.

"No. You watch it," Jackson replied, letting go of my hand and retrieving his phone. "I'm not kidding," he suggested showing Marco and I the screen. Right there in black and white was a live feed of my husband holding our son in the living room of our home. "One text and they're six feet under. You're little whore girlfriend too. Don't screw with me."

"Can you make the stairs?" Salvatore asked.

"I don't think so," I said.

"I got you, *bella*," he offered. "One, two, and up you go. I used to do this with your *Zia* when she was too big to climb the staircase when she was pregnant with Tony." With one swift motion the bull of a man had me cradled in his arms.

Following Jackson to the main floor, a black, unmarked sedan was waiting outside of the back door. The bright sunlight hurt my eyes, but its warmth felt amazing against my skin. It had been months since I'd been in the outside world. My body and brain needed a hot second to acclimate to it. Unfortunately, I wouldn't be afforded that right.

"Get in," Jackson ordered.

Carefully, Salvatore slid me into the backseat. Grabbing his hand I tugged at his wrist. "Don't make me do this alone," I begged, followed by a hearty shriek of pain.

"Let me go with her. We won't do anything stupid. She's scared and you want her to do this alone? Have a freaking heart," Salvatore persuaded.

"No. You'll be recognized. She won't because she's gained a tremendous amount of weight."

"I won't be. I've lost thirty pounds being here. I've also grown a beard and my hair is considerably longer than it usually is. Additionally, I'm not wearing my traditional, signature tracksuit."

"Oh my God. I feel the head," I yelled.

"Get in the car, tubby, and keep that damn kid inside of her until we get to the ER," Jackson demanded.

Roughly fifteen minutes later, the car pulled into the Emergency Room parking lot.

"You're to call me the second that baby is out, Becky Baker. He's your father, Carl Baker. If either of you say a word to anyone about anything, Luca is the first one I go after. Then I'll pick off every single family member and friend you've ever given a crap about. Am I making myself clear?" Jackson warned.

"Crystal. Let's go, Maddy," Salvatore said, opening the door, then supporting my weight until I stood upright.

Waddling into the building I calmly sold the Becky Baker routine, suggesting I felt inconsistent contractions and was roughly seven months pregnant. Out of an abundance of caution, my father, Carl, wanted me checked out. I provided them with my old college apartment address and phone number. After being triaged we were told to sit in the waiting room. We waited a good twenty minutes before Salvatore spoke.

"Did you leave the door unlocked?" he whispered.

"Yup. I did what you told me to do. I let my hand dangle behind your back when you were holding me. I just shut the door and thankfully, Jackson didn't check."

"Show time."

"We've got this," I affirmed.

A few seconds later, Salvatore's eyes rolled upward and his large frame slid out of the chair and onto the floor. Getting up and screaming for a nurse, a team of six medical staff members rushed to his side.

"Pain," Salvatore mumbled.

"Where is the pain, sir?" An older female nurse asked.

"Tight chest. Left arm. Jaw."

"Possible cardiac event. Get him on a gurney and into the back stat."

"Can I go with him?" I asked.

"No. We need to assess and work on him first. Is he on any medication?"

"None. He has no known allergies either. He's as healthy as a horse. Not even high blood pressure or cholesterol problems. Is he going to be okay?" I faked being panicked stricken.

"We're going to do everything we can. Someone will be out to update you soon." With that, Salvatore was rushed behind sealed treatment room doors.

His dramatic performance left me with a small open window. Security was busy filling out an incident report and the triage nurses were with Salvatore. As casually and carefully as possible, I slid out of the door finding myself assessing the parking lot for a vehicle I could steal. As luck would have it, some moron had left his car running in one of the ambulance bays. With authority I entered the Jeep and took off. After a moment, my bearings were collected. The courthouse was a solid half-hour away. Slamming my right foot on the gas, I hauled ass onto the highway. Weaving in and out of traffic the car finally screeched to a halt in front of the building. Instantly, a security guard came running over.

"You can't park there, lady. You've got to move your car," he instructed.

"I'm Madison Santino. My husband, Luca, is in that building right now ready to be convicted of kidnapping and murdering me and four other people. We're all alive and Luca didn't do it, but the others are in danger when Jackson Winters finds out I'm missing. Screw the car. You have to help me," I explained frantically.

The officer simply stood stone still staring blankly at my face.

"Forget this," I snapped, booking it up the steps.

Flying through the security check point not stopping for anything, the buzzer went off. Approximately one dozen guards began screaming and chasing after me, which was exactly what I desired. I needed them hot on my ass, but they couldn't catch me until I made it to the courtroom. Remembering which area Luca was in from watching the trial, my feet kept rapidly racing until I aggressively shoved the doors open.

"Luca," I yelled, once I was safely inside of the space.

Chapter Twenty-Four

Luca

"We presented a strong case, Luca," Jennifer encouraged.

"Yeah," I replied with a shrug. I already had it in my head to spite the sturdy evidence the jury would still find me guilty and I'd be going away for a long time. The fact that Gia would care for and raise Frankie provided me with a great deal of comfort, but knowing I wouldn't be there to watch him grow up killed me. This innocent little boy was going to live a life without his mother or father. He'd never have a chance to know Madison and would think the worst of me once he was old enough to research my name online.

"The trial scientist assured us that he selected the perfect jury," she added.

"Yeah."

"If we lose, we'll appeal. Ally and I will petition the court immediately to have you released under house arrest so you can be there for Frankie."

"Yeah."

"Listen, all eyes are on the Winters now, *not* on you anymore. Our case was airtight and you know it. The prosecution presented weak evidence, none of which is strong enough to pin any of what happened on you."

"Yeah."

"Hey. Snap the hell out of it. Now is not the time to

call it a day. I'll be by your side until you're found not guilty, because anyone with a functioning brain can see that," she said as she squeezed my hand. "I miss her too, but Maddy is tough. She's one badass bitch. We will find her, Marco, and Salvatore. I'd bet my life that they're all still alive. Have a tiny ounce of faith."

"The jury is ready," Ally informed, entering the room.

With a nod I rose and followed her into the courtroom. My body went through the motions of sitting, then rising when the judge arrived, then sitting again, then rising for the verdict.

"In the matter of the state of New York verses Luca Santino, the jury finds the defendant…"

A loud slamming of doors opening caused everyone to pivot.

"Luca," Madison yelled, running into the room. Her hair was as wild as her eyes. She wore an oversized, yellow dress with sunflowers on it. Her white flip flops clopped against the floor, squeaking to a halt. Her head snapped back and forth until she finally spotted me.

"Mads," I whispered in disbelief. Scaling the partition into the gallery I took hold of her to make sure this wasn't a dream, but rather a beautiful reality. "Get the hell off of me," I shouted at the bailiffs who were attempting to pull us apart. Shoving them away, I remained focused on my wife. Several seconds later, the bailiffs, along with three security guards, took hold of Madison and tore her from my arms and cuffed me. With tremendous aggression they began dragging me out of the room, but one thing registered as clear as day. Madison was pregnant, heavily pregnant at that.

My father rose and was now shielding and

protecting Madison from the grabby hands of the security guards. She was safe.

"Are you okay, Mads? Where's Marco? Where's *Zio*?" I hollered.

"Order," the judge screamed, banging his gavel.

"That's my wife," I shouted at the judge.

"Everybody freeze and shut up," Stone ordered.

Once everyone froze and silence fell over the room, he spoke again. "Who are you, Miss? Why are you here, disrupting my courtroom? And, why are you being chased by every single security guard in this building?" he demanded.

"I'm Madison Santino, Luca Santino's wife. I was abducted and managed to escape about an hour ago. Marco Santino, Salvatore D'Angelo, Jillian Winters, and Liam Stevens were being held with me. They're in danger. You have to help them immediately or else they'll be killed. Salvatore is not there. He assisted with my escape and is at St. Frances Hospital. He's not hurt, but he had to fake a heart attack so I could make a run for it. I had to steal someone's car which is parked out front. I'm sorry, but I had no other choice," she explained, through severe panic and tears.

"Are you all right, Mrs. Santino? Do you require medical treatment?"

"I'm eight months pregnant. A nurse examined me a few months ago, but that's the only care I've had. Can I sit?" she panted, struggling to breathe. My father took hold of Madison's waist and guided her to a nearby bench.

"Do you feel like you're going into labor or that the baby is in any type of distress?"

"I don't think so."

"Call for an ambulance and get her a glass of water. Also, see if there are any medical professionals in the building. If there are, get them in here immediately," he instructed one of the bailiffs. Turning his attention back to Madison, he spoke again. "Do you know where you were being held, and do you know who abducted you?"

"Yes. We were all taken to Tag and Miranda Winters home in Sands Point, on Todd Lane. Jackson Winters abducted all five of us. He's been keeping us locked in the basement of a pool house on the property. Please, I'm begging you. Get the police over there now before Jackson, who is watching this trial as we speak— he had us watching it too, that's how I knew where to find my husband, murders them. He also has live feed cameras positioned on my home, and he's using them to threaten Luca and my son. Salvatore is at St. Frances Hospital, under the name Carl Baker. I was triaged as Becky Baker before I snuck out. I can tell you the entire story in great detail, but right now, please, help the other four first."

Madison's words were met with a loud gasp from not only the jury, but from the press as well.

"Uncuff Mr. Santino and get Mrs. Santino to the hospital. Dispatch local police and the FBI to the Winters' estate in Sands Point immediately. I want active BOLOs on Jillian Winters, Marco Santino, and Liam Stevens. I want officers sent to St. Frances Hospital to locate Salvatore D'Angelo/Carl Baker. Mr. Santino will be transported to the hospital with his wife. Officers will be stationed outside of Mrs. Santino's room. Once she's cared for, Mr. Santino will be taken to the nearest police station where he will wait for my orders. When the investigation is complete, I'll contact all parties so we can reconvene. Ms. Newman and Ms. Glick, you're more than welcome to stay with Mr. Santino. In fact, I recommend it. Court is adjourned," he declared, slamming his gavel, rapidly rising, and taking off into his chambers.

I didn't have a chance to actually speak with my wife until after she'd been checked into the ER. Part of me was still in a state of severe shock. I didn't snap out of it until my mother entered Madison's hospital room with Frankie. She and my father hugged and kissed Madison, but gave her space, leaving shortly after arriving. Madison refused to let go of Frankie, embracing him tightly as she cried. When he asked where she had been, she told him she was away but was back now and in a month or so he'd have a little brother or sister. Thankfully, he accepted the answer. I, on the other hand, had questions, but I didn't want to overwhelm her. With no idea over how anything went down over the last six months, I wasn't sure how to proceed. However, I had to be made aware of the truth.

With a heavy, deep breath I spoke. "Did Jackson or anyone of them touch or harm you?"

Sitting straighter she replied. "No. Do you honestly think Marco would've allowed that?" She paused. "This baby is yours, Luca. You realize that, right?"

"I do."

"I'm sorry, babe."

"For what?"

"For not listening to your warnings. For putting you through this. For going behind your back."

"It's over. You're okay. That's what matters." I should've been ripping pissed, but yet I wasn't. Relief that this nightmare had come to a close was all I felt.

That, and deep-seated rage for the Winters. They'd pay. The moment my name was officially cleared, they'd get what they deserved.

Poised to speak, Madison was interrupted by a doctor.

"How are we feeling, Mrs. Santino?"

"Totally fine. Tired, but good." She smiled as she gently rubbed her stomach.

"You're eight months pregnant. That's to be expected. All of your tests and labs look excellent. The baby has developed perfectly normal. I don't see the need to keep you here unless you'd like to stay for the night. It's up to you. However, I want you to follow up with your OBGYN as soon as possible. I sent everything from today's visit over to their office. If you'd like to speak with one of our counselors here or would like a recommendation for an out-patient therapist, let the nurse know, and we'd be happy to provide that information. The only other thing I can offer is the baby's gender, if you'd like to know," the doctor spoke while flipping through Madison's chart.

"Luca?" Madison said.

A fleeting memory took me back to the day when we sat in the doctor's office at Madison's five-month checkup. I was over the moon to find out that we were having a boy. Throughout her entire pregnancy I was beyond excited. Perhaps it was because I was there from day one when the pregnancy test revealed a positive result. Everything about this moment felt strange. The paternity of the baby wasn't called into question. Simple math clearly proved it was mine, but too much had happened over the course of the past four hours. This morning I was ready to be found guilty of a crime I didn't commit. A plot twist later, and here we were. Before I could answer, the door opened and three police officers entered.

"Luca Santino?" One inquired.

"Yeah," I answered, standing.

"We're here to escort you back to the courthouse."

With a nod, I turned to face Madison. "Let's be surprised this time. I have to go. My mother is in the waiting room. I'll send her in to stay with you. When you're released, she'll take you back to her house with Frankie. Stay there, and I mean *stay there*, Madison, until I return, or my father tells you otherwise." Though I wanted my words to come across as soft and gentle, the delivery was the farthest thing from it.

"We have to pat you down and cuff you," another cop informed.

"Yup," I said. Parting my legs and placing my hands behind my head, the cops searched my body, then they restrained my wrists.

A look of deep sadness and guilt hung from Madison's worried face.

"Everything will be fine, Mads. I'll see you soon."

"We'll give you a second to say goodbye to your wife," one officer said, freeing my arms from his firm hold.

"I love you," I said, leaning forward to kiss her forehead, then her swollen stomach. Exiting the room I passed Ally, Jennifer, my parents, two sisters, and son in the waiting area. Instantly, my father, Ally, and Jennifer rose and fell into step behind my police escorts. My mother and Tina headed down the hallway to Madison's room, and Gia sat holding onto my now sleeping son. No words were spoken, but much had been said.

The ride was short but filled with far too many unanswered questions. I honestly had no idea what would happen next. Attempting to figure out what I'd tell a client in this situation proved useless because no real answer presented. In theory, I'd return to the court and the judge would find me not guilty based off of the new evidence, but what if that wasn't the case?

"All rise. Nassau County Criminal Court is now in session. The Honorable Judge Stone presiding," the bailiff ordered.

"You may be seated," Stone said, waving his hands. "Due to recent events, the matter of New York State verses Luca Santino has been dismissed. The Court thanks the jury for their time and is excused. All other parties are to remain here."

"We've got this," Jennifer whispered, pulling me into a firm side embrace.

"Don't say anything unless spoken to," Ally warned. "It's over when this mess is read into public record and stamped closed."

"Your Honor. We'd like to make a motion that the cameras be turned off for this," Lyman requested.

"Ms. Newman, what are your thoughts?" the judge asked.

"We see no reason as to why the cameras need to be shut down now."

"Please, Judge Stone. In light of what occurred before, it's believed what's to come next will only damage the credibility of several of our high-profile witnesses. Without a proper and thorough investigation, any information provided would create a potential public outcry, possibly placing some witnesses in danger. It's been streamed that the charges against Mr. Santino have been dropped. The world is now fully aware of his innocence."

"Ms. Newman?" the judge questioned again, turning his head to face her.

"We feel this decision is up to your discretion." Ally shrugged. I'd seen her use this power maneuver many times. She was humbly stroking Stone's overinflated ego.

"Overruled. The cameras will remain on. If it was allowable for Mr. Santino's good name to be dragged through the mud in a public forum, it's allowable for others to suffer the same fate. What's good for the goose, is good for the gander." He paused to allow his ruling to sink in. "Now that we've cleared that up, Mr. Santino, I offer this court's, the police department's, and the FBI's deepest and sincerest apologies. From time-to-time mistakes are made when evidence strongly compels. However, after personally speaking with your brother, Liam Stevens, Jillian Winters, and Salvatore D'Angelo, the Court and law enforcement are aware of the true perpetrators of the crimes and carefully crafted lies you were accused of. Rest assured, justice will be served.

"I'm confident your legal team will provide the public with a statement of your innocence, thusly clearing you of any wrongdoings. It is not only this Court's hope, but mine as well that you, as a talented attorney—I've read your file which included your tremendous credentials and stellar landmark work, do not lose faith in the system, and that you continue to keep fighting for what's fair, legal, and just. I wish you and your family only the best going forward. Congratulations on becoming a father for the second time. Being a parent is one of life's greatest joys. Court is dismissed." With the slam of Stone's gavel, my nightmare ended.

My body automatically stood. I could breathe again, but for some reason the expected intense relief wasn't present. All I felt was numbness. Ally pulled me into a firm embrace, whispering something into my ear that my brain couldn't seem to process. Jennifer followed doing the same. I can clearly recall thanking them for everything, but the haze remained in place. When I walked out of the courtroom, my father positioned himself in front of me while Tony and Jimmy brought up the rear. The flash of cameras and shouts from reporters assaulted my eyes and ears.

"No comment," my father kept repeating as he continued to move forward.

As we neared the exit, something caught my attention causing my feet to root to the spot.

"*Fratello*," Marco called, limping over. His face was swollen, crusted with dried blood, and adorned with stitches. His clothing was filthy and torn to shreds, especially his pants.

Holding him tightly in my arms, I never wanted to let go. Everything inside of me—fear, anger, rage, grief, and finally relief rose to the surface and poured out of my tear ducts. Truthfully? I didn't think I'd ever stop crying. I could hear the media going wild screaming questions, but I didn't give a shit.

"It's all good, Luca. Everything is okay," Marco assured repeatedly.

I wanted to speak, but I couldn't. No words existed. For the first time in a long time, I knew I was safe and all would be well because Marco was with me.

"I got you," Marco whispered, turning his body slightly. He never released his grip despite the pain he was surely in while he guided us to the car that was parked out front. "*Zio* is at the house. He just got there according to Pop. Maddy will be released from the hospital within the hour. Mom will bring her home." Marco paused. "Hey, it's over, Luca. Those bastards, the Winters, are going to go away for a long ass time. None of them will ever work in politics again," he said as he rubbed small circles on my back.

"What happened to you? Are you okay?" My eyes surveyed his body.

"My shoulder popped out again, but it's back in place. I had a scuffle with a few of Tag's security guards, and I was grazed by a bullet to the thigh. I'm confident I sustained a few hand fractures and a cracked a rib, but I can breathe, so it didn't puncture my lung. That's a win. Liam Stevens is a former Army medic. He sewed me up. Once everyone is home, I'll swing by the ER for Paulie to take a quick look-see. You know, just another day at the office," he answered with a light laugh.

Sitting in the backseat of the car, my hands cradled my head. I was beyond grateful that my father opted to catch a ride with Jimmy and Tony, leaving Marco and I alone. The privacy allowed for me to purge everything that my soul could no longer hold onto.

"What the hell happened?" I questioned.

"After we met with Beau, something clicked. I'd been working an angle with Maddy's help. When I realized that old shit had nothing to do with the picture and note that you were sent, I was confident the grandson was the culprit, but I had no proof. So, Maddy and I went to go obtain said evidence. We figured if we could unearth something that would stick, we'd present it to you for you to do your law shit with. We found some damaging evidence, but unfortunately, Jackson caught me. Maddy called to see where I was, but it was too late. While I was on the phone with her I dropped clues so she'd be able to tell someone—you, Pop, *Zio*, the boys, freaking anyone who wasn't her, where I was. Sadly and stupidly Maddy took it upon herself to find me. The second she entered Tag's property, Jackson nabbed her. He stashed us in the basement of Tag's pool house. When I got there it was just me and Liam Stevens. Then Maddy joined us followed by Jillian Winters and finally *Zio* about two weeks later. *Zio* said he suspected Jackson but kept his gut intuition to himself. He allowed himself to get caught so he could rescue Maddy and me—which in the end he did. It was his plan to fake a heart attack so Maddy could sneak out of the Emergency Room. He made sure when he, Jackson, and Maddy left for the hospital that Jackson was the first one out of the basement door, so Maddy could leave the lock open giving the rest of us the opportunity to escape, which we did. When the coast was clear, we snuck out, but not before Liam sent a time/date IP address stamped email from this old piece of shit computer that he and *Zio* fixed, to the FBI, local police, and your lawyer. Yours truly beat the snot out of Jackson and Tag, locking their asses in the basement for the police and Feds to find. I hotwired one of Tag's cars, then threw down with his bitch ass security.

"How did Maddy and I figure out it was Jackson, you ask? Great question. Whenever a politician is involved in anything follow the money and locate their enemies. Maddy did the first while I handled the latter with the unknowing assistance of Courtney Blackstone—public enemy number one. I'll let Maddy fill you in on all of the details. So, in conclusion, if you're going to be pissed at anyone, direct it at me, *not* at your wife. I dragged her into this. Finding who targeted you and bringing down the Winters family was my obsession and mine alone. They screwed with not only you and our family, but with Courtney too. I suppose it was a personal vendetta. Please know I always protected, kept safe, and was there for Maddy. We may have been detained, but she was never, not even for one second, in any danger. Between *Zio* and I, Maddy was the most watched after person in that pool house hell hole of horrors."

"Who planted the evidence against me? What was Beau, Tag, and Jackson's actual involvement?"

"We were potential threats to Jackson's career. You were easy to pin everything on. Tag was aware of what Jackson was doing. Beau knew some, but not everything because Tag and Jackson were icing him out, only dusting him off when they needed his assistance. Beau hired the cops to plant your hairs in Jillian's and Liam's vehicles. Jackson, through Beau's police contacts, was provided with the copy of the picture of the Lessor/Davis crime scene, and Jackson carelessly scribbled the note attempting to make it look like Tag wrote it. For years Jackson has been forging his father's name on all types of documents. It was a team effort between the three of them."

"How do you propose we attack? All eyes, especially the public's, will be on them. The media is already pouncing on the Winters, digging for whatever scraps of information they can find to be the first to break the true story."

"We wait and see. Under no circumstances does

anyone make any immediate moves. You have to trust me with this. Let the police, Feds, and courts attack first. When the dust settles, whoever didn't receive adequate punishment, I'll deal with them personally. You're benched."

"Hell no. In case you've forgotten I may be perceived as the Santino Family's *consigliere*, but we both know the second Pop is out, you'll promote me to Underboss. Should something happen to you, I take over—with or without Pop. When we both drop dead, my son is up. So whatever you do, I better damn well be included in it. No more secrets," I demanded.

Marco laughed lightly. "Oh, *Fratello*. For as different as we may be on the education map, we're no different with regard to temper and hot headedness. I used to be like you. The way you look and feel right now, I've been there and done that. Gets you nowhere. For once, learn from me. Trust my ways and thought process because they're Pop's. He obtained his knowledge from *Nonno*—the man who started all this. We've already discussed what happens when Pop retires. That plan hasn't and will never change, but for now calm the hell down. Take a frigging breath. In a few minutes we'll be at Mom's. Everyone will be there. The Santino name has been vindicated. We lay low conducting business as usual. When I say we attack, we attack. Not a second sooner. Do you understand me?"

For a brief moment, I clearly saw and heard our father come out of Marco's mouth via words and mannerisms. This happening allowed for comfort and peace to find its way back into my otherwise nearly dead soul.

"Yes. For the record, I do and always will trust you."

"Same. If we don't have each other's back, we've got nothing. Never forget that," he said as he gently slapped the side of my face Frank Santino style.

"I'm taking you to the hospital later. You need to be x-rayed or something."

"Whatever makes you happy. We have one last thing to discuss."

"What's that?"

"Your wife. Cut her some slack. Her actions were out of love and driven by me. Like I said before, if you're going to snap at someone, snap at me, *not* at Maddy. She was dying a slow death without you and Frankie. I want you to act like nothing happened. Tuck your emotions back and be a husband and a father. You've got another kid on the way. Your wife and children are going to need you to show up and be a man."

"I'm trying. I promise, I really am. I'll get there, but I'm going to need everyone to cut me some slack. It's been a rough ride." I reached for Marco's wrist. "Hold up a second. What's the deal with Kelly Greenly? Why didn't you ever tell me about her?" Part of me felt deeply insulted that he hadn't told me about his relationship with a woman who had a direct tie to the Winters family. However, another part of me felt suspicion. When Noah Lessor and Sarah Davis had my wife, Marco had a line in—his girlfriend, but he conveniently neglected to share that bit of information with anyone. Back then I was on my knees with grief, losing my mind, but yet for some reason he continued to conceal his romance.

"She's not one of them so stop thinking that. Courtney was an innocent bystander and a victim of the Winters family. As for why I kept her a secret, I don't know. Maybe I didn't want anyone knowing I was with someone or that I took Nick's sloppy seconds. I'm not embarrassed of her at all, but you know how our mother and sisters can be at times—judgmental. You got lucky with Maddy. Everyone accepted her straight away. Courtney was an escape from this life. A once-a-month retreat from all of the heaviness our lives are forced to carry on a daily basis. I've been a good soldier in the Santino Army. I deserve a break too. You have a good woman to go home to. Our sisters have husbands waiting for them. What do I have? Mom and Pop down the hallway. Don't get me wrong. I love them and I am grateful for all they've done and do—and then there's Mom's cooking which no one will ever be able to top, but I'm too old to crawl into their bed at night for comfort. That would be weird and exceptionally creepy. There's also the whole protection thing. I was going to bring her around to meet the family, then Maddy went missing. It made me realize how exposed we were. I didn't want Courtney to be in the line of fire ever again. *But* after what she did for us, for me, it's making me look at the situation differently. Once Beau and all of them are behind bars, she can safely return to New York and maybe, just maybe, our family will accept her—see her for the amazing soul she truly is, and I'll marry her. I don't know, Luca. We'll have to wait and see how shit plays out. Hell, she could've left the courthouse and hauled ass out of town, never wanting to see or speak to me again. Because of me, all of her dirty laundry is out in the open for the world to criticize. Though that was never my intention, it happened and here we are."

"Wasn't it you who told me that we protect our own no matter the cost? Madison is mine, but you kept her and my baby safe. What makes you think I wouldn't do the same for your girlfriend?" I paused. "She'd be stupid if she didn't want to be with you. Call her," I added, handing him my phone, and exiting the car.

Chapter Twenty-Five

Jillian

Part of me didn't believe we'd pull it off, but here we were sitting in the Sands Point Police Station. The moment Madison and Salvatore left the basement, Marco crept up the steps, straining an ear to hear what was happening in the main area of the home. Once he felt confident we were safe, he instructed Liam to send a group email to the police, the Feds, and Ally Newman. By the time it went through, he heard Jackson returning. Off booking it, Marco slammed the door open shoving the solid wood hutch blocking the entryway aside. He grabbed Jackson by the scruff of his neck and proceeded to beat him within an inch of his life.

"Come near anyone of us or our families again and I'll murder you with my bare hands. Do you understand me?" Marco hissed, centimeters away from Jackson's face. Snatching Jackson's cell phone from his pocket, Marco smashed it against the floor.

Jackson moaned in agony as Marco aggressively kicked him down the basement steps. Shoving Jackson into a kitchen chair, Marco tied him up with some cords that we'd found in the ceiling earlier. Moments later, Tag waltzed into the house and was gifted the same treatment as his son. Though Marco kept ordering Liam and I to make a run for it, we didn't. We felt the need to provide backup if necessary, which it wasn't. It appeared Marco had run this gambit many times over in the past.

"Unlike my authority my patience isn't limitless. The next time we meet, I will kill you. That's a threat and a promise, *Mister Speaker of the House*," Marco warned.

"Hey. It's okay, Marco. You've handled them sufficiently and I'm confident they've gotten the message, but right now I need you to take a breath and refocus the lens. We're not out of the woods yet," Liam said softly. The look on Marco's face was pure insanity meshed with total rage. He needed to get out of the loop he was currently in, in order to regain composure. If he didn't, we were royally screwed. There was no way Liam and I could finish this without him.

"We've got to go," Marco replied, slapping Liam on the shoulder.

Curiously, while sprinting to Tag's vintage car garage, Marco grabbed hold of my hand, using his body as a shield to protect mine. After being the target of his arrogant, nasty treatment these past months, I'd have assumed he wouldn't have given a rat's ass if I was shot or not, but for some reason he appeared to care about my safety. Within seconds he'd successfully broken into the garage, skillfully disarmed the alarm, and used his elbow to shatter the driver's side window of a Chevy Impala from the late sixties. His eyes scanned the area landing on a toolbox in the far-right corner. Rapidly retrieving several items, he returned to the car, aggressively yanked the plastic from under the steering column off, put on a pair of gloves, and began messing around with wires. The car impressively sprang to life.

"Let's go," he ordered.

"Hold on. Do they employ any armed guards, Jill?"

Liam asked deeply concerned.

"Maybe. I don't know. I can't recall seeing any when Jackson brought me here, but the Winters, especially Tag, are huge on security."

"It doesn't matter. I'll handle it," Marco said.

"How? There's a very real chance there are multiple men with guns and knives out there who more than likely possess formal military training," Liam said.

"Do you know where the police station is, Jill?" Marco asked, ignoring Liam's fears.

"Yes."

"Can you drive a stick shift car?"

"Yes."

"Awesome. Count to forty-five, slowly. One, pause. Two, pause—like that. Then meet me by the gates. If I'm dead, slam through the gate at full speed. This car is made of solid metal. It'll get banged up, but you'll be able to get out. Make sure to brace yourself for the impact. If I'm alive, but compromised, do the same. Got it?"

"I'm not leaving you behind," I insisted.

"You have kids to get home to. Liam too. They need you. Please do as I say, Jill," Marco ordered, walking out of the garage.

Liam climbed into the back of the car; this way when we collected Marco, he could jump in quickly. I positioned myself in the driver's seat. Steadily we began counting. In reality, three quarters of a minute is nothing, a blink of an eye, but in this situation it felt like an eternity. Finally reaching the target number, I placed the car in reverse.

"Go slow, Jill," Liam urged. "We don't know what's waiting for us. You can always smash the gas if necessary."

Bang.

A gunshot sliced through the otherwise still air.

Bang.

Another blast fired.

Disregarding Liam's warning, I sped down the driveway to find Marco skillfully engaging in hand-to-hand combat with two men in uniform. Unsure what to do, my instinct took over. Out of the corner of my eye I saw a handgun on the ground. Marco must've wrestled it away from one of the men and now it lay unclaimed.

"Don't do it," Liam begged.

"Sorry," I replied getting out of the car and retrieving the discarded weapon. Aiming it up in the air, my index finger wrapped around the trigger, then pulled it. All attention turned to me.

"This is how this plays out. You two lick your wounds and go back to your security booth, making sure to open those gates. Call the cops, call whomever you want. I really don't give a shit. They're looking for us anyway. He gets in the car and you do not stop us from leaving this property, because if you do, I will shoot you myself. I have experience with murdering and maiming which means I'm not afraid to do it again if need be, and I can assure you that I will not lose any sleep over ending your lives or making it so you never walk again. Try me," I threatened, pointing the weapon at them.

Without a backwards glance, the men took off at a full sprint for safety. Marco limped as quickly as possible to the car, slumping into the passenger's seat. As my eyes scanned his body, multiple blood stains on his shirt and pants appeared. His left cheek was swollen. His lip was split.

"You're bleeding pretty bad," I said, passing through the now parted gates.

"Punch it, Jill," he slurred harshly through tremendous facial inflammation and anguish.

"Were you shot?" Liam inquired.

"Grazed," he responded.

"Where?"

"Right thigh. My shoulder is dislocated, I've got about a half dozen lacerations on my face and hands that will require stitches, and I'm fairly sure I've got a few broken bones and at least one fractured rib. Once we get to the police station, I'll pop my shoulder back in. The rest can wait," he answered.

Ripping the arm off of his shirt, Liam handed the material to him. "Tie the area, tightly. Try not to move it. The rest I can triage quickly when we're safe. Do you feel faint?"

"This isn't my first ride at the rodeo. I've been here many times, but I appreciate the help."

"We're almost there. Two minutes tops," I stated, driving like a woman who had just held up a bank.

"Where'd you learn how to fight like that? Were you in the military?" Liam asked in an attempt to keep Marco focused and conscious.

"Occupational hazard. Some people are book smart, while others are street smart. I'm the latter."

"Can you walk?"

"Yeah, slowly. Go ahead. I'll catch up."

"Go, Jill. I've got Marco."

"No. We're in this together," I stated, slamming the car into park in front of the entry doors. Leaning over, Marco pulled the wires under the steering column apart. The Impala died immediately.

With Liam's assistance, Marco was able to stand. Before entering the building, Marco paused.

"Don't even think about it," Liam urged, turning Marco around. "On three. Relax the shoulder. Stand straight. Deep breath in. One, two."

The loudest crack I'd ever heard, accompanied by a guttural grunt came out of Marco.

"All better," Liam said, taking hold of Marco's frame again.

"Can I help you?" a desk sergeant asked.

"I'm Marco Santino. This is Jillian Winters and Liam Stevens. We're the subjects of the Luca Santino trial. We were abducted along with Madison Santino and Salvatore D'Angelo," Marco explained in an unnaturally calm manner for a man who'd been beat up and shot moments ago.

A cop passing by stopped dead in his tracks. "You're Marco Santino?" he questioned.

"Yes."

"Someone get the chief now," he barked. Several officers scurried away. "Come with me."

"I need a first aid kit, as many ice packs as you can find, and someone has to call the paramedics. This man has injuries which require immediate assistance," Liam ordered, getting Marco to a chair.

The officer grabbed a large red box from behind the front desk and tossed it to Liam who went to work at a rapid fire pace. With the assistance of the cop, Liam was able to stitch Marco's gashes and bullet graze, assessing the damage as not as bad as expected. Marco's jaw was covered with bags of ice. With his head leaning back against the wall, his eyes closed. Without looking, he reached for my hand which shook from nerves and concern over his wellbeing.

"I'm okay, Jill. This is nothing," he assured, not flinching at all. The fact that he had no topical lidocaine while being sutured and didn't move a muscle revealed his true inner discipline and his tremendously high threshold for pain.

"We called for EMS. They should be here shortly," the policeman informed.

"Your shoulder is back in place. The graze and cuts are handled. Be careful not to bust those stitches open. Your vitals are stable and strong. I'm going to have you stand and I'll bind your ribs as best as I can because I'm fairly sure they're fractured. However, since you aren't struggling to breathe, nothing pierced your lungs. You more than likely have various breaks, tears, pulls, and fractures, but without an x-ray my hands are tied. It doesn't appear there's anything else going on such as internal bleeding, but you need to be seen by a doctor," Liam told Marco. "How's the pain?"

"Five by five. Thank you."

"Are you ready to give your statements?" the officer asked after Liam bound Marco's torso.

Reaching for my hand again, Marco clutched it. We followed the cop down a hallway into a private office. Initially, he wanted to separate us, but Marco wouldn't allow me to be alone. Instead of arguing, the cop shrugged, suggesting that we all take a seat. A few moments later several uniformed cops and a few in suits entered the room, closing the door. For some reason I didn't feel safe or like the victim of a crime, but rather like I was the criminal and in some sort of trouble. A nervous energy seeped in causing my body to go rigid.

"I got you," Marco whispered. "I won't let anything

happen to you, but you have to trust me." As he squeezed his fingers around mine, a sense of comfort found its way back inside of my core.

After being questioned for what felt like forever with a short break for the medics to examine Marco who insisted he didn't need to go to the hospital and that he'd go later, we were fingerprinted for identification and re-questioned by the FBI. Thankfully, Special Agent Timothy Wilder, an FBI Agent who'd worked on my husband's case, recognized and positively identified me. Liam and I were forced to be checked out by the paramedics even though we swore we were fine. Eventually, we were transported to the building Luca's trial was being held at. Never once did Marco leave my side. He kept holding my hand and protecting me from everything from the police to the fly that landed on my arm outside of the courthouse. He even stayed with me until Nick arrived when he probably should've bolted to be with his own family. Though the introduction was brief and awkward, the two men kept their personal opinions to themselves.

"Marco," I called after him as he limped out of the room.

"Yeah?" he said, stopping and turning around.

"Can I please take you to the hospital?"

"I'm okay, Jill. I've been hurt far worse than this, but if it will make you feel better, I'll swing by the ER later for a checkup and I will have someone update you. Right now, I need to be with my brother."

"I understand. I'll be waiting for that call and thank you."

"*Thank you*," he said with a slight smile.

"If you ever need anything, anything at all, even if

it's just someone to share a cup of coffee with, reach out."

"Likewise. The door is open twenty-four seven."

"Good luck with Courtney."

"I hope I don't need any luck, but I appreciate it. Be well, Jill," he said before hobbling out of the room.

"Are you sure you're all right?" Nick took hold of me, squeezing me so tightly that I couldn't breathe.

"I'm fine. Are you okay? Are the kids okay?"

"The kids miss their mom and are excited you're coming home. As for me, I suppose justice was served. Had I thought for one second that Jackson had you stashed in the poolhouse basement I would've broken down the door with my bare hands to rescue you. I was in that damn house, Jill. I can't believe I didn't put two and two together."

"It's over. We're all alive and well."

"This may be over, but the shit show we're in for because of my family is only beginning."

"True, but you've always distanced yourself from them in the past. I doubt the public will blame you for anything. Plus, we have a team of PR people who handle crap like this. If we lose the show, we lose the show. Who cares? We'll move along and do something else."

"Oh, Jill. I'm so sorry." Tears rolled freely down his ageless cheeks.

"There's nothing to be sorry for. We've weathered worse, Nick. Right now, I'd like to go home, see our children, hug and kiss them, take a long shower, eat a decent meal, and attempt to return to our normal life."

With a nod, he pulled me into his side. As we walked out of the courthouse, hundreds of cameras snapped pictures and recorded our every movement. Reporters shouted all kinds of questions, but we kept going until we reached Nick's Lexus.

"Doctor Winters, what do you have to say about what your family has done? Did you have anything to do with it? Are you involved in any way?" a young female reporter bellowed.

"We realize you have many questions, and we'd love to stand here and answer them all. However, after the ordeal my wife has recently endured, and in light of statements made during the Santino trial, for now, I'll have to humbly say, 'no comment.' In time Jill and I will make a statement, but for the moment, we'd like to go home and spend some time with our son and daughter. We hope that you can appreciate the shock, exhaustion, and emotional overload we're experiencing," Nick explained calmly, flashing his classic megawatt smile coupled with his expression of understanding. It seemed to have worked because the reporters backed off and were focusing their attention on Liam and Kendra who were now leaving the building.

Taking advantage of the opportunity, we got into the SUV and went home. Seeing Jordyn and Ethan filled my heart with love, replacing intense fatigue with endless hope. Of course we didn't share what happened with the children. We told them I was working on an assignment for the station that took far longer than I expected, which in the end wasn't a total lie. Though the network kept *This Just In* on, and surprisingly enough our ratings went through the roof upon my return and thereafter, Nick and I decided to clear the air and write a book about our lives and all of the ugly truths in it. For the most part the novel humanized us, drawing people who had pulled away from us due to our last name back in. They understood and sympathized with our situation, praising the strength of our honesty and marriage. As for Nick's two sisters, we never heard from them again. They both resigned from their political positions and faded into the background. Maris and Miranda did the same. Beau, Jackson, and Tag were all awaiting trial and to be frank, it didn't look good for them. The once mighty and powerful political Winters family had fallen from grace, never to rise again.

Chapter Twenty-Six

Marco

"Whoever performed your emergency triage did an excellent job, Marco. You were lucky. A plastic surgeon couldn't have stitched you up better, and your shoulder is completely back in the socket. As for the rest of you, you've got a fractured right hand, two fractured ribs, multiple contusions, and a nasty sprained ankle. Your labs look fine, and there's no internal bleeding. I don't need to do a thing about the sutures, but you'll need to come back in ten to fourteen days to have them removed. As for the other injuries, I'll be casting your hand, you'll have to wear a rib brace and use a Cam Walker Boot for the ankle. Other than that, you look good. You're going to be sore as hell for a while, but you'll heal," Paulie informed me as he closed my chart.

"See? I told you I was fine," I said to Luca.

"You're *not* fine. If you were, you wouldn't be leaving the *hospital* with a cast, a brace, and a surgical boot. I also wouldn't be bringing you back here in two weeks to remove the three dozen plus stitches you've got," Luca replied as he rubbed his temples.

"True, but I'm not dead, so that's a win."

"How are you feeling, Marco?" Paulie asked.

"Not bad," I lied for Luca's sake. The truth was, every ounce of my body was done with me and screaming out in agony.

"I can write you a prescription for pain killers if you'd like. Tomorrow morning you'll more than likely feel like an eighteen-wheeler slammed into you at full speed."

"That's not necessary. I'll be fine."

"You don't need to be a hero. If you're in pain, take something. To err on the side of caution, I'll send you home with a script. Hang tight and a nurse will come in to cast and brace you up." He paused thoughtfully. "Listen, Marco. We've known each other for a long time now. You're not a young man," he said, holding up his hand to stop me from talking. "In your mind you might believe you are, but internally you've taken many beatings which have left unrepairable imprints on muscles, tendons, bones, and so on. I also saw previous gunshot damage on your films—most of which I've treated you for. It's not my place to tell you how to live your life, but I strongly advise that you slow down. Take a breath. Experience a little less excitement. Right now I want you on bedrest for at least a week. When you're back up and running again, you can meet me at Gabriel's Pub and buy me that drink you stiffed me on, but this time try not to get abducted beforehand."

"I will personally make sure he gets the rest that his body requires. Thank you, Paulie," Luca spoke for me.

When the door closed and we were alone, Luca felt the need to open his mouth, again. "Paulie is right. You have to slow the hell down, Marco. You might be willing to sacrifice your life for whatever, but I'm not willing to lose you. You're in your fifties for Christ's sake."

"The ocean is as old as time and it will still drown your sorry ass, Luca. I know what my age is. I'm especially aware of it on days when it rains or it's cold outside. The pain my body experiences from past mistakes made out of carelessness is always present. However, you, Paulie, not even Pop for that matter are going to tell me how to carry on. Bones break. Muscles stretch. I'll survive," I snapped. I hated when someone mentioned how old I was.

"I'm not ready to be without you," Luca whispered barely holding it together.

"Stop. Please. No one is going anywhere," I insisted, not wanting to witness him cry again because it would break my heart. We should be celebrating the end of this nightmare, but for some reason he refused to let shit go.

"I've got you and Gia."

"And Tina, Marie, Mom, Pop, your two kids, *and* Maddy—plus Salvatore, Tony, Jimmy, and the list goes on for days."

"You and Gia are my closest allies."

I didn't like where this conversation was going. Sitting up as straight as possible, refusing to wince from the pain, I spoke. "What's going on with you and your wife?"

"Nothing."

"Bullshit. You were going out of your mind to get her back, and now it seems like you're ready to call it quits."

"I'm not," he shot back, His voice was laced with venom.

"It sure seems like you are, and I can assure you that it will be the biggest mistake of your life. Shit happens all day, every day, Luca. Suck it up and move along. You've got one baby at home and another on the way. Grow the hell up and be a damn man. This crumbling under pressure, this intense fear of losing us—cut the crap. Enough. Yeah, sure, what we all just went through was awful, but everyone is totally fine and will remain that way. It's over. Get that fact through your thick skull."

Before he could answer, someone knocked on the door. Assuming it was the nurse, I settled back down and Luca regained his composure.

"Marco?" an all too familiar voice questioned.

"Court?"

"Oh, thank God," she said relieved, sprinting towards the bed, throwing herself in my arms. "I'm sorry. Did I hurt you?" she added in response to my involuntary grunt.

"You have no idea how good it is to see you, to feel you. It's been way too long, *dolcezza*," I replied, squeezing her waist tightly to spite the pain.

"Never do that to me again." Her tone was sharp and harsh. "You scared the shit out of me, Marco Santino. I've been sick with worry for months. My eyes have been glued to the television and any online articles I could get my hands on. Then some lawyer calls because of your brother, and yes, I'm sorry I outed myself and the identity you created for me, but what other choice did I have?"

"You didn't do anything wrong," I spoke softly, brushing whisps of hair away from her beautiful face while wiping her falling tears with my left thumb. "The man sulking in the corner, wringing his hands in worry like a little old Italian lady is my brother, Luca. All he's missing is an apron and Rosary Beads. I believe you two haven't officially met yet. Luca, this is *my* Courtney. Court, this is my baby brother, Luca."

"It's nice to meet you—face to face; not in a

courtroom," Courtney said, turning to him.

"Same. Thank you for coming forward and for agreeing to help with my case. That must've been difficult," Luca answered.

"Of course. Your wife—is she all right? Is your baby okay? How is your other son doing with all of this?" The fact that she showed genuine concern for Luca and Madison, two people she didn't know from a hole in the wall, caused my heart to swell with intense love.

"They're all good." He paused. "You don't have to hide anymore if you don't want to. Now that we know about you, you're one of us and we will, as a family, keep you safe and protected."

"I appreciate that."

"Hey, *Fratello*. Would you mind finding the nurse so we can get out of here?" This wasn't the time or the place to be discussing private family business. Though I fully understood where Luca was coming from and I commended his full acceptance of Courtney without question, I needed to know exactly where she stood before we could figure anything else out.

With a nod, he left the room.

"What are you doing here? Not that I'm unhappy you are here, but I would've come up to visit you this weekend." Taking her by the wrist, I pulled her to the bed.

"The second we hung up, I threw some clothing in a bag and ran to the airport. The plane only landed an hour ago. Once I got to Kennedy Airport, I called Jennifer Glick. While I rented a car she did a little digging and told me you were here. What did the doctor say? Are you hurt badly? Luca said Madison is fine, but how is your uncle?" Traces of panic danced in her sweet, brown eyes.

"First, thank you for coming. It means the world to me. Second, take a breath, *dolcezza*. All is well. A few stitches, a sprained ankle, and some fractures aren't going to be the thing that takes me out. Third, Salvatore is fine. Salvatore is always fine. When you meet him you'll understand that statement. Nothing ruffles that man. Fourth, what are you doing for the rest of your life? Would you possibly like to spend it with me?"

"What?"

"You and me—together, here in New York, living in the same house as Mr. and Mrs. Santino."

"Are you proposing?" Her voice shook with disbelief.

"Yeah, I am. I don't have a ring and I currently cannot get down on my hands and knees to make the request, but we can go to the jeweler tomorrow and get whatever you'd like and whenever I can bend down without wanting to punch a wall, I will ask you properly."

"Are you sure?"

"I've never been surer of anything in my life."

"Yes. Oh my God, yes. One million times yes." Throwing herself into my arms, she kissed my lips with a passion only she could provide, something I'd missed terribly.

Upon my discharge, I took her back to the house, figuring if she agreed to marry me it was time for her to meet my family. Plus, I refused to spend another moment without her. Introductions were short and sweet with an air of welcoming vibes for Courtney. It was a relief to see her sitting on the couch, relaxed, and chatting with Madison. Would they fully accept her, taking her into the Santino fold in the same fashion they had with Madison?

I had no idea, but I was sure she'd be all right. We'd be all right. Luca, on the other hand, I prayed to every god known to man that he'd pull it together. If not for him, then for his wife and kids. Bringing him into the family business was a risk I wasn't willing to take. I'd told my father countless times to deny Luca's request. He didn't have the mindset to be a part of what we did. Did Pop listen? Of course not.

"*Damn it*," I hissed, slamming the refrigerator door shut.

"Stop it. I'll handle it," Gia warned, pausing from whatever she was doing on the stove.

"Handle what, Gia? The Winters? Luca's bullshit? You're our bookkeeper and secretary. Please, stick to what you know. I don't have the time or strength right now to be bothered cleaning up any more messes."

Raising a wooden spoon, she shook it while charging in my general direction exactly like our mother would when we pissed her off. "Listen to me well, future *il capo*. None of you could wipe your asses without my help, so when I say I will handle it, I will freaking handle it. Period. Case closed. I dare you to challenge me. The last person who did is six feet under. The Winters will be taken care of and I'll stabilize Luca. Until then, back off. Focus on that girl in our living room and on healing."

"I believe you've forgotten who is in charge here. In case you have, allow me to remind you. It's Pop, Salvatore, then me," I fired back.

"In case *you've* forgotten, without me you're all as good as dead. I might not be the face or the brawn of this family, but I'm most certainly the brains. While you and Salvatore were missing and Luca was being charged with abduction and potential murder, who was Dad's right-hand man? *Me*. Enough."

"Look at me, Gia. I took one hell of a beating so that no one in that house had to. I protected my family. I did my damn job. No one has a scratch on them, and I'd do it again if necessary. So, if you want to stand there all high and mighty over how you stepped up to help Pop while I was off trying to finish what the Winters started, then fine. You can have your moment in the sun, but don't get too comfortable there. And for the record, I warned Pop and Salvatore to leave Luca the hell out of this life, but no one listened. If you have the pull that you suggest you have behind the scenes, why didn't you get that kid out of the line of fire? Why did you throw him to the wolves?"

"I am looking at you, Marco, and I too begged Dad to decline Luca's request. I also pleaded with him to leave Madison out of it as well." Tears streamed down her aging cheeks. "Do you know what it's like for me every time the phone rings late at night? I hold my breath praying it's not the call I fear most—that one of you idiots was killed. And now you have a chance at the life I always wished for you. A beautiful wife and possibly kids. The white picket fence, the minivan, and the dog. I want you to live to enjoy that."

"Gia," I whispered, pulling her into an embrace. Never once over the years did I ever consider how she, my other sisters, and mother might've felt. Watching her cry broke my heart. Hearing her fears twisted my gut. "Hey. Do you remember when we used to sneak out of your bedroom window when we were in high school so we could run to the corner and smoke the cigarettes that we stole from Mom's secret stash in the kitchen?"

"Sure. Why?" She sniffed.

"We should do that again."

A tremendous laugh erupted from Gia's throat. Tears of sadness were replaced by tears of levity. "If I tried to squeeze my fat ass out of that window and climb down that tree today, the tree wouldn't stand a chance and I'd end up in a full body cast. But…" her voice trailed as she made her way over to one of the cabinets. Opening it, she reached her hand inside, finally extracting a soft pack of smokes imported from Italy.

"She said she quit years ago," I said, examining the opened package.

"Mom lies." Gia snickered, extracting two cigarettes. "After everyone goes to bed. Same time, same place, but this time we use the front door," she added, handing me one.

Before I could respond, Madison walked in. Her green eyes surveyed the room. "We're going to head out, but goodbyes can wait until whatever is going on in here is finished."

"Everything is good, Maddy. Marco and I were taking a trip down memory lane. Are you feeling okay? Can I get you anything? Do you want something to eat?"

"I'm tired, but happy to be home, and stuffed from the amazing dinner you prepared," she answered, gently rubbing her pregnant stomach.

"Mom and I thought maybe you, Luca, and Frankie would like to spend the night here. You're more than free to go back to your house, *but* we feel it's best if everyone stay. You know how Mom is. She needs to make sure that you and Luca are all right before she can set you loose with peace of mind. I pulled a few of your old maternity outfits out of the guest room closet. You can stay in Luca's old room and Frankie can sleep in my old room."

"Sure. I'll let Luca know," Madison replied, backing out of the kitchen. Man, she'd become a faithful Santino soldier, taking orders without question.

"Courtney can stay in your room with you. You're a grown ass man. It's no secret neither of you are virgins. Plus you're engaged. Tina and her husband will bunk in her old room, same with Marie and her husband. The kids will sleep in the attic apartment. Me and my pain in the ass will use the pullout couch in the den. All of us will shelter in place until Dad gives us the all clear. Is there anything else you'd like to discuss?"

"Aside from apologizing for underestimating you earlier, we're good," I said, kissing her cheek, and exiting the kitchen.

With a tremendous sigh of relief, I thought how fantastic it would be if someone else took the lead on the cleanup crew this time around. What was the worst that could happen? She'd screw up and Pop and I would fix it? Perhaps it was Gia Santino-Russo's time to extract her pound of flesh, to seek her justice, to have her voice heard.

Chapter Twenty-Seven

Liam

It worked. I was still in a state of shock over that fact for days once I was back home. We'd been gone for six, long months, but Kendra never gave up hope. Neither did the kids. However, being I'd been dragged into Jillian's nightmares twice now, I made the decision to retire. Kendra and I had stashed away a nice chunk of change over the years so we could afford for me to call it quits. I'd consult or fill in on the side for the network, but I was far too old for this shit. I stayed on with Jillian and Nick's show for a bit post return until I found them a suitable replacement. Though initially she fought me on my decision, I stood my ground, making sure that I didn't blame her for anything. While I was packing up the car with Kendra three months later, a heavy sense of relief was felt. The second my Subaru crossed the Maine border, my once tense body finally relaxed.

I did regularly keep in touch with Jillian, often reminding her that all of our adventures together were precious and that I regretted nothing. I also kept an eye on the news for any updates on any of the Winters trials, but it wouldn't surprise me if one of the Santinos got to them before a court of law did. After a few months of living in Greenville, I ran into Marco and Courtney at a local farmer's market on a beautiful spring day. Initially, I didn't recognize them. He was clean shaven, toner, and wore drastically different clothing then he had when we were locked up. He also appeared well rested and calm. Long gone were the heavy bags which once resided under his dark, warning eyes.

"Liam Stevens," he said, approaching me, and sticking out his hand.

"Marco Santino," I replied, accepting the gesture.

"How the hell are you? What the hell are you doing way up here?"

"I retired. Kendra's sister lives locally. Since we love the cold and were desperately craving a slower paced life, we moved a little while ago. What are you up to? You look great by the way."

"First, this is Courtney Blackstone. Court, this is Liam Stevens."

"It's so nice to meet you. I've heard quite a bit about you," she said beaming. A sizable diamond rock sparkled off of her left ring finger.

"Are congratulations in order?" I inquired.

"I guess so," Marco said, grinning like a content man in love. This new version of him was a total change from the one I'd known.

"That's wonderful. I'm happy for you two." And, I was. This kid deserved it.

"Thank you."

"I assume you're all healed up?"

"Five by five. Always, five by five. The ER doctors were impressed with your fieldwork. They said your stitches were better than a plastic surgeon's. The shoulder was fine, but I had a few minor hand and rib fractures, and a sprained ankle. Nothing too terribly serious. Court was a tremendous help with my recovery. Thank you for patching me up as well as you did."

"After what you did for us, it was the least I could do. How is Maddy? Salvatore? Luca? Your family in general?"

"Maddy had the baby—a boy, Marco Salvatore. Salvatore is Salvatore. Nothing shakes him. He threw on a tracksuit and jumped right back into work as if nothing happened. He lost about one hundred pounds though. He looks fantastic and twenty years younger. Luca struggled for a little bit, but he's okay now. Our sister, Gia, slapped his ass back into place. Other than that, we're all good. How's Jill?"

"She's doing well, actually. Nick too. Those two always seem to find a way to land on their feet while coming out on top. God love them for that. I won't keep you. Please send my best to Maddy, and especially to Salvatore. Congratulations, again. I'm really happy for you, Marco. If you need anything, just want to talk, or Salvatore would like to reach out, here's my card. Give me a shout—day or night," I spoke, handing him my contact information.

"Thanks. Same goes. If you ever require anything, or find yourself in a situation, call me. I'm glad to see everything ended well," he replied, scribbling his number down on a receipt.

"Keep your nose out of trouble kid and it will remain that way," I warned.

"Impossible. Be on the lookout for an invitation to our engagement party and wedding. You and Kendra should try and come." He smirked before fading into the crowd with his fiancé.

I wanted to believe he'd stay far away from Beau, Tag, and Jackson, but I couldn't. He had an axe to grind for many reasons, and Marco Santino wasn't the type of guy to let shit go no matter how in love he was.

"Hun?" Kendra said, tapping my shoulder.

"Huh?" I turned, snapping back to reality.

"Is everything all right?" Worry hung from her beautiful, brown eyes. She was just as gorgeous as the day that I met her.

"It's wonderful."

Pecking her full, red lips, I took her hand in mine, shoving the past and everything in it back into the box in my mind where it belonged, locked away for good, and placed my focus back on what mattered—the here and now. Whatever Marco had up his sleeve was his problem, not mine. Whatever Jillian decided to do with her life was on her, not me. I'd earned my peace, and damn it, no one was going to rob me of it again.

Chapter Twenty-Eight

Madison

I don't want to sit here and lament over the past. I also have zero desire to relive either abduction or to discuss what happened in between and after. The Winters family would be dealt with and when that happened, Luca would spring back to his old form. I was confident of this. Sure, some days were more trying with him than others, but it was a waiting game; one I was more than willing to see through. The Santinos would get their pound of flesh for the Winters' crimes. How or when? I had no idea, but for the moment, we were all told, Marco and Salvatore included, to lie low and stand down. When orders like that came from the top you listened. There was no debating, no questioning, nothing. You fall into line. Period.

Not every moment was a white knuckle one. Marco had proposed to Courtney, and I gave birth to my second son—Marco Salvatore. I saw the name as fitting. I still do and always will. Between all of the wedding preparations and being a mother of two active boys, time flew. Roughly six months after having Marco, while celebrating my father-in-law's birthday, Big Marco, since his namesake was born we began referring to him this way to avoid any confusion, handed me his phone and walked away. Glancing at the screen it read that Beau Winters had passed away peacefully in his sleep. A massive, sudden heart attack was being labeled the cause of death. Showing Luca the headline, a flicker of a smile broke the permanent tension which resided daily on his face.

Some weeks later, while I was in the city with my mother-in-law, sisters-in-law, and Courtney, dress shopping for her wedding, a text message including a link from Big Marco came through. Pressing the screen, a picture popped up revealing a flipped over sports car and a snapshot of Jackson Winters under it. He'd passed away from injuries sustained from the crash. A few minutes later Luca called from the Yankees Game he was at with our sons, his father, brother, uncle, and cousins to tell me that he loved and missed me, and that he couldn't wait to see me later. A little more of him had returned.

Two weeks after Jackson Winters had died, while wrestling my two boys into suits, trying to get Luca ready, and finish my own look, all while racing against time before we had to leave for Big Marco and Courtney's engagement party, both Luca and I stopped dead in our tracks, slowly turning around to face the television screen in our family room. Tag Winters' body was found in his Sands Point home hanging from a beam with a belt around his neck acting as a noose. He'd killed himself. Apparent suicide, the media was calling it.

"They're all gone. It's over," I whispered to no one in particular.

Glancing at my husband, his mouth was agape. His eyes were wide.

"Did you…," my voice trailed off. Honestly, I was too frightened to finish my thought, and even more terrified to know the answer.

"No." He shook his head.

"Do you think…"

"Yes, but I have no idea how or who. We were together and in public for each death."

"Are you okay," I asked, softly touching his forearm.

"Never better, *vita mia*."

Everything I'd lost because of the Winters reappeared in an instant. All it took was for the Winters to end so spring could return.

Chapter Twenty-Nine

Luca

"Push, Madison," a young, energetic nurse urged.

Sitting up, her feet in stirrups, her white knuckled fists clutched the railings of the hospital bed she was in.

"I am," she grunted while bearing down.

"Excellent job, Mom. Dad, I need you to support her back. One more good push and you're done. Come on. You can do this. You're seconds away from meeting your baby."

With a final scream, all sounds of pain vanished as the cries of a baby filled the space.

"Congratulations, Mom and Dad. It's a boy," Madison's doctor informed us.

Reaching for her son, she quickly secured him on her chest, finally taking a breath for herself. After bearing witness to this miracle twice, I still had no idea how the hell she, or any other woman for that matter, did this.

"He's perfect," she whispered, stroking his full head of dark hair.

Words escaped me due to the heavy purge of emotions I, myself, was experiencing. I had everything any sane person in the world could ever desire, but yet this intense sense of gloom and doom resided inside of my brain refusing to release its hold.

"Just like his mother and brother," I managed to say

as I kissed her forehead. Leaning closer to Madison and my new son, my fingers stroked his cheeks.

"Does the newest member of the Santino family have a name?" the nurse questioned.

"Marco Salvatore Santino," Madison answered.

"Are you sure?" I asked. It's not that I didn't approve of the name, we simply hadn't discussed it. I figured she'd want to name him after someone from her family, being our first child was named after my father and grandfather—Frances Luca. With everything that had gone down, we had little time to ponder potential names. I felt lucky I was able to get the nursery ready in time.

"Yes. They're the reason we're still here. Can you think of anyone better to name our son after?"

"No."

"Why don't you go and share the good news with your family in the waiting room, Dad? We'll clean up Mom and get Marco Salvatore off to the nursery for some newborn testing. By the time your wife is checked into her room, your baby should be ready to spend some quality time with his parents," another nurse suggested.

I hesitated. Splitting the baby and Madison up into two separate areas terrified me to the core. How could I keep an eye on both of them at the same time?

"Go. We're going to be fine. Call Gia so you can tell Frankie he's officially a big brother," Madison encouraged, in an attempt to sooth my nerves.

"I'll be right back," I replied, before exiting the delivery room.

Removing my foot covers, hair cap, and scrubs, I found my parents in the hallway. Madison's parents were present as well, but they kept a fairly sizable distance from mine.

"It's a boy. Marco Salvatore Santino. Madison and the baby are both fine," I said, lacking any excitement whatsoever. Two of the most important people in my world were exposed to God only knew what. An anxious edginess consumed my every movement.

My parents were thrilled, but it was Marco who picked up on my elevated stress levels. With a nod, he took off towards the double doors, heading to where Madison was. He'd, without a doubt, stand guard making sure my wife and child were safe. Smiling weakly, I excused myself to call Gia.

"Hey, G," I said into the phone while grabbing a cup of coffee in the cafeteria.

"So?" she asked excitedly.

"Madison and the baby are both fine."

"Name?"

"Marco Salvatore."

"Because that won't feed into Marco's ego at all." Gia laughed.

"Yeah."

"Length? Weight?"

"I have no idea. Big? He's about the size of a Thanksgiving turkey."

"What's the problem, Luca?"

"Nothing."

"You have a wonderful wife and now two sons—the only two grandsons in this family. What more do you want for Christ's sake?"

"What do you want me to say, G?"

"I want for you to cut the shit and be happy."

"Cut what shit? I am happy."

"There was once this devastatingly handsome,

279

exceptionally charming, brilliant man who I knew. The second life got hard he lost himself within the storm which was beating down upon him. Because of that, life's simple pleasures eluded him. You see this man was an amazing son, uncle, and brother, but by the time he got married and created his own family he was a miserable son of a bitch. The story ends with him losing everything and everyone he loves, but not because of death, but because they upped and left him due to his inability to get a damn grip."

"I have to go."

"No. No you don't."

"I don't have time for this."

"Well you better make it."

"I have to get back to Madison and the baby," I practically shouted. The anxiety inside of me had reached its peak. I felt irritated, sweaty, edgy, and way too many other emotions to list.

"You need to calm the hell down. Marco is with her. He literally just texted the group chat a picture of your baby."

"I can't damn it. Get off my back. You're not my freaking mother, G."

"This is our life, Luca. You're not the only one who lives with regular fear. We take orders from Dad and spend time with our families, because that's all we can do. It's all we can control. Case closed. If it's too much for you to handle, that's okay. Talk to Dad and go back to your old law firm. No one is forcing you to be a part of the family business."

"Twice, G. Twice I couldn't protect my wife, and now I have two sons to worry about," I admitted.

"Neither time was your fault. The Winters were to

blame for both occurrences. Madison is all right and she will remain that way. So will the boys."

"What if they return for a third go at it? You know, to finish what they started, but this time Frankie and Marco are thrown into the fire?" I could barely breathe. The thought of losing my family terrorized my brain.

"Stop it. Get a hold of yourself. Don't you dare shed a single tear in front of me when no one is dead, Luca. You're a God damn Santino man. Act like one. The Winters are being handled *without* your involvement. Period. Discussion over."

"I have a right to know —"

"No. The only right you have for the moment is to act as our lawyer. Worry about our legal problems."

"It doesn't work like that."

"Yes, it does. Do your damn job and let everyone else do theirs. Keep your nose out of shit it doesn't belong in," she warned.

"G," I started.

"Don't G me. I'm telling you what to do and you're going to freaking do it or else. Go be with your wife and son. Enjoy them. Enjoy the moment. I'll bring Frankie up to the hospital in a few hours and you better be cured of this nonsense. If you want to speak to someone, I'll find you a doctor, or go bitch and moan to Marco. This conversation is over," she informed, slamming the receiver down so hard people who were on the roof could've heard it.

****

Six months to the day after Marco's birth while at my father's birthday party, Madison handed me Marco's cell phone. A major news outlet was reporting how Beau Winters died in his home after suffering a major heart attack in his sleep.

Some weeks later, I was sitting at Yankee Stadium with my family. Marco passed me his phone. The screen read that Jackson Winters' sports car had flipped over in a tragic accident causing him to lose his life.

Two months after that, Tag Winters had been found inside of his Sands Point home with a belt around his neck, hanging from the ceiling—an apparent suicide.

I remember that night as clear as anything. Madison was riding my ass to get ready for Marco's engagement party. I was having a hard time getting it up to attend an event that would leave my wife and children exposed. With well over two hundred people in a decent sized space with the lights dimmed, keeping eyes on everyone felt like an impossible task. One I wasn't feeling ready for. Reaching for the remote to turn the television off, the sound of a reporter speaking stopped Madison and I dead in our tracks. Tag Winters was gone.

The hold that had been strangling me and beating me into the ground instantly vanished. Though Beau went from natural causes, Jackson from a traffic accident, and Tag from suicide there was no talk suggesting foul play was involved, but I knew better. This wasn't fate or Karma in action. This was the work of someone from my family, but exactly who and how remained an unknown. For each death every Santino could be easily tracked down to a public place or event. We all had tangible alibis. The hits were flawless. The true act of an evil genius.

"I told you I'd handle it, *fratellino*," Gia whispered casually into my ear while I waited for the bartender to pour me a scotch on the rocks.

My head instantly turned to face her. I could feel my

eyes broaden. I wasn't sure if I should hug her or fear her.

"You wanted revenge. You needed retribution. It's yours," she said, before kissing my cheek and heading back into the main ballroom.

Would a part of me always be on edge causing me to protect my family with the ferocity of a starving lion? Yeah, of course, but the Winters had fallen and would never get back up again. Vengeance was finally mine.

Chapter Thirty

Salvatore

What can I say? All's well ends well, I suppose. We all lived to drop dead another day. Did I have concerns and worries over the future? Sure, but who doesn't? I could sit here and bitch over what transpired, but why? Shit goes down every single day. You can either find a cave to die in or fight. I'm a fighter. You deal with the cards you're dealt. Period. Perhaps that's the wrong way to approach things, but it's the only way I know how to, and it's worked so far.

Everyone bounced back and returned to work except Luca. He took some time to find his footing. Once Beau, Jackson, then Tag bit the big one, the kid sprung back to life. I'm not going to lie. Watching him live in survival mode was rough. He was constantly riddled with debilitating anxiety. It had to have driven his wife insane, but she never showed it. Never-the-less, Luca pulled through and in my humble opinion, he's better than before. He appeared calmer these days. As for what happened to Beau, Jackson, and Tag? I couldn't tell you for sure. If the Santino clan had something to do with it, that was news to me, but it wouldn't be surprising or shocking either. Ignorance is bliss, right?

After faking a heart attack, I took a long glaring look at myself in the mirror and began making changes. I lost one hundred and twelve pounds and I've never felt better. Of course I still and always will don my coveted, iconic tracksuits, but at least now said outfits are actually seeing walking tracks as opposed to racing ones. Jimmy took back up with the nice Italian girl he had broken up with, and Tony met someone, a real sweet southern girl who'd recently moved into the house across the street from ours. As for my beautiful Donatella, well she's still the best and the love of my life. She always will be.

I found it flattering that Maddy used my name as her son's middle name, and I was even more touched when Marco gave me Liam's contact information after having run into him up north. I shot Liam an email and we've been chatting weekly since then. It was nice being able to converse with someone who wasn't attached to 'the family.'

I've got nothing left to comment on. Everything I could ever need or want is mine because never once did I ever allow myself to lose sight of who I was and what mattered most.

Chapter Thirty-One

Nick

"Where's my wife?" I yelled at a security guard on the steps of the courthouse. I'd been watching the trial daily and after seeing Madison Santino fly into the courtroom, boldly declaring Jillian was alive and well stashed at my father's home, I jumped in the car and drove straight to where I thought she might be.

"Who's your wife?" he asked.

"Jillian Winters," I said in disbelief that this man had no idea who I was.

"She's currently being transported here now. If you go inside and tell them you're the husband I'm sure they'll be able to tell you where you can go to meet up with her when she arrives."

Without thanking the man for his time, I pushed past him and did as instructed. I was placed in a room with a long glass window and told to wait. About twenty minutes later, I saw Liam supporting Marco Santino's beaten-up body while Marco held Jillian's hand. Anger coursed at first, then panic replaced that sentiment. Why were they sharing an intimate exchange? How dare he think he was good enough to touch my wife? Who the hell did he think he was? Wasn't it bad enough that *my* name was dragged through the mud multiple times during *his* brother's trial? That I had to publicly admit to having an affair with his now cheap tramp girlfriend? Or, was Jillian so mad for having to relive my infidelity, she decided to do something with someone she knew I would loath?

I paced the room for at least another two hours before some random, middle-aged man entered, telling me to follow him. My anxiety reached an all-time peak as we made our way down several corridors, then into an elevator, and finally to a set of double cherry wood doors.

"Mrs. Winters is in there. She's waiting for you. The police, FBI, and the Judge have all questioned her, but she's been told to not leave the state or country until this case is officially closed. If you need further assistance or have any questions, she's been given a packet with all of the required information. If you cannot find your answers in there, you or your attorney can call the provided numbers," the man stated.

"Thank you," I said rushed, shoving the doors open.

There was my lovely, brilliant wife sitting at the end of a long conference room table alongside Marco. Her head rested on his shoulder. Her eyes were closed. He appeared to be comforting and protecting her. I couldn't hear what he was saying, but it was soothing and safe enough for her to feel she could let go and relax.

"Jill," I spoke.

"Nick," she said, springing up and throwing herself into my arms. She never felt better than she did at that moment.

"Are you all right? Do you need to see a doctor? What do you need, babe. Tell me." My hands inspected her form. To the naked eye, she seemed whole and fully intact.

"I'm fine. I swear. This is Marco Santino. Marco,

this is my husband, Nick."

Using the table for support, he limped over to where I stood. He looked like he'd taken one hell of a beating. "It's nice to meet you," he said, offering up one of his banged up hands.

"Same. Are you okay? Should I get someone in here to help you?" I asked.

"Like I keep telling your wife and Liam, I'm five by five, but thank you for asking. I'm going to head out to catch up with my family." He paused. "I hope you realize how amazing your wife is and how lucky you are to have her."

"I do." A part of me wished to thank him for enduring whatever smack down he had, leaving Jillian without a mark on her, but I couldn't bring myself to. There were too many negative emotions swarming around inside of my mind to find a positive one.

Jillian exchanged a few additional words with him before he left. Once we were alone, one simple glance at her chased away everything horrible that had accumulated inside of my soul since she vanished. As expected, leaving the courthouse was insane, but we managed. To my tremendous shock, not only did the network keep our show on the air, but the ratings went through the roof. We were back on top, which was great. However, we both felt it prudent to clear the air and tell our story our way. A major publishing house signed our book before we even finished pitching the idea. About a year later, it hit the shelves and we began a family tour. All in all it went better than expected. We were revered as the victims of unfortunate circumstances and were celebrated for coming clean.

The downside to everything was any contact I had

with my family of origin no longer existed. To be honest, I had nothing to say to any one of them, even my grandparents. There were no words to describe how I felt about them. Even if I could muster something to say, I doubted it would be anything nice.

Some months after Jillian returned, I heard on the news that my grandfather had passed away in his sleep. A couple of weeks later, Jackson was in an awful car wreck, succumbing to his injuries. Not seeing the need to create a media frenzy, I opted to not attend their funerals, but rather to grieve privately. To this day, I have yet to make a public statement on the matter.

Then, an invitation arrived for Jillian and me to attend Marco and Kelly's engagement party. Initially, I saw it as an olive branch of sorts. It was their way of suggesting it was time to leave the past in the past with regard to my affair with her and our family's bad blood. However, hours before the event I received word that my father had died by suicide.

Though the now dead three men were all awaiting trial for their crimes, and I was hopeful justice would be served, I couldn't help but to think the Santinos had their hands all over this. Unsure what to do—despite being at odds with my family, I never wished for them to meet their ends the way they had, Jillian thought it was best that we still attend the event because Liam and Kendra would be there and it was time to move along with our new life. In all fairness, the party was classy and nothing like I imagined it would be. Peace was brokered between the Winters and Santinos via Gia Santino-Russo. Her words and sentiments were kind, but behind her sweet smile rested a woman I would never dream of screwing with.

If you would've told me that day I was sitting in Charles Downey's office arguing with Jillian over our impending divorce that this was how my life was going to play out, I never would've believed it. But a strong case could be made that karma had been received for all parties involved. I was finally free from the shackles that had held me back, which had been hindering me from living my best life. Enduring what we had, I had all of the confidence in the world that Jillian and I would be fine because we were an unbreakable team.

Chapter Thirty-Two

Gia

When I make a promise, my word becomes my unbreakable bond. I never agree to do anything if I know there's no chance I can't complete the task fully *and* well. So, when I told Luca, Marco, and my father that I'd handle the Winters, they *never* should've doubted me. Marco took a step back, focusing his attention on Courtney. My father also took a step back, but only a slight one and he was sure to keep me on what he believed to be a short leash. Luca, on the other hand, made my life a living hell. Watching my little brother become a nervous wreck hurt me deeply, but since I couldn't speed up the plan of attack, I kept a firm eye on his ass, having Jimmy, Tony, and the others report back to me daily. Whenever he'd steer off course, I'd slam him back into place. He had to remain cool until the deeds were done.

Now, I won't share exactly how I was able to pull off three inconspicuous deaths, but I did, and every single one of my family members had a rock solid alibi. When Beau corked off we were all together celebrating our father's birthday, which I made sure went on well into the early hours of the morning, ensuring maximum extended public visibility. When Jackson's number was called, all of the men were together getting fitted for tuxedos for Marco's wedding and then went to a double header Yankees game. The women were in the city at a bridal shop with Courtney helping her pick out her gown, then we were off to see a Broadway show and have dinner after. As for Tag, we were all getting ready for Marco's engagement party—an event I went out of my way to plan so I could control where we'd be at precise times. Hell, I even invited Nick and Jillian Winters. I knew they'd come even with Tag's passing earlier that day. Pulling them aside, I peacefully discussed how our families should interact going forward to which they agreed. We shared a drink and no one—no one meaning any other Santino, was the wiser.

Do I regret what I did? No, and I never will. I did what I had to, to keep the Santinos together. Marco's engagement party wasn't just a celebration of his union with Courtney. It marked the end of an era and the beginning of a new one. Never underestimate a woman who has everything to lose. She'll win every time. Besides, the world needs more soulful savages in the form of women.

A word about the author…

A lifelong storyteller, JP Barry specializes in crafting heart stopping, compelling, unique, emotional page turners for a variety of genres. A New York native, Barry is always on the hunt for ideas for her next novel. When not writing, Barry enjoys spending time with her family.